NO BODY
NO CRIME

NO BODY
NO CRIME

A Novel

TESS SHARPE

MCD ⊛ FARRAR, STRAUS AND GIROUX   NEW YORK

MCD
Farrar, Straus and Giroux
120 Broadway, New York 10271

EU Representative: Macmillan Publishers Ireland Ltd,
1st Floor, The Liffey Trust Centre, 117–126 Sheriff Street Upper,
Dublin 1, DO1 YC43

Library of Congress Cataloging-in-Publication Data
Names: Sharpe, Tess, author.
Title: No body no crime : a novel / Tess Sharpe.
Description: First edition. | New York : MCD / Farrar, Straus and
Giroux, 2025.
Identifiers: LCCN 2025000322 | ISBN 9780374614423 (hardcover)
Subjects: LCGFT: Thrillers (Fiction) | Romance fiction. | Lesbian fiction. |
Novels.
Classification: LCC PS3619.H356655 N63 2025 | DDC 813/.6—dc23/
eng/20250107
LC record available at https://lccn.loc.gov/2025000322

Our books may be purchased in bulk for specialty retail/wholesale, literacy, corporate/premium, educational, and subscription box use. Please contact MacmillanSpecialMarkets@macmillan.com.

www.mcdbooks.com • www.fsgbooks.com
Follow us on social media at @mcdbooks and @fsgbooks

10 9 8 7 6 5 4 3 2 1

For my friends in the Trifecta,

I am so grateful for all of you, your friendship, your advice, and

your perspectives on life and craft.

Also, I am sorry for talking about feral peacocks pretty much

nonstop for two years.

Part I

THE CRASH

1

MEL

FORTY MINUTES AFTER THE PLANE CRASH

The first thing Mel thinks is: *that is not the plane ceiling.*

She stares up at the blue sky and pine trees that shouldn't be there, trying to make sense of it all. Her ears ring and her head aches like someone's taken a baseball bat to her temple.

What in the world? She blinks slowly. Then more rapidly, her eyes stinging, tears leaking out the corners.

Smoke. It's smoke. Choking, black and thick, acrid in her nose and mouth. She coughs, raising her arm to protect her face.

They're on fire.

No. That isn't quite right.

Another furious batch of blinking, her nose clogging against the toxic pour of black surrounding her and funneling through the front. No flames yet.

But the smoke. The plane . . .

Oh, shit.

The plane crashed.

And then Mel's not thinking anymore.

She's just surviving. Struggling to get out of her seat, only to be jerked back by the still-buckled belt. She claws herself free, aware of how the floor of the plane is tilted dramatically to the left and unsteady under her weight.

Get to your feet, Tillman. She can practically hear her old high school coach's voice in her head as she pushes herself. She lurches to the side, her legs shaking uncontrollably.

Mel looks down, her pulse beating in her ears like a snake's rattle. A dark wash of blood spreads down her calf and the harder she stares at it, trying to comprehend, the more aware she becomes of a dull throbbing in her leg. She tilts her head to the right and, *oh*.

There's a steak knife stuck in her leg. From lunch. They'd been eating when . . .

The chicken. There'd been something in the chicken.

But she doesn't have time for tracing back steps. She's been stabbed and drugged. The cockpit's on fire. The plane doesn't have a roof—or a ceiling, or whatever you call the top of a plane—anymore.

How the hell is she still alive?

And where is everyone else?

Pilot. Co-pilot. Attendant. Chloe. She'd done a head count before she'd stepped onto the private plane. A seven-seater Cessna. Forty-two feet. Five passengers, including her.

Chloe. Her heart hammers as her name floats through her fuzzy head.

"Chloe!" she yells. "Chloe! Are you in here?"

No answer.

Did she get out? Mel looks around frantically. She'd gone to the bathroom during lunch. That was the last time Mel remembers . . .

Fuck. What was in that chicken they served?

Breathe, Tillman.

She needs to un-stab herself. First and foremost. Then she needs to find Chloe. The smoke's thickening fast. If the fire reaches the fuel tank . . .

Mel stares down at the knife, embedded a good inch into her calf. Her fingers wrap around the edges of the hilt. Bracing herself is pointless, so she yanks it free, her scream filtering through her gritted teeth. Fresh blood streams down her leg as pain lances and then dulls to a throb.

She'll bandage it later. She needs to get out first. Tucking the knife into the waistband of her jeans, she stumbles into the aisle, toward the bathroom. But when she gets there, the bathroom's empty.

"Chloe!" she yells, staggering down the aisle, past her seat, toward the emergency lever. It's to the right. She'd made a note when she did her sweep. She just needs to get to it . . .

Her foot catches against something. She barely has time for a "Fu—" before she crashes to the ground. Her elbow catches painfully against a seat, but she doesn't have time to think about it because, this low and this close to the ground, Mel can finally see what she tripped over: A body. Blond hair.

Please don't be Chloe. Please don't be Chloe.

"Chloe?" Mel touches the woman's shoulder, pulling her closer. She hates herself for the relief that floods her when she recognizes the flight attendant. Blood trickles down the woman's forehead. She must not have buckled into her crash seat in time.

Mel's fingers slide to her neck. No pulse. Mel's heart swoops, a sickeningly familiar sort of drop.

This is not her first dead body. But it is her first plane crash, which is maybe why she kneels there, desperately trying to find a pulse for way too long.

You need to get up, Tillman.

She can't just leave this woman here to burn. Mel knows all too well the pain of having no body to bury, of headstones over empty graves. So she grabs the attendant under the arms and begins to drag her toward the front. Smoke is billowing around them, tears making it hard to see until she realizes: the smoke is funneling *out*.

The emergency lever's already been pulled. The door's open.

Chloe. She got out. It has to be.

"C'mon," she says, half to herself, half to the corpse as she drags them both out of the plane and onto the ground. It's a drop. It's not pretty. On the edge of vomiting, she fights to get control of herself. She needs to get away from the fire and wreckage.

Fifteen feet. That's as far as she gets dragging the body before she collapses on the ground, retching into the dirt, the horrible tang of jet fuel, smoke, and blood in her mouth.

"Chloe!" she yells.

Smoke spins up to the sky from the cockpit. She stares helplessly at it, trying to make out *something* through the smoke. Did anyone else get out? The pilot? The co-pilot?

Is she the only one left?

No. Chloe's okay. She has to be.

"Chloe!" She struggles to her feet once again, the world spins, a lazy sort of dip that makes her feel like she's in a fun-house-mirror situation. But she bites the inside of her lip and the burst of pain focuses her, clearing her mind of the fuzz for just a second.

She shuffles her feet forward. One step. Then two. Then she's moving away from the wreckage.

All she can see is pine. They landed right in the trees. Probably why the top of the plane was missing. Sheared off going down.

These are old-growth trees. Staggeringly tall. She's somewhere logging hasn't touched in a long time. National forest, maybe? She turns in a slow, limping circle, trying to gauge an idea of *where*. She'd closed the shutter on her window when they took off. It always made her feel queasy to watch the landscape grow smaller and more stamp-like.

They'd been in the air for what . . . three, four hours? That would put them . . . where, exactly? What forest was this? What *state* was this? Had they even made it out of Canada?

Her head throbs as the questions tumble inside it, finding no purchase and no answers.

"Chloe!" She cups her hands around her mouth this time, hoping her voice will carry. She has to find her.

Mel looks toward the plane. Had she missed her somehow? She has to check. To make sure.

She stumbles toward the flaming wreckage.

"Hey!"

Mel freezes. Her eyes slam shut against the flooding wash of tension. They pop back open, bulging with adrenaline.

She's a rabbit caught in a trap. *Run, little Red, before the wolf gets you.*

Nat Parker, the PI who taught Mel everything she knew, used to tell her that fear is a gift. Once you experienced real fear, it left a scar. One that ached when you were about to step into some shit. Her body knows enough to recognize it at the start, instead of in the middle.

When you realize the danger at the start, you can fight back. When you realize it in the middle, you're screwed.

"Hey," says the voice again.

It's a male voice. Not Chloe.

The pilot? No. He'd been British. The co-pilot, too.

She'd checked them both out. She'd done her job. She was great at her job. She'd met the crew. Memorized their faces and voices and mannerisms. She'd secured the plane before Chloe even stepped inside.

Mel's hand curls around the steak knife tucked in her jeans.

Fear is a gift, Tillman. Now the voice in her head is a mix of her old high school coach and Nat Parker. Their voice is going to be the last thing she ever hears.

The knife's in her fist. Tight to her side. It's useless as a throwing knife. The weight's all off.

Goddamn it, have the last eighteen hours *sucked.*

Mel turns slowly and yup, there's a guy standing there. A guy who was definitely *not* on the plane.

And her brain starts doing that *thing* it does. A ticking time bomb of a list, building rapid-fire in her mind as her eyes dart from his hat—*knit and pulled tight over his ears*—to his jacket—*there's a dark spot on the arm, he pulled a patch off it recently*—to his shoes—*sneakers, not hiking boots, bulge at the ankle.*

Like ice spilled into a glass, it tumbles together in her head in a rush: He's got a vehicle stashed somewhere. Four-wheeler or dirt bike, with this terrain. Otherwise he'd have better shoes on. It's parked far enough she didn't hear an engine. And that bulge at his ankle is a gun. This is rifle and shotgun territory. A handgun means shit against a bear.

You're either a criminal or a cop with an ankle holster in the middle of the woods. And this guy's facial hair is all wrong for a cop.

"Hey, you okay?" he asks, his dark brows scrunching together in concern as Mel's blood thrums *Run, run, little Red*, but her feet stay frozen because: *Chloe.* Where is she? Does he have her?

"I saw the smoke from my hunting cabin. Shit. Did you . . . did you crash? Are you hurt? Are there other survivors?"

Semi-plausible story. She should believe it, but they're too deep in the woods for hunting cabins. He's scanning the area too closely.

And he hasn't even reacted to the flight attendant's body.

That tells her everything. His focus isn't on rescue. It's on something else. His eyes sweep over Mel's head, tracing the tree line.

The details don't line up and she's remarkably lucid. It makes her want to laugh and then she does, because it's kind of absurd. Even a plane crash can't shut her brain off. The way she noticed things and asked questions drove her father crazy when she was a kid and then it drove Bob's fist into her kidneys once or twice or maybe dozens of times and then she just stopped going home to the trailer park until she was sure he was fast asleep.

"You're gonna be okay," the man assures her as she continues laughing. "Why don't I—"

He steps forward, and as he does his right hand moves toward his back.

Run.

Her muscles tense and then her entire body *jerks* as something whizzes right past her, so fast and so close she can feel the air kick up against her ear. It's a *zip* through the air that startles her back and out of the way.

There's a certain *thunk* an arrow makes when it hits its target.

Mel knows the sound well. Even after all these years apart from her.

A second arrow sails past, neatly embedding in the man's chest, clustered tight against the first arrow.

Chloe always knew how to group her shots.

The man jerks, falling to his knees. When he pitches over, the gun he was going for falls from his hand and Mel's brain lights up like a strongman game at a carnival.

Ding, ding, ding. Another win for fear is a gift.

Mel turns.

And *finally*, there she is: lit by flames and backdropped by smoke like a goddamn action hero, her blond hair a messy halo around her head. There's a gash on her cheek, but she's alive. She just shot a guy— *Jesus Christ, Chloe*—but she's *there*.

Mel wants to clutch at her like they've been through a war, because haven't they? But Chloe's all business. She's got a third arrow nocked in her compound bow—where the hell did she have that stashed? Did it fold down into her backpack or something?

"You good?" Chloe's eyes sweep down. "You're bleeding." Her voice softens. It almost breaks through Mel's anger. *Almost.*

"The plane crashed," Mel says. "I woke up with a steak knife in my leg. I'm pretty sure there was something in that chicken they gave us. And you just shot some dude. So no, I'm not *good*, Chloe."

Chloe ignores the slow rise of Mel's voice and walks right past her, toward the guy.

"He dragged me out of the plane. He wasn't here to rescue us."

"Chloe—" Mel steps forward, but Chloe just kicks the guy over and Mel feels some of her anxiety dissipate because yeah, dude's super dead and that's probably a good thing, all guns considered. And then that anxiety spikes right back up because Chloe steps on the guy's chest and grabs the arrows' hilts with one hand, yanking them out with a visceral *squelch* that sends blood and bits flying. Mel grimaces, trying to quell the sick churning in her stomach.

"We need to move," Chloe says, stashing the bloody arrows in her quiver and kneeling down next to the dead dude. She sticks her hands in his pockets, searching. She comes up with nothing but an extra magazine, so she grabs the gun and holster. She pockets the bullets and gets up, holding the gun out to Mel expectantly.

Mel stares at her. Then at the gun. Then back at Chloe.

Her eyes squint. Her head pounds.

God, this has been a shitty week.

"Melanie." Chloe kind of shakes the gun. "Take it. We need to move."

"Are you fucking kidding me right now?"

Chloe frowns. And then! She *growls*. Like she's the goddamn wolf and Mel's standing in the way of her dinner.

That just sets Mel off completely.

"You"—she points at Chloe—"are going to explain the last eighteen hours. And then, you're going to explain the last six years."

"I—" Chloe starts.

"Nooooo." Mel drawls it out, partly because she probably has a head injury and partly because she is pissed. "Eighteen hours ago, I had to ford a river like I was a pioneer on the Oregon Trail only to find your place was *booby-trapped* to the gills like you're growing reefer in the seventies. And to my surprise, once I've gotten through all the booby traps, I find that you don't have some grand cannabis operation going on. You're not running even a little grow. No. It's just you! Living in the middle of bumfuck nowhere Canada like you're Nell from that Jodie Foster movie. And you keep refusing to contact your family, which is why they hired a private investigator to come get your ass!"

Chloe frowns, rubbing at her forehead. It smears blood and soot farther across her skin.

"I can't believe they hired you."

Mel glares at her, wishing that she could set fire to things with her mind. "They didn't. They hired my boss Nat Parker."

Chloe's eyebrows snap together. "You work for Nat Parker?"

Mel grits her teeth and grinds the toe of her boot into the dirt. "Things got complicated after you left."

"Nat Parker accused you of murder!"

"Like I said: complicated."

"That's not what I wanted when I left," Chloe says. "Mel, I promise, that's the last thing—"

Crack.

She flinches as the sound sends a cold trickle of dread across her skin.

Chloe's bow goes up, nocking the arrow in a smooth movement. Blood drips from the tip. She moves in a slow circle, trying to track the source of the noise.

All is silent but the furious crackle of the plane burning.

"We need to go," Chloe says. "I will explain. On the move."

When Mel was seventeen, she knew Chloe's face better than the back of her own hand. Every curve and freckle, that shine in her eyes that glinted into razor-sharp focus when it settled on her.

She made you feel seen in a way that cut you if you got too close.

And Mel got too close, over and over. Cut herself to ribbons on Chloe's sweet sharpness and asked for more. Begged for it. Loved her for it.

She was the one who got away. Not just with Mel's heart. With everything.

"Mel," Chloe says. "I need you to trust me. Like I trusted you when I agreed to come home."

She holds out the gun.

Cut me. Take me. Love me.

"I am the same person I've always been," Chloe says.

Mel takes the gun.

She thinks: *that's what I'm afraid of.*

Their fingers brush as she pulls away.

She thinks: *your skin is as soft as I remember.*

Mel releases the magazine, checks the rounds, snaps it back into place.

She thinks: *I should've never gone to Chloe Harper's sweet sixteen party.*

2

CHLOE

It's still under her shredded fingernails, a shadow underneath remnants of pink polish. When Chloe turns her hand around, there it is: blood tingeing brown.

She thought she'd gotten it all. She dips her hands back in the creek, scrubbing furiously even though it makes the tips of her fingers raw, and the nail she almost pulled out throbs under what's left of her skin.

Two days ago, her mom had taken her to get her nails done. It had been a special treat for her party. Mom got her nails done with Olivia twice a month, but she rarely took Chloe. There was no use, Mom said, because she was always chipping the polish at the stables or at the archery range Daddy had set up. Olivia didn't waste her time with such things, so she got manicures and spa dates.

Chloe lets the water stream through her fingers, wishing it could carry her away, too.

What's to come is almost as terrifying as what she just survived. But she can't run anymore.

She hears the *slide-clunk* of Mel's footsteps across the rocky creek bank, the water-smoothed rocks shifting under her feet. Chloe gets up, shaking the water free.

"The car's all ready," Mel says. "It'll take both of us to push it off the ridge."

Chloe looks over Mel's shoulder, where Chloe's brand-new BMW is parked up on the ridge. Mud-streaked and already half-destroyed, one of the headlights and the windshield are shattered.

"My dad's going to kill me." It's the one thing she can think to say.

"Well, he won't be the only guy today who's tried," Mel says.

Chloe's eyes startle to hers, locking onto Mel's golden brown. The words hang there for a moment. Mel's mouth twitches the longer the silence reigns. And then it's too much, it builds and builds in her chest until laughter burbles out of Chloe. It rises in the graying predawn, Mel's unhinged giggles twinning up with hers. The chill comes off the creek and her body shakes with laughter, making her bruised skin pepper with goose bumps.

When Mel's hands close over her wrists, her laughter fades. Mel's touch is so gentle, and the goose bumps spread for a whole different reason.

"We stick to the story. I convinced you to take the car out. I hurt my hand and we decided to go to the ER." She pauses and it takes a second for Chloe to realize Mel's waiting for her to finish.

"On the way there, I swerved to avoid a deer," she says, her voice hoarse. Getting choked out does that to you. "We spun out, off the embankment and crashed. When we came to, we got turned around in the dark. Finally, we found the creek and followed it until we got to a road."

Mel nods, but she worries her lower lip, gnawing it bright red. "We can't be seen together," Mel tells her. "Once they start asking questions and realize Toby's missing. We have to go back to normal."

"I know," Chloe says. "I know," she says again, not to make it real, but to taste the bitterness in her mouth. To learn it. She's gonna have to get used to it.

Mel's hands tighten around her wrists. No longer a suggestion, but a reality. Mel's warmth against her bruises. She could power a whole town through the winter.

This is the last time she touches me. Chloe stares down at Mel's fingers, wondering when the first time was—just hours ago—so it shouldn't matter that now there's a last time.

But it does.

So much.

"It's gonna be okay," Mel assures her.

But it's not, because this is ending. This terrifying, endless, life-changing night.

She's not the same girl she was at five o'clock yesterday. When the first guests arrived at her party, she'd been a glimmer of who she is now.

But it's familiar, to change so much in so little time. It's what happened to her on the road last year, the tragedy that set all this in motion, that put her in Toby's path. And now she's here. Brand-new again.

Now, she's a girl who grasped something good while being hunted.

Now, she has to let it go.

It's the only way to save them both.

"Are you ready?" Mel asks.

Chloe wants so badly to tell her *no*. She needs to know why. She always needs to know the why of things. And this one, this is certainly the biggest why of her life. Because she cannot even begin to understand.

Why the hell did Melanie Tillman risk everything, for *her*?

She opens her mouth to ask, but Mel starts to pull her hands away from Chloe's wrists and she just . . . can't. It can't be over. Chloe's hands scrabble, desperate to keep the connection, and their fingers wrap and entwine, careful of Mel's burnt skin and how all of Chloe's fingertips are rubbed raw.

The feeling punches the breath out of her: palm to palm, scrape against cut, bruise against blister.

This girl bled for her. Fought for her. Broke fingers for her.

Now she has to leave her alone. For good.

Tell me why, I need to know. Why didn't you just walk away?

Chloe licks her lips. Copper tangs on her tongue as she gathers her courage to ask.

"Mel, I—"

It's too much to ask. It's too much to know.

Everything about tonight is just . . . too much.

She steps forward, crowds into Mel's space, their clutched hands coming up to press between their bodies, the only barrier between them. Her tongue feels like cotton in her mouth, her heart hammers under her battered bones, and if she thinks anymore, she's going to scream.

So she stops thinking.

Her thumb strokes Mel's wrist, because that skin isn't bruised and Mel's eyes sweep down, following the movement, and when she looks back up, Chloe doesn't look away.

She moves forward, until she doesn't think there's any closer to get, but when her lips touch Mel's, she realizes that yes, there is closer. There is more.

There's *her*.

It's just this time, Chloe tells herself. *We can't speak after this. I'll never touch her again.*

Her breath hitches into Mel's mouth, an angry sob at the ugliness of the truth in the beauty of *this*.

It's the only time.

(It's not, though. It's the first time. Of many.)

That's the funny thing about murder.

It can bond you like nothing else.

3

MEL

Mel had gotten the text when she was walking in Miller Park, before she'd even done the morning coffee run.

It's time.

She'd driven straight to the hospital. She hadn't come until now. She'd wondered if it was her place.

There'd always been an uneasiness between her and the Parker family. Nat's youngest daughter, Tiffany, had been in Mel's year at school. She'd known Toby. Even dated him for a few months. Tiffany had watched it all go down and Nat never explained why she'd done such a 180 on Mel and there had to have been questions at home about it. A lot of them. Nat was never one to provide answers. Not unless you were paying for her to ferret them out. Mel knew this all too well. She had a feeling Tiffany and her older sister, Claire, did, too.

"Nat Parker's room, please," Mel says to the receptionist at the front desk.

"Room 245."

"Thank you."

Mel takes the stairs, maybe to draw it out a little. Having to face the gauntlet of Parkers grouped around Nat's bed isn't going to be fun. But when she was called, she came. That was her and Nat's deal.

Mel had feared her once. Hated her even more and then she loved her, and now she's losing her.

God, cancer is such a fucking bitch. Robbing the world of a woman who is crotchetier than kind, but who'd go after any child abuser or woman beater with a baseball bat.

Her hand trembles as it closes over the door handle leading out of the stairwell. It takes her three deep breaths before she can pull it open. Nat's room is halfway down the white hall, lined with medical carts and rooms with the doors open, but the curtains around the beds closed.

Mel hesitates in front of her room. She peers inside, surprised to find it empty and not full of Parkers.

"Nat?" she calls softly, stepping farther inside, twitching back the curtain.

She hasn't seen her in six weeks, so it's a shock. A gut punch that forces her to scramble to keep her expression neutral. Nat's lost so much weight, her hospital gown's hanging off her shoulders. The oxygen cannula is strung under her nose, tubes going into the port in her chest and stomach.

Mel comes closer to the bed, not wanting to wake her if she's sleeping. But as soon as she reaches the end of the bed, Nat's eyes fly open, those honed senses of hers still going strong.

"Kid," she says, her cracked lips stretching into a smile. "You came."

Mel hurries to her side, looking around. There's a cup of half-melted ice chips on the side table and she fishes one out, running it gently across Nat's lips.

"Where's your family?" Mel asks.

"Made the girls go get lunch. Didn't want Tiff to bitch at me about you. She's gonna be mad enough when the will's read and she sees I've given her sister the Mustang."

Mel frowns. "Don't talk like that," she says. "You're gonna—"

"They're moving me to hospice tomorrow," Nat interrupts. "End of the line, kid."

Mel doesn't dare sit down on the edge of the bed . . . she doesn't want to disturb Nat. So she grabs the chair in the corner and drags it close.

"I've got a week, I think. Maybe a little more. But I don't want you to see me in there, okay?"

Mel bites back her protest and nods instead.

"It's okay," Nat tells her, and Mel sniffs, trying to hold back the angry wash of tears, because it's *not*. "I needed you here," Nat continues slowly. Every word is an effort, but she's holding strong in the importance of it. "The safe code is 2319. Petty cash and all my active cases are in there. Along with the deed to the building."

"I'm sure your girls will take care of the business—" Mel starts to say, trying to reassure her.

"Agency's not going to them. It's going to you."

Mel's glad she's sitting because she would've been on the floor right now in shock otherwise. "Nat, no—"

"Don't argue with a dying woman," Nat snaps, her cranky tone so familiar it makes the back of Mel's throat burn.

Tiffany Parker is going to kill her. First her sister gets the Mustang and now Mel gets her mother's business? Tiffany's sure to at least slash her tires and throw a drink in her face. She's that type.

Fuck, Mel's going to need to sleep with one eye open for the rest of her life.

"I've got more to say," Nat insists, but she takes a deep breath, like she's trying to get enough air to do it. Mel takes her hand gently, squeezing encouragingly.

"Remember when I started chemo?"

Mel nods. Nat had made her wait outside to pick her up. Mel used to sit in the parking lot with paperwork the entire time anyway. She wasn't gonna leave her.

"I made a friend at the clinic. Jackson Harper."

Stern face. Marlboro-man tough. Staring down the barrel of his rifle. What are you doing on my land, girl?

Mel only met Chloe's parents once—that time Jackson caught her waiting for Chloe at the archery range she had set up in a lonely corner of the ranch. She'd pretended to be a hitchhiker, just looking for a place to crash for the night. She never knew if Jackson had believed her or not. But he had let her go after he marched her past the house, Chloe's mother watching from the porch.

They had to be extra careful after that.

"Jackson asked me to find Chloe for him."

Mel pulls away at the words, her heart kicking up like a horse pushing into a gallop.

This isn't part of their deal.

But deals don't matter much anymore. Just truth.

"You—" Mel licks her lips. "You didn't."

Nat's blue eyes burn bright against her pale skin. "I don't regret the path I took with you, Mel."

"You protected me," Mel says. "You taught me everything you knew."

"I did," Nat agrees. "But I've been trying to figure out for almost eight years what happened to you and Chloe Harper on her birthday."

Mel had known, on some level, that *this* was the conversation Nat had wanted to have. Their relationship started with an interrogation and now it'd end with one. It's fitting. She never could leave a case unfinished. And Mel was her last mystery.

"We've talked about this," Mel says slowly and carefully. It's a line she knows like the back of her hand. "I was in a car accident with Chloe. We hiked back to the road and it took all night because we were hurt and we got turned around in the dark. That's it."

Nat chuckles, her eyes drifting shut. "You were always a brilliant liar. I thought you must've come up with her escape plan, but considering Chloe's been so hard to find, maybe she was the brains." Her eyes pop open, alight with curiosity. "Were you the brawn, Melanie?"

Mel stares at her. "You really want to do this? After all these years of working together? You want to spend our last time together playing *this* game?"

"You were the one who came to me and asked me to find Chloe first."

God, Nat has always been brutal.

"I was a kid."

Nat smiles, her face sharpening with fondness. "You know, it's how I realized how smart you are. That mind of yours . . . I could've conquered the world if my brain worked like yours."

"Global Empress Parker would've been quite a sight, I'm sure," Mel says, and Nat laughs so hard that she grimaces as her oxygen cannula gets dislodged.

"It's okay," Mel reassures her, helping her adjust the cannula with shaking hands. "It's gonna be okay."

"Never knew how you could be such a good liar and a bad one at the same time," Nat huffs between harder breaths.

Mel presses her lips together, the pang in her too great to speak for a second. "Talent, I guess," she says finally, and it's what she can give her. Crumbs, and pitiful ones at that. "You should rest," she tells her. "I'll stay here until the girls get back."

"I could make it my dying wish," Nat says. "For you to tell me."

"That seems like a shitty dying wish to me," Mel says, fussing with the blankets that had gotten tugged up, away from Nat's feet.

"I found Chloe this time."

Mel freezes.

"You didn't ask," Nat continues. "Wasn't sure if you're interested."

"It doesn't matter to me," Mel lies, the cotton blanket clutched between her stiff fingers.

"It wasn't easy. Girl's got a talent for disappearing. I always wondered if you'd known where she was this whole time. But if you knew, wouldn't you have gone to her by now?"

"You're the only one here who knows where Chloe Harper is," Mel says, which is the truth. She's never looked for Chloe after that time she showed up at Nat's door, demanding she find Chloe. Nat had laughed at her. When Mel had burst into tears, Nat had stopped laughing and brought her inside and sat her down at the chipped Formica table for the first—but definitely not last—time in Mel's life. She'd made her tea and made her drink it even when she made a face.

She had told Mel she had a choice. Sink into the loss or use it.

And then she offered Mel a job.

Even after she worked her hours and became a PI, Mel never looked for Chloe. She couldn't bear knowing and not going. And if Chloe had wanted her to follow all those years ago, she would've left breadcrumbs. Mel's sure of it.

"You wanna know where she is?"

Yes. No. Always.

Mel finally looks up from the blankets, meeting Nat's eyes.

"Why are you doing this?" she asks her. "You and I made a deal—"

"I didn't know back then what you'd become," Nat interrupts. "I didn't know I'd—" She stops. "I love you, kid. Like you were one of my own girls. And I've watched you all these years."

"So what?" Mel demands shakily.

"You've been through some shit and you came out of it. But you're not happy," Nat says simply, and if she'd prettied it up, maybe Mel could run from it. But you can't run from three words when they hold that much truth.

She can't stand the pity in Nat's eyes. She takes in a shaky breath and wipes away the held-back tears. In the hall, she can hear a distinctly squeaky voice talking to a nurse. That would be Tiffany. Nat's daughters were coming back.

It's time for her to go. She isn't family. Not really.

"Your girls are back," Mel says, leaning over and pressing a kiss to Nat's forehead gently. "I've got to go."

Nat grabs Mel's arm, surprisingly strong all of a sudden.

"The information's in my safe. It's up to you what you do with it. But Jackson would really like to see his daughter before he goes. And I would really like it if you were happy.

"That's it," Nat says, tears trickling down her face. "My real dying wish. I'll haunt you if I don't get it."

Mel leans over and presses her forehead gently against Nat's cheek. "I love you, old woman," she whispers through the clog of tears in her throat. "You changed my whole life."

The pressure of Nat's hand against her head makes her start to cry as the older woman cradles it for a moment. "You did it all yourself, kid. Now go do as I say. One more time."

"Momma—oh. Melanie. It's you."

Mel clears her throat, pulling away from Nat. "Hi, Tiffany," she says. "I'm just leaving."

Tiffany doesn't even look at her further, hurrying over to her mother. Claire at least gives her a nod and a slight smile.

Mel walks over to the door and turns. The Parker girls have positioned themselves on either side of their mother like knights ready to fight the reaper.

"Bye, Nat," Mel says, knowing in her gut it's the last time she'll get to say it.

She's right. Nat's gone six days after they move her into hospice.

By then, Mel's read through the entire Harper file at least twenty times. She only stops to buy a black dress and attend the funeral.

Afterward, she checks on her brother and lets Teddy know she'll be off on a job. Six hours later, she's on the Harper family's private plane, on her way to British Columbia with just a crude map, all of Nat's methodical notes, and a fuzzy picture of a twenty-four-year-old Chloe Harper that she can't stop looking at.

4

CHLOE

Everything goes back to normal.

That's the problem.

Chloe's stepped into an alternate universe of her own life and no one knows and all she's doing is waiting for the rest of reality to ripple and reset.

Her grandpa would call it *waiting for the other shoe to drop.*

Her dad is absolutely furious about the BMW being totaled, but the anger is canceled out with worry over her, which is a relief. Even her mom fusses over her, and Olivia stays home an extra week from Stanford and barely leaves her side.

We were so worried when we couldn't find you, her sister told Chloe, patting her gently on the tops of her feet like it's the only place she's sure Chloe isn't bruised.

She'd be wrong: Chloe's bruised there, too. Running through the woods in cowboy boots does that to you.

Her parents keep her home for a week before letting her go back to school. She's antsy by the third day. By the end of the week, she's losing her mind.

But it's even worse when she returns. Gigi and Whitney stick to her like twin burrs. And there Mel is, in the halls, in her classes, across the courtyard where everyone eats lunch. Mel's where she always was, but Chloe never noticed before, and now she can't escape her.

Deep down, she doesn't want to.

"Chloe, are you even listening to me?" Gigi asks.

Chloe tears her eyes away from Mel, who is reading her book in the corner of the courtyard. "Yes," she says. "Sorry. What were you saying?"

Gigi lets out an annoyed huff, flicking her white-blond hair over her shoulder. The strands are held in place by a pink tweed Alice band that matches her skirt. Around her neck is a gold acorn pendant. "I was saying it was lucky you had your accident *now* instead of in a month. You'd be all bruised and purple for homecoming."

"Yes, way to perfectly time your horrific car accident," drawls Gigi's twin, Whitney, from next to Chloe. "Ten points, Chlo."

"I didn't mean—" Gigi protests. "You always think the worst of me!"

Whitney stretches out on the bench. Her pants can't even be called pants. They can only be described as *trousers*. Wide-legged and billowy when she walks. Chloe could never pull such pants off. She'd trip on the cuffs.

"I do not think the worst of you," Whitney says patiently to her sister.

Chloe rolls her eyes at both of them. The twins love to bicker, which makes having a built-in partner to argue with handy. She can't imagine what it would be like being friends with just one of them. She'd get steamrolled in every argument.

"How are you feeling, really?" Whitney asks.

"I'm fine," Chloe says, popping a chip in her mouth, one eye still on Mel. Mel's turned the page in her book. She doesn't have a lunch. Was she not hungry? Or did she not have one to pack?

A prickle of worry snakes inside Chloe's stomach. She's always at Miller Park when Chloe goes there to run. Not just sometimes. *Always*. Almost like she lives there. But she knows that's not true. Mel lives in the River View trailer park. So why does she spend so much time sitting at the picnic tables in Miller Park?

What is she running from?

"And the doctor said you weren't gonna scar! That's great!" Gigi chirps, breaking her spiral of thoughts. Chloe just blinks at her, trying to remember what they were talking about.

"Oh my god, Gigi, cut it out." Whitney sighs. "Don't focus so much on looks, please."

"I'm just saying," Gigi protests. "It could've been a lot worse. Chloe careened down the Bluffs at full speed. She could've *died*."

Mel's gotten up. Chloe watches her pull her backpack strap over her shoulder and head toward the exit that leads to the hall.

"I'll be right back," she says to the twins, walking off before she can hear their protests, because they're supposed to help her to class.

She's still moving kind of slow. Her entire body is one big bruising throb, especially her shoulder, even though Mel had done a good job popping it back in after it dislocated. The doctor at the hospital said so.

Harper's Bluff High is tiny—there are less than five hundred students in total. It still takes her way too long to get across the courtyard. She's tempted to call her name as Mel disappears into the girls' bathroom down the hall, but instead, she follows.

The school hasn't been updated since the seventies, when the town actually had money, so everything is severe concrete, with beige stalls. Mel's standing at the sink, washing her hands with the shitty powdered soap that dries the hell out of your skin. Her eyes flick up to the mirror when Chloe steps inside, and then shoot right back down when she sees who it is.

Someone flushes and one of the freshman cheerleaders comes out of the stall, her bouncing ponytail secured by a green-and-gold bow. She washes her hands next to Mel and brushes past Chloe with a "So glad you're okay, Chloe!" before leaving like Mel wasn't in the accident, too.

Red crawls along her cheeks, her heart thudding as Mel's mouth quirks in the mirror.

"You need something, Chloe?"

"I—" She loses her words halfway to her mouth. There is so much Chloe needs and even more that she wants and she's pretty sure she doesn't get any of it. Just another thing that night took.

Mel still won't turn around, but she does turn off the taps, her eyes focused on Chloe's reflection in the mirror.

"You okay?"

Finally, a question she has an answer to.

"No."

Mel doesn't say anything. She just shakes water off her hands and then reaches for the dispenser for the scratchy towels that are more paper than towel.

"Are *you* okay?" Chloe asks, torn between wanting her to say no so there's proof she's not alone in this and wanting her to say yes so at least one of them came out of this unscathed.

Mel finally turns, the towels wadded and stained dark with water in her hands. She stares down at them like they're the most interesting thing in the world and for the first time, it strikes Chloe that maybe it's as hard for Mel to look at her as it is for Chloe to look away.

"No," Mel says. "I'm not."

It's like the words break her free of whatever's holding her there. She bolts forward and so does Mel and just when they're about to—

"Chloe!"

The door bangs open and Chloe skids to a halt, her hand still outstretched, ready to curve around Mel's waist, to haul her body against her own, *anything* to get closer.

Mel whirls away, stepping toward the sink, turning the taps back on as Whitney rushes into the bathroom, followed by Gigi.

"You just ran off. You know we're supposed to watch you!" Whitney scolds.

"You missed the whole thing, Chloe!" Gigi tells her.

"What whole thing?" Chloe asks.

Mel's still methodically washing her clean hands, pretending she's not listening, as good as invisible to Whitney and Gigi.

Mel was never invisible to Chloe; how could she be? Mel stood out in the way take-no-shit girls did, and Chloe may have envied it when they were kids and then realized she was a little attracted to it when they were teenagers. But Mel wasn't important until eight days ago, and now it's like Chloe's entire universe is spinning on Mel's axis.

"Tiffany Parker came screeching into the courtyard about how Toby Dunne's *missing*," Gigi says. "No one knows where he is. He was supposed to be at his grandparents' house in Grants Pass a *week* ago, but they just figured out he never showed up."

"His parents are freaking out," Whitney adds. "They thought he was in Oregon this whole time. He texted them he got there. I don't think they should worry too much. He probably just lied and took the travel money his parents gave him and went to Vegas or something. He's the worst of the senior boys. He's drunk in some shitty motel, I guarantee it."

"Come on." Gigi tugs on Chloe's hand. "I want to get the details from Tiffany."

"I'll be there in a second," Chloe says. "I need to . . . to . . . change my tampon."

"Aww, there should be a rule that you don't get your period after a horrific car crash," Whitney says, tsking sympathetically. "I'll get you some chocolate from the vending machine."

Chloe smiles. "Thank you."

But her smile snaps off her face when the twins leave in search of chocolate and gossip. It's just her and Mel, and once again, Mel's unwilling to face her.

They're right back where they started.

"Mel," she says softly.

Mel says nothing. Instead, she turns.

And without a word, she walks out of there.

Just like they promised. No contact. That way no one would connect them.

Chloe has to follow the rules, too. No more chasing after her.

But she wants to. She has to go over and splash water on her face so she doesn't go after her again. What is wrong with her?

You're a killer now. You're definitely not just queer in theory now. You're a mess maybe forever.

Chloe splashes more water on her face.

Eight days ago, she could list exactly three things she knew about Mel Tillman.

1. Mel had a single pair of boots. She wore them everywhere. Chloe was pretty sure they were her only pair of shoes other than her cleats.
2. Mel was a killer softball player. Rumor was Coach Thorne paid for all of Mel's gear, because her dad certainly wasn't going to shell out for it.
3. Mel seemed to spend more time in Miller Park than at her own place, because every time Chloe went there to run, there was Mel, doing her homework on the benches, walking the paths by herself, wandering the river trail that ran along the bank, hanging out with the homeless guys at the park that Chloe's mother would put together packs of toiletries, snacks, and twenty-dollar bills for each Thanksgiving and Christmas.

Those were the things Chloe knew then.

And now . . .

Now there's so much more than three things. Too many to list.

That's what happens when you survive with someone.

That's what happens when you kill with someone.

5

MEL

Mel flies into Vancouver and rents a camper van off a camping app. The gas is going to cost a fortune, but the Harpers are paying and there's no motel.

Zeballos. Population 121. It's not really a town. More like a village. A cluster of buildings and fishing boats and a river snaking through the mountains and forests.

It looks like NorCal up here. Familiar terrain, just colder and foggier. Mel gets why Chloe chose it. Feels like home.

She pulls into the campground around seven, checking in with the gray-haired woman in the little log-cabin-style kiosk and scoping out her lot before she heads back out for dinner.

Nat's notes are meticulous. Chloe's address is unknown. She lives somewhere in the vast woods in the area. Zeballos isn't the only town she's been reliably spotted in, but it's the only one that she goes to more than twice a year.

Her visits don't follow a schedule—that would allow someone to do exactly what Nat tried to do: use her patterns to reliably track her and get the drop on her. But Mel has another plan and there was one note in the file that made Mel's senses clamor: under the town's diner Nat had written *great apple crumble*.

If there's one thing that you can't change, it's a sweet tooth. And back when they were teenagers, Chloe's favorite thing was apple crumble. They'd even served it instead of cake at her birthday party.

So Mel parks and strolls into the diner. It's not kitschy, that would make it self-aware. It's practical, a space that uses every bit of its square footage, with booths along the windows, a counter lined with stools, and stand-alone tables creating a maze to navigate. The narrow kitchen crammed in the back has everything stored vertically on shelves, and the serving window is still lined by ancient neon.

"Sit anywhere you'd like," the older waitress calls from the register as she rings up two women.

Mel takes a booth with a perfect view of the door and the parking lot and orders a burger when the waitress comes by. She's the only one in the restaurant now, which suits her just fine. She's got information to gather.

"You traveling through?" the waitress asks when she brings Mel's drink. Her name tag, chipped and old, says *Peggy*. Her hair is big and boldly plum colored, matching her eyeshadow.

"Camping," Mel says. "It's gorgeous out here. And I hear the fishing is fantastic."

Peggy smiles. "That it is," she agrees. Then, after Mel places her order, "Food'll be right out."

Mel waits. The key to getting people to open up is creating a sense of safety and comfort. You've got to be familiar but unassuming. Friendly, but not too interested. Asking too many questions will make alarm bells go off.

She moves into the next part of her plan: laying the bait. Mel pulls out her notebook and flips it open, where the one photo of Chloe she has is tucked. For a moment, she stares at it, trying not to be taken in and failing. There Chloe is, eighteen and beautiful, smiling at the camera, her sweater falling off her shoulders, her blond curls blowing out like a crown, and her hand reaching toward the photographer— toward Mel.

Mel had taken it just weeks before Chloe was meant to leave for college—which turned into her leaving them for the wilderness and whatever life she's put together here instead.

For years, Mel wondered what kind of life that was. She spun herself stories of Chloe disappearing into a European city sprawl overseas, reveling in the anonymity only a crowded population can give. Or Chloe in some farmhouse in the middle of nowhere, married with three kids, no one the wiser to her life before. In her dark moments, she wondered if Chloe was dead in a ditch and they just didn't know it yet.

The idea of getting an answer *from* Chloe, not from a file filled with Nat's sparse assumptions, made Mel want to bolt out of this booth and keep running until she hit the border.

She had tried to put it past her. But it had never been easy. It wasn't like she could go to therapy and talk about it. Who knows if it even would've helped. Her problem wasn't very solvable without Chloe.

You're not happy. Nat's voice echoes in her ears.

"Here you go." Peggy sets the platter with her burger and fries down in front of her. "Need ketchup or ranch?"

"Ketchup, please."

Peggy returns with the ketchup, setting it down next to the notebook. She frowns, her eyes catching on Chloe's photo. Just like Mel wanted.

"Sorry," Mel says, hastily moving the notebook and photo out of the way.

"You know Marie?" Peggy asks cautiously.

"Marie? No, that's my cousin Cindy," Mel says. "Last I heard, she was in Whistler. My mom told me to look her up if I got up that way. But I haven't had the chance yet."

"Oh, my mistake," Peggy says, with a faltering smile.

"They say everyone's got a doppelgänger or whatever," Mel says cheerfully.

Peggy walks to the counter and Mel watches her discreetly, munching on fries and scrolling the digitized file of Nat's notes Gigi created for her.

C.H. spotted in three different vehicles over the period of a year, Nat had scribbled. *Silver 2000 Jeep. Black truck, possibly American in design. White Range Rover. Likely she has more vehicles/sells them for cash every few months to keep anyone off her trail.*

Mel pages to the file with the map Nat had marked with possible locations. Chloe certainly wasn't living in town, wherever she was. She was somewhere in the Canadian equivalent of the boonies, coming into town only when she needed supplies.

The thing about remote living is that unless you're good at everything, you've got to foster community in some ways. Chloe would know that. Which is what Mel's counting on.

"How's everything tasting?" Peggy asks.

"Great," Mel says.

"You said you were at the campgrounds?" She takes Mel's half-empty Coke, holding it as she waits expectantly and a little too obviously.

"Yep," Mel says. "These forests remind me of home."

"Oh yeah? Where are you from?"

"Portland," Mel lies.

"Like that funny TV show."

"Exactly like that."

"I'll get this filled up for you."

Mel finishes her fries, pretending not to watch as Peggy goes over to the drink machine and pulls her cell phone out of the back pocket of her jeans and makes a call. She has a hurried conversation, one eye on Mel, who keeps munching on her fries and blithely scrolling on her own cell, pretending she isn't being cased like she is.

Mel's phone screen switches to an incoming call, her phone vibrating in her hand. When she sees it's her best friend, she picks up.

"The international charges are gonna kill me," she says into the phone.

"Do you really think I'd let you go to Canada and not add international calling to your cell plan? I'm the one who dealt with the Harper family jet and all the arrangements, remember? You'd be lost without my administrative skills," Gigi bitches back at her. "Did you get there safe?"

"Yep."

Peggy finishes her call and brings Mel's soda over.

"Anything else?" she asks.

"I'm good, thanks," Mel tells her.

Gigi huffs so loudly into the phone it crackles. "Are you ignoring me?"

"No, Gigi, I'm being polite to the nice lady who served me my food. I just finished up eating."

"I can't believe you're doing this."

"Eating dinner?" Mel asks, even though she knows what Gigi's on about. Sometimes winding her up is too easy.

"You know what I mean. I can't believe you've gone chasing after Chloe."

"Really? 'Cause you've been saying it's exactly what I'm gonna do every time you get too drunk and go on a nostalgia tirade," Mel points out, keeping an eye on the parking lot as a red truck pulls into it. A group of men get out. Her brain ticks the facts off as she glances them up and down: tackle boxes in their hands, waders in the truck bed, along with beat-up Igloo coolers full of ice and most likely fish. These guys knew what they were doing.

"I didn't mean to become a fortune teller or whatever," Gigi says.

"A prophet," Mel says as a red SUV drives down the street.

"Yes, that," Gigi says. There's a weighty pause. "Have you seen her yet?"

Mel admires how level Gigi keeps her voice. Mel's been unraveling ever since she got within a hundred miles of this place.

"No, but she's here," Mel says.

"What if you missed her?"

Then I'll search every inch of these woods until I find her.

"I don't think I have," is all Mel can say without sounding crazy.

Mel knows the feeling when Chloe's heading toward her, no matter how far away she is. Mel forged it during one night in the forest with her—a skill born out of the necessity of survival—and then honed it over two hopeless, over-a-cliff years before Chloe disappeared.

"Call me when you find her," Gigi says.

"Mmm," Mel agrees vaguely as she keeps one eye on the street.

"I mean it," Gigi says. "The *second* you find her. You call me. So I can talk you out of whatever crazy plan she's gotten you to agree to within five seconds of seeing her again. Actually, you should call me *before* you talk to her. Have me on speaker when you confront her."

Mel bites back a retort about being treated like a child with no control because Gigi is her best friend. It's sometimes strange to think that—when they were kids, if someone had told her Gigi was who she'd end up with as her ride-or-die, she'd probably have wondered what the fuck they were smoking. Hell, three years ago she would've laughed at the idea.

But here they were. Best friends. Colleagues. Opposites. Brought together by too many choices by too many people and too much loss and Mel's always-needed PI skills.

Life is weird. And fucking tragic. But she's grateful to have Gigi for so many reasons. People always underestimate Gigi. And that is as good as gold in the PI game.

"You're being ridiculous," Mel says, stirring the melting remnants of her soda ice absently. The group of older men had entered the diner, setting their tackle boxes by the door on a shelf painted with cartoony fish that seemed reserved for that exact purpose. They take the booth farthest from her and she's glad, because she can whiff the fish guts from here.

"I'm being smart," Gigi says, so sincerely it's got Mel flushing hot. She looks away from the phone, back toward the window, grateful Gigi's in Harper's Bluff so she can't see the guilt stained red under Mel's expanse of freckles.

"I want you to remember something," Gigi says suddenly and too intensely, and for a moment she sounds so much like Whitney instead of like herself that it's a gut punch. Mel has to swallow around the rising grief. "Remember how far you've come. How you picked up the pieces. What you've made of yourself. The life you built for you and your brother. Okay?"

Mel licks her lips, thinking she should've packed ChapStick. "Okay," she promises.

"It's important," Gigi continues, and she keeps talking, but Mel's not listening anymore. It all fades to background noise as her eyes fix on the road.

That black truck . . . had she seen it before? It'd passed by when the waitress had slid her burger down on the table. She'd made a note of it. The bumper was warped in the middle, like someone had used it to haul something too heavy and it was never the same again.

The truck slows down as it drives across the road from the diner. Mel tracks it as it passes, trying to see the driver, but she can't get a good look. Her hand grips the phone so tight she's afraid she's going to Hulk-crush it. Gigi will never let her hear the end of it if she has to expense another phone to the office.

"Gigi, I've gotta go, my dessert's here," she lies into said phone, not looking at the very finished plate in front of her. "I'll text you before I go to bed, okay?"

"Ugh. Fine. You better. Be safe."

Mel pulls on her baseball cap, tucking her ponytail into her oversize jean jacket and scarf. Slipping on a pair of sunglasses, Mel leaves two green Canadian twenties and a blue five on the table and grabs her purse, hurrying out before she can even ask for the check. Luckily, the waitress is distracted by the fishermen and just glances over and nods when Mel calls back, "Money's on the table."

She bolts down the diner's wooden stairs, her feet hitting the pavement with a *thump* she feels through her whole body.

Mel stands there for a moment, letting it prickle over her skin, up her arms and down her chest, settling in her gut.

You don't get far in the investigative game if you can't tell when you're being watched. But Mel came into the job with that instinct already carved deep.

You grow up with someone who hits you, you get really good at knowing when they're watching you, ready to explode. It's a sixth sense violence gives you.

Where are you? She barely resists turning in a circle, holding out her arms in mockery. *Come and get me, sweetheart.*

Instead, she turns toward the diner and then digs in her purse, like she's worried she's forgotten something, then pretends to find her wallet and sighs in relief. Then she moves toward her camper van, gets inside, and drives off.

Mel doesn't see the black truck in her rearview all the way back to the campground, but it doesn't matter. She doesn't know these roads. Chloe would. And she'd know where Mel was going just by her vehicle.

That's why Mel chose it. Obvious sometimes worked for a woman.

She parks in her camping spot and pops the camper top up, inflating the mattress pad and arranging the bedding that came with the rental. She sends Gigi a good night text, because she won't hear the end of it if she doesn't. Literally. Gigi will call her until she picks up. She can't blame her—Gigi is about as traumatized as you can get when it comes to missing people. And not just because of Chloe.

She turns off her phone and then the lights in the van. She lies back, but she doesn't go to sleep.

Lying there on the too-squishy mattress pad, hands folded above the blankets, she waits.

Her mind, it can't help but work. Will she come? If she does, what will Mel say after years of silence? Mel has always been patient, but this is agonizing.

The hours tick by. First one, then three, and then it's 2:00 a.m. and she's still waiting.

But she's no stranger to darkness. When she was a kid, Miller Park's streetlights were never maintained, so as soon as it got dark the expanse of trail and scrub oak along the river became a different place. A shadowy expanse that revealed the truth: no matter how the town liked to pretty it up, it was much more forest than park.

She'd spent years doing homework or reading by flashlight on the benches or tucked in the cubby behind the child-size tic-tac-toe wall in the play area that was good for sleeping in when the deputies were doing park rounds and she didn't want to go home.

She used to see Chloe there after school. It used to be their only interaction in the before time. Chloe in her hot-pink jogging shorts and headphones firmly snapped over her head. A clear message: *leave me alone.*

Mel always did. They didn't belong in the same world back then. But she watched her out of the corners of her eyes. Maybe she admired the fluid grace of Chloe's run from time to time, the bounce of her ponytail. Maybe she wondered what music Chloe played. But she studiously avoided thinking about Chloe Harper in the before except at Miller Park. Straight girls like that were forbidden fruit . . . they didn't . . .

Well, she had been wrong about the straight thing. Wrong about Chloe. Clearly she needed better gaydar. But she'd been right about the forbidden part.

She still walks in Miller Park every morning before work. It's out of her way now, but it doesn't matter. She picks up trash from the trails and creek twice a month and probably walks the park more than the deputies—much to their annoyance, since she keeps working to stop them from rousting the homeless camp out.

Gigi's right: she made something of herself. But who the hell knew what she was walking into with this. Gigi was right again: she was playing with fire.

Scrape. Click.

In the oppressive hush of a late night in an empty campground, Mel's senses are primed for the sound. The van door slides open as quietly as one can manage, relying on Mel being asleep.

But she's not.

She holds herself still, blood rushing through her body. She breathes in and out, proud of how steady it is.

The weirdest thing about the PTSD is that she's usually fine in the woods. It's like her body's already resigned to expect death and terror in the trees.

She doesn't know what to expect here. *Who are you now*, she wonders as she listens to Chloe's feet shuffle quietly down the narrow aisle that splits the camper van.

Mel breathes in. The ladder creaks. The third rung is the one that creaks. Four rungs to go.

Mel breathes out. She grips the extra pillow, wondering if it's possible to love someone you don't even know anymore.

She breathes in, eyes skittering between the gap leading to the main level and the pillow in her hands. It's full of real feathers. She can feel the ends of a few poking at her skin through the material. It's probably goose down plucked from Canadian nests or something. The expensive stuff. It's got a lot of weight to it. It'll work.

Two more rungs and then she's vulnerable. She's not just talking about in a fight.

Now or never.

She breathes out.

And flings the pillow violently down.

6

MEL

Her pillow hits its intended target. Kind of.

She'd intended on keeping hold of the pillow. But there's a flash in the moonlight and her mind says *knife* before her body fully understands. The pillow's tugged out of her hand with the force of the blade sinking in. It slices the fabric and then: feathers, floating everywhere.

What the hell is she doing with a knife?

Mel slaps the light switch on as white feathers rain down on her. Her eyes tear up in the sudden light, but she pushes forward, half hanging out of the little sleeping cubby. She stares down at Chloe, half up the ladder, one hand on the rungs, the other clutching the knife.

"Mel?!" Chloe shouts, her eyes widening as Mel pushes her hair out of her face.

"What the fuck, Chloe?" she shoots back. "You broke in here with a *knife*?"

Chloe's eyes drop to the knife and she lets go of it with an uncontrolled shudder, like she can't believe it's still in her hand. It clatters to the floor. Mel can't help but note it's not a butcher knife. Eight inches. Bowie knife. Antler handle. Lethally sharp. The kind of thing you use to hunt. A practical weapon. Substance over style. That was Chloe.

Mel looks back up with a jolt when she realizes Chloe's not staring at the knife anymore.

"Mel," Chloe repeats, so flat with shock that the jolt turns into a seconds-long tug into realization.

Chloe climbs down from the ladder, landing on the floor with a *thump*. Mel's eyes slide to the knife, wondering if she should grab it. Just in case.

"What are you doing here?" Chloe demands.

"Camping," Mel grinds out furiously, trying to make it make sense. Peggy the waitress had warned Chloe, just like Mel had hoped she would. Chloe had taken the bait. But this reaction . . .

This isn't what she expected. She assumed Chloe would realize it was her. What other tall brunette was looking for her?

"Bullshit," Chloe says. "Why are you here?"

Mel climbs out of the loft and jumps down the last two feet, landing on the floor with enough force to rock the van slightly. The knife spins toward her and suddenly they're both looking at it.

When Mel glances back up, Chloe's watching her instead, fascinated. Her eyes rove over Mel's face with rapt hunger. Mel flushes, inside and out, and she tries to breathe through the heat on her cheeks, though she knows it's no use.

"Do I look that different?" Mel asks.

"You look spooked," Chloe says. "You scared of me, Tillman?"

Before Mel can even answer, Chloe advances, stirring the fallen feathers. She closes the space between them in two steps and it takes everything in Mel not to back up until her hips slam into the camper's tiny sink. Instead, she remembers she's a grown-ass woman and plants her feet.

This is *Chloe*.

Chloe, who came into her van with a knife, probably thinking she was someone else.

What the hell have you gotten yourself into?

"I'm not scared of you," Mel says quietly, refusing to be cowed or to flinch or flush further. Chloe wants a reaction. One *she* can react to and spiral off.

It gives her some sort of hope. That it's as weird for Chloe as it is for her.

She's different than before, but also the same. She'd always been strong, the shoulders and the arms of an archer, but now—

Now she looks like she could bench-press Mel, and Mel has never been the pocket-size one when it came to the two of them. It's . . . different.

The lizard part of her brain coos *it's fucking hot* but now is really not the time.

Or maybe it is, because Chloe takes another step, then another, and if Mel doesn't move, she's going to be flush against her and then it's all over. So she does. She moves.

But Chloe doesn't stop. She walks forward, pressing against Mel, and all Mel can do is shudder farther into Chloe's touch. All she can think about is that gray light above Harper's Creek the day after the birthday party, Chloe's jagged fingernails and her own bruised skin. That first teenage kiss that tasted like blood and triumph.

All she knows is: *I missed you.*

Chloe's hand slides up Mel's neck—not soft, but terribly present. Like she'll leave a mark only Mel can see as Chloe's fingers bury in the frizz that gathers at her nape, and when they tighten, Mel trembles against her.

It's just like before. That need zips across her skin, jerking parts of her awake that have been asleep for years. Tears should gather in her eyes as her long-dormant heart shudders back to life, but she's cried too many tears for Chloe Harper. Mel's done giving them to her.

Chloe will have to come and take them from Mel with her hands and her mouth and her words.

Her forehead presses against Chloe's, and Chloe's fingers grip her baby hairs tighter, greedily unable to let go. Mel stays still, refusing to close her eyes. Instead, she watches Chloe touch her like she's finally got the grail and all that's holy in her hands. Part of her is transfixed, swaying into her, into the thick of the feeling. But part of her holds back from leaning into what will become a kiss, if she lets it. The part that whispers in Mel's ear: *There's a job to be done.* The part that needs to slip the micro-tracker into Chloe's back pocket.

"Why did you come?" Chloe whispers like it's some damning character trait of hers.

"Why did you leave?" Mel whispers back, because if she's damned, it's because of her.

That gripping ache of a question—it makes Chloe stiffen. For a second, she's still holding on to Mel, close enough to kiss, and then she pulls away completely. Reluctantly.

"Christ," Chloe mutters, rubbing her hand over her face. "I didn't mean— Fuck, Mel." She stares at her like she can't help herself. Like Mel's some forbidden fruit she can't resist going for. Even now, her eyes keep dropping to Mel's lips.

It makes her feel all sorts of things, but mostly like crap, because this is the way it always was with them. Irresistible. Secret. Hidden. Not because they were ashamed, but because they were surviving.

What are you trying to survive now?

"You need to go," Chloe says. "Leave tonight. Don't come back here. Don't tell *anyone* you found me—"

"Your family knows where you are," Mel interrupts. "They sent me in the jet."

Chloe's eyes widen.

"They hired a private investigator—my boss—to find you. I was sent to bring you in."

"Bring me in?" Chloe shakes her head. "Like I'm a wayward calf or something."

"Your people are ranchers, not mine," Mel reminds her.

Chloe shakes her head, her barely-there blond brows are drawn together so strongly Mel can actually make them out.

"Go home, Mel," she says. "Tell them I was long gone when you got here. No trace of me. Forget you ever found me."

"I can't," Mel says simply. Sometimes the truth is that simple.

"You have to."

And sometimes it's that complicated.

Mel shrugs. "Guess we're at odds, then."

Chloe folds her arms and crosses her feet. Mel's mouth twitches, even though she fights the smile. In a second, she's gonna start tapping her foot. It's what she always did, when they were kids.

And sure enough, there she goes. So different, but still *Chloe*, even after all this time.

"Then I'll leave," Chloe insists.

"You do that," Mel says.

Chloe's eyes narrow, that brilliant blue that she's never seen in anyone else's face sparkles in annoyance at her. "You can't follow me."

"You know me," Mel tells her. "I haven't changed." Another complicated truth. "So what do you think I'm gonna do?"

"You don't know what you're messing with, Mel."

"I don't," Mel agrees affably, because she can tell it's pissing her off and she forgot how fun it was to piss Chloe Harper off. Almost as fun as touching her. "Because *you* won't tell me. I'm gonna find out, though. That's what I do these days. Find people. Find things. Fix problems." She leans forward and Chloe rears back like she's a sparking wildfire. "Do you have a problem, Chloe?"

"Yeah, my ex-girlfriend tracked me down after years with no warning, like a psycho," Chloe drawls.

"Wow," Mel says. "What a coincidence. Mine showed up with a knife like a criminal."

"I wasn't going to stab *you*," Chloe sneers.

"No, just whoever you thought I was," Mel says, and Chloe sucks in a breath. "Who are you after?"

"I'm not after anyone," Chloe says.

"Then who's after you?"

The foot-tapping stops. *Bingo.*

"You're just doing that thing you do, where you make giant assumptions that defy logic," Chloe says coolly.

That hurts, Mel's not going to lie. Chloe had been the first person to marvel at her ability to observe and retain all sorts of information. It had been nothing short of glorious irony to be valued for the thing that got her in so much trouble at home. Coach had appreciated her knack for holding stats in her head, but that's about as far as it went.

But Chloe had seen her. And she hadn't turned away. At that point in Mel's life, not many people had done the same.

So it's hard to keep her voice level when she says: "Whatever you want to think, Chlo."

"I'm leaving," Chloe says. "Don't follow me."

"I'm not going anywhere but back to bed," Mel says. "I'm tired and you took your sweet time breaking in."

But Chloe doesn't move despite her declaration.

"Please just tell them you couldn't find me," she says, her voice cracking.

The sudden desperation almost breaks her. She sounds so scared. It's written all over her body, too. Her shoulders tense, defensive and discouraged. She's a rattler, poised to strike.

Mel is the one who closes the space between them this time. She slides her hand up to cup Chloe's cheek like she'd done hundreds of times as a girl in love. Now she's a woman on the edge and Chloe's face fits into the cradle of Mel's palm like she remembers, but this Chloe—a woman sharpened into something that makes Mel's stomach jolt in part fear, part attraction—she doesn't lean into Mel's touch the same sweet way.

She pushes into it like she's goddamned starved for it.

How long has it been since anyone's touched you?

"Tell me why I have to lie," Mel says. *Tell me what's wrong.*

"Please just trust me," Chloe murmurs.

Mel's thumb strokes down Chloe's jaw, hovering on her pulse point, where she can feel it wildly kick up against her skin.

"Trust is earned," Mel says, and she can't hide the pain behind the words. She doesn't want to.

Chloe's mouth twists. "You're gonna be the end of me." She turns and stalks toward the van's sliding door, feathers swirling in her wake.

"Yeah, well, love's a bitch," Mel calls, and Chloe freezes, her long-ago spoken words shot at her like arrows, and for a second, Mel thinks she's got her. She allows hope to grow that it'll be this easy. That Chloe will just fall back into her arms and they'll go home and she'll tell her why and it'll be okay, somehow.

But Chloe Harper's never taken the easy road. Her shoulders square and her chin tucks and Mel's hope goes *poof* just like that.

Love really is a bitch.

"Go home, Mel," Chloe says. "While you still can."

She disappears into the night, leaving Mel standing there, her entire body buzzing back alive for the first time since she was eighteen.

7

MEL

Mel doesn't go home. She gets back into bed, just like she said she was going to. She pulls out her phone, bringing up the micro-tracker. She's almost positive Chloe won't find it—it's so small, the size of a pinkie nail and just as thin. The kind of tech that's only accessible in certain markets, with people who have certain licenses. If Chloe's been off in the woods this whole time, running around armed with a knife of all things, Mel has to wonder if she even has an internet connection out where she is.

The knife might just be because it's quieter than a gun, her brain singsongs back, ever her best debate partner.

Mel shakes it out of her head. She focuses on the little dot that is Chloe, stopped about half a mile down the street from the campground. Probably waiting to see if Mel gets on the road immediately like she demanded.

Instead, Mel lies back and watches the dot, her own personal game of chicken.

Mel's spooked her like she intended—Chloe will head back to wherever she calls home, grab her stuff and go. And she'll learn her lesson because Chloe *always* learns from her mistakes. Which means Mel might never find her again. This is it. Her only chance. She stares at the unmoving dot half a mile away.

You're gonna have to blink first, she thinks.

Finally, the dot starts moving.

And so does Mel.

She focuses on the task at hand. If she starts thinking about anything else, she's going to spiral and she's already tempted to drift into the memory of her touch that's so recent she can still feel it.

Chloe looked so different, but still, fundamentally, the same. That's growing up, she guesses. It hurts all of a sudden, that she didn't get to grow up with Chloe. Mel didn't get to see her at twenty-one, ordering fancy cocktails at a bar, or at twenty-two, graduating from college.

They missed each other's finishings. The roundings-out that made you a person as your frontal cortex fully matured or whatever. The experiences that they should've had together—first apartments and first real jobs, proposals and adopting rescue cats and arguing over which curtains were best for the living room.

Mel just let Gigi buy stuff for her apartment because she doesn't spend any time there anyway. She practically lives at the office since her brother, Ted, got his own place. She's always been crap at making a home.

Chloe wouldn't have been crap at that. Chloe would've made anywhere a home because she was there with her.

What is your life like now? She tries to imagine it. A cabin in the woods. Maybe a little farm? No. No. She wouldn't risk having to leave livestock behind if she had to run. Once a ranch girl, ever a ranch girl.

That must be difficult for her. Chloe loves animals. She always had a dog or two tagging along with her when Mel would sneak through the back forty to get to Chloe's archery range. Their secret world was built there, alongside the hay targets and the romping dogs. Tucked away, hidden from everyone as the world raged on. Weeks and then months stretched by with no sign of Toby—but rumors spread and Nat Parker started to circle.

She tries to shake off the memories, but the past's heading away from her and she needs to catch up.

There's a special kind of dark the forest gets when there's barely any population. Her headlights will stick out like a warning. So she takes her time packing up the van and stops at the gas station to fill up, one hand always on her phone, her eye on the screen as Chloe moves north and heads off the main highway.

Chloe's got at least a twenty-mile jump on Mel by the time Mel hits the road for real. She speeds down the highway, glancing at the paper map she unfolded at the gas station.

The miles blur, her focus splits from the road to the tracker's journey on her phone to the map, and when she takes the exit Chloe did, she finds herself heading straight down a single-lane road lined with trees for another thirty miles. She glances at the tracker—Chloe's still moving, heading northeast now. She's taking an uneven, winding path through the expanse of forest surrounding them. Timber roads, Mel bets. Or maybe old mining roads. Something not a lot of people have access to.

How in the world had *Chloe* gotten access?

Mel almost misses the turn, the road is so hidden, tucked away in the trees and fading into rough, potholed dirt almost immediately. The kind of road only locals know, that's blocked in the winter by the snow. The van rocks back and forth as she navigates down it, her headlights cutting through the dark, making the shadows of the trees stretch in front of her menacingly. She grits her teeth as the plastic dishes rattle out of the cupboards in the tiny kitchen. The van is not built for this—this is the kind of road you need a truck on. The kind of road Chloe grew up on.

But she pushes ahead anyway. Slowing down as much as possible, inching forward like she's in LA traffic. Dawn's starting to streak high enough in the sky that it filters through the canopy of the trees when she has to pump the brakes, the van shuddering to a halt in front of the rushing water ahead.

Mel gets out of the van and walks up to the creek. Or maybe it's more of a river. Whatever it is, it's a body of swiftly moving water, and there's no bridge.

"How the hell did you get across?" Mel asks under her breath, looking to her right and then her left. Her eyes snag on a spot fifty feet down the bank. The foliage is jagged and when she hikes over there and starts to pull it away, she sees why: it's a camo cover, big enough to hide a vehicle, overlaid with branches. Chloe's black truck lies underneath it.

"Fuck," Mel says.

She checks the truck: it's completely empty. She tries to puzzle it out as she replaces the cover, laying the branches back, and then walks over to the creek bed. Did she *swim* across? Mel dips her hand in the water and bites back a groan of displeasure. It's not *freezing*, thank god, but it won't be pleasant.

"There's gotta be a bridge," she says, mostly to convince herself. She traces her steps from Chloe's hiding spot, searching for signs of her. *There.* Footprints in the wet dirt. The bridge has to be upstream.

Mel heads back to her van, shoving her stuff in her backpack and locking the van up before moving out on foot. It's a slog, the crunch of her footsteps and the waking forest a riotous soundtrack to her displeasure as the walk gets longer. Thirty minutes pass. Then an hour. Worry swirls in her chest. Did she follow the wrong set of footprints?

"Oh, your paranoid ass better *not* have laid down a false trail," Mel mutters as she spots another divot in the earth—a heel print. "I am going to *kill* you if you've made me—" She stops abruptly, her eyes snagging on where Chloe's footprints end. And then she swears even louder, her annoyance spiking like a volleyball.

The riverbed narrows ahead, and strung across the length of water is a thick rope, with buoys knotted along it every three feet or so, each end secured to a tree on either side of the bank.

Chloe's version of a bridge.

Mel has done a lot of crazy shit in her life. Some of that shit she willingly tangled herself in, and some of it was against her will. And then she kind of made crazy shit her job, which says a lot about her, she knows. But this?

"Utterly batshit," Mel says. The birds and trees—her only witnesses—don't add anything to the conversation. But if they could, she is sure they'd agree with her.

She eyes the water, pacing back and forth in front of the rope. She's utterly reliant on sheer strength and force of will, and no wonder Chloe is so buff if this is the only way to get to her place.

"I'm going to drown," Mel says, and she hates herself a little that it's not even a question, whether or not she's going in.

She's glad she emailed the tracker link to herself before she left. That means when she drowns and goes missing, Gigi will dig and find Chloe's path mapped and at least have an idea of where Mel went.

She won't let Gigi linger in the wondering. That path is already too well trod with her. Gigi's lost too much. If Mel puts her into a state of wondering and searching again, Gigi's gonna lose her goddamn mind more than she already has.

Her body to bury is the least Mel can give her if everything goes south. Grim? Yes. Realistic? More so.

Mel plunges into the water, her hands gripping the rope as the current tugs at her body. The cold makes her let out a *motherfucker* under her breath, but the river thankfully doesn't take offense. She sloshes forward, each step a fight the deeper she gets. She's up to the middle of her rib cage, teeth starting to chatter as she grabs the next foot of rope and tugs herself forward. The bottom drops off deeply and suddenly—her feet float up and free of the riverbed and she can't get her footing back. Water sloshes into her mouth, choking her as the current drags her body sideways. She pulls herself forward purely by arm strength, her shoulders protesting mightily as she struggles foot by foot, panting. This was definitely the kind of workout Tiffany Parker would pay a trainer three hundred dollars an hour to give her. Maybe Mel will suggest it to her. If she survives.

The opposite bank seems to be getting farther away instead of closer. Mel reaches forward, fingers grasping, her legs dangling and knocking uselessly against each other in the rush of the water. Her right hand slips, losing its hold, and time stops as she's flung into the current, only her left hand gripping the rope. Her bicep and shoulder strain under the pull as she heaves herself forward, slapping her right arm through the water and toward the buoy anchoring the rope, fingers scraping and then finally grabbing.

She yanks herself forward the remaining five feet and throws her body onto the muddy bank. For long minutes, she lies there, breathing hard, the tang of exhaustion and river muck in the back of her throat. When she struggles to her feet and pulls her pack off, she winces as water drips from it. Thankfully, everything inside is still dry.

She checks her phone. Chloe's tracker's stopped. Three miles ahead. Almost a straight line through the trees. Mel searches for a trail but doesn't find one. No footprints, either. But that doesn't mean she didn't go this way.

Mel slings her backpack over her shoulders and squeezes the water out of her ponytail, wishing futilely there was some way to dry her clothes. The chafing is going to be a bitch.

Three miles is nothing, she tells herself. She'll be fine. She'll be there in an hour. Chloe won't be happy about it, but Mel will deal with that later.

She gets twenty feet into the trees when something strikes her cheek, a sharp sting that goes from a prick to *painful* in a second.

"What the—"

Mel stumbles back, her eyes blinking furiously in reaction as wet trickles down her cheek.

Her hand comes up to slap at the sting and she yelps as her finger makes contact with the metal hook stuck in her skin.

"Fuck." Blood drips down her cheek as she yanks her hand free. She prods the fishhook embedded in her cheek tentatively, wincing as it digs deeper with each prod, no matter how gentle. "Oh, *fuck*."

She doesn't keep trying to dig out the hook in her cheek—there's no way she's going to be able to without some tweezers, a mirror, and a few shots of vodka for good measure.

"The not-a-bridge wasn't enough?" she demands to the nearest pine tree. "She had to booby-trap the forest?"

What the hell are you hiding from? Every single move Chloe has made speaks of extreme behavior.

Or extreme danger.

She grabs a stick, three feet long and sturdy, and starts whacking it ahead of her as she walks. She just needs to make sure she doesn't get a hook to the eye.

Mel gets about thirty steps before her makeshift sword snags on clear fishing line Chloe's strung through the trees, the little hooks dangling at eye and groin level for a special puncturing touch.

"You're really guaranteeing a pissed-off assailant, Chlo," Mel mutters, having long given up not talking to herself when she's making her way through unfamiliar, booby-trapped Canadian wilderness. If she didn't stay sharp, Gigi would end up sending the Mounties to save her and would never let her live that down. She'd be getting Mountie-themed birthday gag gifts until she was eighty.

She grabs the knife Chloe left behind in the van and cuts the fishing line free and continues her slow journey forward.

There are four more hook traps to dismantle in the first mile. Every step is a not-so-fun adventure, because as soon as she gets through the hooks and stops encountering them, her mind goes wild with: *What the hell does she have in store for me next?*

Mel steps tentatively forward, still using the branch as a sort of booby-trap detector. She scans ahead, searching for disruptions in the dirt. She can't help but filter through all the known booby-traps she's ever read about. The hook traps are basic. Child's play, really.

Chloe isn't basic. And they haven't been kids for a long time.

This is about surviving. Mel has to keep that in mind. Whatever she's running from, whatever traps Chloe's got set, it's about survival.

That means lethal measures.

She starts walking a lot slower with that thought in mind. Chloe probably couldn't get her hands on the materials to build a land mine, but a steel bear trap—one of those clamper ones with teeth—is a good way to stop someone in their tracks—literally.

Something echoes in the distance—an animal call, maybe? Mel's head jerks toward the right, her ears straining, but there's no other sound.

She taps along the edges of the undergrowth, the piles of leaves and browning pine needles making the path hard to detect. The entire time, she's split between keeping aware of her surroundings and trying really hard not to think of Gigi getting a call about her going missing. The guilt's sharp in her gut, but she has to ignore it. She can't turn back now. Not that she would.

She's all in. She's been all in since the moment Nat told her she'd found Chloe.

You're not happy, kid.

She'd been, once. In the midst of the chaos and the worry and the suspicion, she'd been happy.

She'd been in love and she's stayed in it, even when it put her at risk. Even when she was abandoned. She really didn't know when to leave something well enough alone. She's mired so deep that it's a permanent state. She has brown hair and freckles and bruises like a peach but can take a punch like a boxer and she is forever fucked in love when it comes to Chloe Harper.

Those are the facts. This is her life. Totally pitiful, really.

She steps forward, her mind on her pitifulness and not on the ground.

Big mistake.

Mel stumbles.

Huge mistake.

Her foot punches through the carefully arranged leaves covering the deep hole dug in the ground.

Downright lethal mistake.

8

CHLOE

Chloe didn't have *save Mel from the tiger pit* on her to-do list today. Chloe had a plan. Get home. Get her stuff. Get out.

So when the intruder alarm triggers and her boots hit the ground, she tears out of her cabin and races through the trees.

Fuck you, Mel, she thinks furiously as she sprints. She hops over the two trip wires, nearly misses the third before she rounds the corner. And there Mel is, stepping right toward the goddamn tiger pit.

It wasn't her finest moment, digging the tiger pit. It's an awful way to die. Not that she knows from personal experience, but still. Wooden impalement is pretty medieval.

But you've gotta be kind of medieval out here.

She doesn't even shout—just in case she startles Mel into the pit— she just runs toward her, full speed, her hand outreached.

She snatches the collar of Mel's jacket, yanking her backward just as Mel pitches forward. Mel lets out a shrill scream, half surprise, half *oh shit I'm falling*. The momentum forces them both forward. Exactly what she didn't want.

Chloe plants her feet as they skid toward the edge of the pit that's eight feet deep and, every six inches down, has a five-foot branch sharpened to a killing point embedded in the dirt.

Chloe's really regretting digging the pit now.

"Pull me up!" Mel shouts.

"I'm trying!" Chloe grunts back, throwing her entire body into the movement of hefting them backward. Her shoulders slam into the dirt, Mel sprawled on top of her, shivering either from fear or the fact that she's soaking wet or maybe because she's spread on top of Chloe like a blanket. Maybe all three.

"You are crazy!" Mel spits out. "What the hell are you thinking, building shit like this out in the woods?"

"Me? You had to slap a tracker on me to find me out here!" Chloe says, wriggling out from underneath her because she's not going to get trapped into a *sharing body heat* sort of situation. She's got to guide Mel through the booby traps and then get out of here. Fast.

"What else was I supposed to do?" Mel demands, getting to her feet. She looks over her shoulder at the now-uncovered pit. "You gonna explain why you built a goddamn tiger pit?"

"Nope," Chloe says, making sure to pop the *p* because she knows it annoys her. "Come on. Follow close."

"Does the next pit have *actual* tigers in it?" Mel asks, but she does what Chloe says as they skirt around the pit and start down the path.

"Watch it." Chloe stops her from triggering the first trip wire. Mel looks down, and then her eyes follow the path of the wire, spotting the net of rocks Chloe's rigged. And then she arches her eyebrow at Chloe, but says nothing, which is maddening.

When a woman sets up booby traps, she doesn't expect to be psychoanalyzed because of them. She expects her enemies to trigger them so she can flee.

The silence grows as Mel spots the second trip wire—Chloe doesn't even have to point it out, and by the third, Mel just silently hops over it. And Chloe gets more and more nervous as the quiet stretches and her thoughts spin.

The thing about having an extraordinary mind is that it makes people smart enough to realize they've been outpaced nervous. And Chloe is smart, but Mel has the extraordinary brain. Chloe used to admire it, and then she had to run. So she lived in fear of it, that Mel would put her focus on finding her.

But Mel never looked for her. That first year after Chloe left, when she was in Colorado, she thought she might go insane because the days were so painfully quiet and slow. She thought she knew rural life, but she had known ranch life. A ranch is always busy, there's always something to do, always something happening, there's always an animal making trouble.

Not the same for a cabin high on a mountain and a scared eighteen-year-old with nothing but books to learn from as she tried to survive that first winter and counted down the days until Mel found her or she found a way to come back.

Chloe had been a foolish girl once, wishing someone else would save her. But not anymore. It cost too damn much, being foolish and having hope. She knows the only thing that's left for her is revenge, and she's got a slim chance at it. Not that she's going to stop trying. She's just had to get selective with her attempts through the years as the Dicks rose in power and prestige.

Well—some of them did.

It pleases her how Rick Newell's been denied the pomp and circumstance awarded the rest of his family. Once a black sheep, always a black sheep. But all three of them after her were deadly shitheads, really. Each in their own special way.

It's classic small-town in-fuckery, if you actually zoom out and look at the situation she's found herself in: a drug dealer, a state assemblyman, and a mayoral candidate, all in the same family. All named Richard, because of course they are.

The one thing she knows about the Newell men is that their obsession with finding her is rooted in their obsession with pleasing the Newell family patriarch. Big Daddy rules them all like he's got a magic ring. And the Dicks will do about anything to make him happy.

Including chasing her for six years just because he told them to.

Chloe is forever stumbling into nightmares and having to find a new self in the moment, because what she's learned is there's never an aftermath. There's just another nightmare. The Newells were a whole other level.

But now Mel showing up is the kind of mess Chloe can't contain. She shouldn't be here. Not after all this time.

Why after all these years?

It drifts into her head, a horrible, unbidden thought she banishes as soon as it sputters to life: *Did they get to her? Do they know?*

No. Mel would be dead already if they knew she'd been involved. And she wouldn't work for men like the Bag of Dicks.

Seriously, who names *all* their sons *Richard*? It's so confusing.

"Up here," she says, breaking the silence as they turn the final curve in the path and the cabin comes into view.

This, too, is a skin-crawlingly vulnerable moment. No one's ever been out here. No one's ever seen this cabin, the one she built with her own hands.

"Come on," she says. "You're hurt."

Mel reaches up absently, touching the fishhook in her cheek like she's forgotten it's there. She always could power through pain. Every time Chloe thought of the *why* behind that, her fists would curl, a skin-biting clench that was entirely rage.

Mel had shown up at the archery range once, half of her face bruised and not even covered with makeup and she'd tried to make an excuse, *I fell*, and Chloe had been ready to take her bow and arrow and march down to the trailer park and kill Mel's dad. The only thing that stopped her was the fact that she wouldn't get away with it a second time. She wasn't that lucky.

She learned later that she was wrong about that. Pity she didn't learn on Bob.

She walks up to the cabin door and pushes it open, letting her step inside. Mel's still quiet, but Chloe can feel it: the almost hum of her mind putting pieces together.

"Nice place," Mel says finally, turning in a slow circle as she takes in the one-room cabin. The little corner kitchen that's mostly a tiny fridge and toaster oven. The couch she made out of pallets and cushions rammed against the other wall near the woodstove. The tiny bed with the quilt that Peggy made Chloe—the reason she'd come back, because she didn't want to leave it behind. Peggy had always been so nice to her and look at where that sentimentality got Chloe. Stuck in a cabin in the woods with the girl who . . . no, woman, she was a woman now.

Girl. Woman. She was still Chloe's biggest weakness. Still the most brilliant person Chloe knew.

She was very screwed here. And not in any of the good ways.

Mel stares at the bed and Chloe's cheeks heat. She used to dream about what it would be like to sleep beside her. Mel always ran so hot. Would they need separate blankets or would Mel's heat envelop her, cradling her into sleep as much as her body did?

She never got the answer. She never did get to sleep next to her. There was the one time they fell asleep in the hayloft and Whitney almost caught them. But there weren't any linen comforters or crisp sheets or endless pillows or a big bed—all the things that Mel deserved—the soft, safe, and good things Chloe so desperately wanted to give her back then and couldn't.

Her eyes rove over Mel's face in the light, trying to absorb all the differences. She's got crinkles near her eyes Chloe's never seen and when she straightens, her necklace falls out from where it's been tucked under her shirt. Chloe's breath hitches, a painful inhale when she sees the gold acorn pendant swinging from the delicate chain. She'd know that necklace anywhere. Whitney and Gigi never took them off. Their dad had gotten them made special, so there are only two in the world.

She clears her throat, unable to ask if it's Whitney's. Not wanting to go down that road. Too painful. Too dangerous. She goes over to the kitchen cupboard and grabs the first-aid kit. "If you sit down, I can . . ." She trails off and gestures to Mel's face.

"You gonna tell me the reason behind all the traps?"

"You gonna let me take that fishhook out of your pretty face?"

Mel opens her mouth to snap back, but it digs the hook farther into her cheek. She winces and Chloe's had enough.

She never could stand watching her get hurt.

"Maybe I want a cool scar," Mel mutters as she sits down on the couch and crosses her arms, grumpy and ruffled and a little bloody and it's so viscerally familiar Chloe almost stumbles on her way over.

She sits down across from her, cross-legged, and she's careful to not let their knees touch.

"Well, you're probably gonna get a scar, so stay still." She pulls the clippers out of the kit and clips the first barb of the hook so she can start to pull it free.

"Done this a lot?" Mel asks as Chloe clips the second barb free.

"I fish a lot."

"I can smell that."

She shouldn't laugh, but she almost does. It's like no time has passed. How is that possible when years yawn between them, all that time they've missed?

She'd been telling herself for years it was trauma that bonded them. It was her mantra. It was trauma, it wasn't anything else. The secrets. A night that only they knew the truth of. That would bond anyone.

That would break anyone.

But they'd never actually broken. Chloe had just left. And it hadn't faded. It hadn't even needed to roar back to life the second she saw Mel in the van, armed with that pillow and a scowl.

It was always present, burning in her chest, the knowledge that she'd touched God and soulmates and whatever else you want to call that thing that sizzles between two people so hot it marks them for good.

She just got excellent at pushing it down and now she kind of can't because Mel's right in front of her.

Her hand settles on Mel's face, cupping under her chin. She clips the final barb free and the sharp piece of metal falls into the cup of her palm, stinging her skin.

She sets the barbs to the side, grabbing the tweezers. She has to lean forward then, and their knees brush, and it shouldn't mean anything. But it does.

"You're freezing," Chloe says.

"You gonna just keep stating the obvious?"

Chloe twists the de-barbed hook expertly out of her cheek as Mel scowls at her.

"Ouch! Give me a warning next time."

"Hopefully there won't be a next time. Since you're leaving."

She should pull away. But instead she leans forward even more on the word *leaving*, like her body can't stand the thought.

Mel bites down on her lower lip when Chloe presses a wad of gauze against her cheek and holds it there, even when Mel's hand comes up to hold the gauze herself, their fingers tangling.

Then it's skin against skin and then Chloe's just as lost again, because how long has it been since someone's touched her?

"Are you hurt anywhere else?" Chloe doesn't know why she's whispering. Her words brush against Mel's cheek, and then her breath does, when Mel takes her free hand and places it right over her heart.

"You broke this," is what she says, and Chloe's fingers curl into a fist, involuntary, such a betrayal of her body, and she can *feel* it, the way Mel's heart picks up against her hand. Against the mutual pain.

"Drama queen," Chloe drawls, trying to lighten it.

But Mel refuses. Stares her down. "Doesn't mean it's not the truth."

Chloe had been strong for a long time. She'd been weak in the van. She can't be again. But she can't pull away. And Mel doesn't move. She just breathes against Chloe, practically in her lap on the couch.

"Are you coming back with me?" Mel prods, because she can't let go of anything.

"I told you—"

Mel takes her hand, the one over her heart. She holds it for a long moment in both of hers and then she brushes a kiss across Chloe's knuckles.

It's a cold shock of horror when Mel's eyes rise and there's pity in them.

"You haven't thought this through," she says gently. "Ask me why your parents sent me," Mel says, and fear builds in Chloe's throat, choking her, threatening to spew forth like black bile, some pure sci-fi shit, that's how toxic it feels bubbling inside her because she *knows*.

Maybe she's known since the second she saw it was Mel instead of one of Rick's minions and she just hid it from herself.

Her hand twists in Mel's until it's her gripping Mel instead of Mel holding her. Mel stares at Chloe and there's so much sadness in her sienna eyes that Chloe just says it. So it'll be real, just to get it over with.

"Who's been killed?" she blurts out. "Is it Gigi or Olivia?"

Mel blinks, her gaze shifting from steady to puzzled in a split second and Chloe jerks back, away from her, off the couch in a burst.

"Killed . . . what are you talking about?"

Chloe swallows convulsively, the dread churning together with a horrible hope. "You said my parents sent you. So they're not dead. And you're here. So you're not dead. That leaves my sister or Gigi. You're wearing the acorn necklace. That belongs to one of the twins. What happened to Gigi?"

Mel touches the pendant around her neck, staring at her like she's lost the plot, which makes hope spear through the horror even more and she can't . . . she can't hope.

"It's not Gigi's," she says. "Do you . . ." She stops. "Gigi's fine. Your sister is fine. Whitney . . ."

She doesn't seem to be able to finish. She doesn't need to.

The relief almost buckles her knees. But she can't give in to it. Not without the full story.

"I know about Whitney," Chloe says, because it just hangs there, the terrible unspoken truth. "If everyone at home is okay . . . why are you here?" She said something about investigators. Had she figured it out herself? Did she know?

"Your dad is sick," Mel says. "He has cancer. He wants to see you."

At first, the words don't make sense, because she's been poised for an entirely different reality. And then they catch up and her eyes tear up and she's suddenly fucked up in a way she's not prepared for.

"Cancer," Chloe says. "He has cancer." She breathes out, a sound that isn't a laugh and isn't a sob, but some horrible twist of both. It digs in her chest like catching your hand in razor wire. He hasn't been murdered but he has cancer and wow, does the universe really have a terrible sense of humor. She leaves so everyone will be safe and look! No one's safe, Chlo! Not from their own damned cells.

She's so angry her breath catches in her lungs, refusing to expel. She's choking on the fury. She wants to shoot something. Preferably a cancerous cell. Which she knows is not actually possible, but she couldn't give a fuck right now.

"Is he . . . is he dying?" Chloe hears herself ask. Her voice doesn't sound like hers. It's all high-pitched and tinny. Panicked. She doesn't get panicked anymore.

Living in the wilderness, panic will kill you, every time.

"He didn't respond to the last round of chemo," Mel says, trying to make it gentle, but you can't make that gentle. "He doesn't want to do another."

"He wants to die at home on the land," Chloe says dully. "I bet Mom and Olivia are driving him crazy, finding all these medical trials for him to do."

"That sounds like what he told my boss," Mel says.

It's two against one. That's what Chloe's left him to. He used to joke that it always balanced out in family decisions: that Olivia took Mom's side and Chloe took his and so they could never actually decide anything and always had to find a compromise. She broke all that when she left. But she had to. If her father knew the Newells were involved . . .

If Rick Newell had gotten to Mel. If he *ever* found out about Mel . . .

Well, she already knows what the Newells will do. They already tried it once, when they thought they found her accomplice. There had been so much blood. She never knew how much blood one person could hold. It's so abstract until you're covered in it.

She presses her hand against her chest, trying to calm the pounding in her heart. The regret and bloody memories.

"He loves you, Chloe," Mel says, like Chloe needs the reminder. "He's scared and he's got maybe a few months and take it from me, they'll go by like that." She snaps her fingers. "There's a private plane waiting. All you have to do is get on it. I will drive you to the ranch myself when we get off the plane. I will make sure you're safe. Even if you saw him for five minutes—" She stops. "You'll regret it if you don't," she says, a blunt weapon of a girl grown into a battering ram of a woman. "That's the truth and that's all I've got. You'll regret it so much it'll eat you alive."

"I've learned to live with those kinds of regrets," Chloe says.

"This will kill you," Mel says with such faith that Chloe searches her face for the answer behind that assurance.

"You lost someone," she says in slow realization.

"I've lost a lot of people," Mel says. "Starting with you. Are you going to lose your father without saying goodbye?"

Chloe doesn't say anything. She wishes there was a tiger pit between them and no way to cross it. She wants to run. From this knowledge. From the grief. From this girl she lóved who's a woman now, standing here and offering things when she doesn't understand the risk, but she can't.

"Are you coming home with me?" Mel demands. "Simple question, easy answer."

It's not, though.

No means safety but heartbreak because Mel is right. She can't live with herself, not saying goodbye.

But if she crosses that town line, she's never going to leave Harper's Bluff alive.

"Yes or no," Mel says.

Chloe could never say no to her.

That's the problem.

That's why she ran.

"Yes," she says.

9

CHLOE

EIGHT MONTHS BEFORE CHLOE'S SWEET SIXTEEN PARTY

For almost sixteen years, Chloe was a princess in a tower—or in her case, a princess in a ranch at the bottom of a mountain—with roots so deep the town ten miles north is named after her family.

She was protected. She was privileged. Loved. Cared for. Coddled.

She was never hungry or worried for more than a few days and the only time she was really scared was when she was little and thought monsters lived in the old barn or when she was thrown from her horse.

For a long time, Chloe believed in right and wrong. That good triumphed over evil. She thought justice was meted out through courts with lawyers arguing passionately and the bad guys always going away.

She believed her father was the strongest, most honest man who ever lived and that someday, if faced with true evil, she would be just as righteous.

It happened on a Sunday morning. She runs every morning, even on Sundays. She gets up early so she can go before church. Usually, she runs on the land, down the long roads and paths that weave through the foothills of her family's land.

But that day, her mother had left a note on the fridge: *Please pick up some milk at the store before church!*

So she'd jogged south and out the ranch gates instead, toward the general store. It would only add an extra mile, after all.

It had been beautiful—blue skies, the smell of hay and a smudge of woodsmoke. It was getting colder at night and it was cheaper to fell a tree or two and season the wood than pay for the propane.

She loves this stretch of road. It's the one she's driven down most days of her life, toward school, toward town, toward the valley that lies below the mountain the ranch nestles at the base of. Yellow grass, dotted brown with cows and green with scrub oaks, rolling hills, the jut of mountains beyond.

It's home.

It had been so ordinary—her feet pounding on the pavement, her mind and body aligned. The only thought in her head was maybe she'd get a candy bar when she picked up the milk for Mom. Her foot slips in her shoe and when she glances down, she sees her laces are loose.

She walks a few steps farther away from the road and bends down to fix them before she hits the curve around the hill. She can hear the sound of a truck coming up the road behind her, she doesn't really pay it any mind.

Chloe's still bent when the truck passes by her. She sees it out of the corner of her eye. Silver . . . or maybe gray . . . she'll curse herself later for not noticing. For not memorizing every detail. All she really thinks is *wow, that guy's going fast* as he disappears around the curve.

There's a *screech*. Brakes hit too fast. The sound of rubber against road. A horrible *thud* that Chloe can't place, but sends shivers down her spine.

She's running without even thinking it through. Her body reacts. Like it knows because her princess mind can't imagine yet.

Yet.

The incline makes her thighs burn as she sprints, she crests the top as she hears the truck take off, speeding away with a squeal. She makes the turn just in time to see it disappear around the next curve, silver or gray, maybe an American make. Was that an *I* or a *J* or a *1* on the license plate? She's too far and then her eyes snag on the bottle of orange juice on the side of the road and then they lie on the little hand the bottle belonged in, barely visible in the tall grass.

And then she's screaming and running toward the kid that truck just hit.

She's not in her body, she's down on the ground, she's babbling, her hands scramble, there's so much blood. The boy is maybe nine or ten and she knows him, *she knows him*, he's the Hendersons' grandson and she can't remember his name, oh no, what's his name?

She can't ask, there's blood everywhere, he's dying, she knows it, she doesn't understand how, but she does. His brown eyes are roving up at the sky, trying to fix on something and then her face is there and his eyes meet hers.

"I'm here," she says. Her hand lies over his on the ground. She's so afraid to touch him anywhere else. "I'm gonna get help," she promises.

But it's too late.

She is a country girl. Death is not a stranger.

But murder is.

He is so small. And he is gone so fast.

Part II

THE PARTY

10

MEL

"I need to pack," Chloe says, and without another word, goes to her bed and the tiny chest of drawers tucked next to it.

Mel is content to watch her from the couch. There's part of her that marvels at it—that they're in the same space. Chloe moves around the one-room cabin like she's mapped every inch of it for security and practicality.

There's a knife stuck in between the couch cushions. Mel would bet the entire PI firm that there's another tucked under her mattress. One of her bows is hung on hooks by the door, but she's got to have more. It's always been her weapon of choice.

The cabin is sparse on the decoration side, but there are touches here and there that make her stomach clench with regret and realization.

"You know, this is the first time I've ever been in your bedroom," Mel says.

Chloe's hands still, a worn T-shirt in her grip. "I guess that's true."

Mel doesn't have to guess. It is. She'd visit Chloe at her little archery range on the back forty of her parents' land. In the summer they'd meet late at night at the park under the bridge, and in the winter in the car that Chloe's father got to replace the BMW they'd pushed off the bluffs.

Mel couldn't be with Chloe in public. In front of Chloe's parents or friends. She couldn't be anywhere near her house. The archery range was already risking it.

As far as anyone was concerned, they barely knew each other.

But they knew all of each other. Deeper than you usually get with another person, even someone you love. There is something about surviving with someone.

Now she's twenty-four and she's finally in Chloe's room. Well, her cabin. Dimly lit by exactly two lamps plugged into extension cords. She's running on generators out here. No power lines. It must get cold in the winter.

But she's made it cozy. There's a quilt on her bed, handmade, and there's a brass figure of a bird, which is the only thing she picks up from the rough-hewn mantel and puts in her rucksack and Mel's brain goes *that's from home*.

God, nothing is right. Mel wants to push her up against one of the walls she built and pour all her frustration into her and she *can't*, she absolutely can't.

She really wants to.

"How long have you been here?" Mel asks as Chloe continues to shove things into a rucksack.

"In Canada or in this cabin?"

"Both."

"I've been here for almost three years. Built the cabin the first year."

"You built this?"

"I planned on staying here for good. But you've fucked that plan up. Anyway, butt and pass cabins are pretty simple once you learn. People have been making them for hundreds of years. It's like playing with real-life Lincoln Logs," Chloe says, and Mel can't tell if she's joking or actually serious. She's not sure of this new Chloe. How much has changed.

What she is sure of is that she's taking Chloe away from her home and Chloe's acting like it's for good. And Mel's under no delusion that Chloe's staying long in Harper's Bluff.

She's gonna run again. The thought sends alarm bells ringing in her head and sickens her heart.

"How have I fucked your plan exactly?"

"Not getting into it. You just have. You said you used the plane, right?"

"Is someone tracking your parents' plane to find you?" Mel asks. That's one of the first things she would do: look at all the Harpers' flight records and see where they were flying.

"Not getting into it."

"Have you done something illegal?"

Chloe draws her rucksack closed and looks over her shoulder at Mel with such irony that Mel flushes.

"If you tell me what you're hiding from, I can help you—"

"I don't want your help." It comes out so fierce that it startles them both and Mel gets up off the couch.

"Don't," Chloe protests, but it's so weak and Mel keeps moving toward her until the back of Chloe's knees hit the bed. It's not like Chloe's Lincoln Log cabin is very large. It's just a big room.

"Why don't you want my help?"

"This has nothing to do with you. I did do something illegal. I'm on the lam, as they say."

"Is that what they say."

"Well, it's what I say." Chloe's chin juts out, pure stubbornness and it's so familiar and so long-lost to Mel at the same time. She wants to hold it in her palm like a child cups a tadpole in a stream, trying to grasp on to something determined to wriggle free.

"What'd you do?"

"You were right before," Chloe says. "I am growing weed. It's just far away from the cabin. I've gotten into a disagreement with the men who move my product."

It's entirely unconvincing and they both know it.

"Mm-hmm," Mel says. "And how big is this weed field? How far? Because it's height of summer, which means I should be able to get a big ol' whiff of something. It's not like I don't know what a grow smells like, Chloe. I grew up in the dirty 530 with you, remember?"

"Mel," she says, begging, but Mel's not having any of it.

"This isn't about some drug dispute. Don't insult my intelligence. You've been running from something since you left home. Running from me, from your parents, from our entire town. That's what I thought, at least."

"Just keep thinking that," Chloe says.

"Now I'm starting to think you ran to protect all that."

"I'm not doing this with you," Chloe says, grabbing her pack from the bed. "I'm ready. Are you?"

"You could tell me," Mel says. "I'm good at what I do. I found you, didn't I?" A little white lie couldn't hurt in this instance.

"*I* found *you*," Chloe corrects.

"In the campground? That doesn't count," Mel says, outraged. "You didn't even know it was me! You thought it was someone coming to kill you. So why don't you tell me about that. About who would be sending people to kill you."

"Let's go," Chloe says. "We've got to avoid all the traps and cross the creek."

"Please tell me there's another way out of here," Mel says. "There has to be. How else did you get this stuff up here?"

"There was, but the road washed out last year," Chloe says. "We're going the way you came in."

"Your not-a-bridge is batshit," Mel tells her. "I almost got sucked into the creek."

"You would've been fine," Chloe says. "There's a few boulders about half a mile down that you would've slammed into."

"How are we gonna get this across?" Mel asks, nodding to the bag.

"There's a pulley system a ways down," Chloe says. "I'm surprised you didn't notice."

"I was a little busy trying not to drown, getting a fishhook in my face, and cursing your name," Mel answers.

Her mouth quirks up, just for a second, but Mel notices. That hot thrill inside her is like a memory faded, crackling to life again. They need to get out of this cabin before she goes all weak and soft and does something she probably won't actually regret, like kissing her.

She has very few regrets when it comes to Chloe Harper. That's the problem with being in close proximity with her.

"I bet you got a cherry of a deal on this land," Mel mutters, and follows her out into the daylight. "Sorry I fucked it up."

"I forgive you," Chloe says, and Mel has to duck her head so Chloe doesn't see her smile, because it's real, not sarcastic or edgy or any of the things she needs to be with her.

You can't trust her, Gigi had reminded her before she got on the road.

Mel's got to hold on to that.

Otherwise, *she's* fucked.

11

RICK

SIX HOURS BEFORE THE PLANE CRASH

They come in the mornings. He's started getting up at the ass-crack of dawn to observe the enemy. Most of the time it's just yellow grass, the heat starting to shimmer on the horizon as the sun rises. But just as you start to relax, they spring forth like the earth opened up and spat them out.

Can't even get down the road to the gate without them trying to cause trouble these days. Rick will never forgive the Baylors who live five miles down the road for thinking that peacocks were good live-stock to raise. A few of them got free about eight years ago and the en-tire gaggle have bred and spread up and down this stretch of the bluffs.

Feral birds are a fucking menace, and Rick knows menaces: he is one.

Sometimes he thinks about setting a fire and running the entire gang of them off the bluffs just to be done with them, but that's a bit extreme, even for him. He can control a lot of things, but he's not dumb shit enough to think he can control fire.

Target practice it is. Only problem is that they've gotten smart. Their leader outthinks the rest of them but the idiot birds follow her lead. Doris, Vinny's named her. He says she looks like one and Rick can't disagree there. She does. Mean little bitch of a bird. If he gets her, the entire pack falls apart. He's sure of it.

He's coming down the road right now, Vinny is. So Rick grabs his shotgun and goes out on the porch, waiting for them to show themselves.

They can't seem to resist Vinny. He's great bait. It's like they recognize the threat of him and know if they take him down, their real target—Rick—is more vulnerable. Vin is his muscle, after all. And loyal as fuck, which is important, after the shitshow that was Toby Dunne.

Movement along the ridge, he spots it through the dust Vin's kicking up. The ungodly screeches send shivers through him. Fucking hell creatures, peacocks.

"Come on," he mutters, eyes fixed on the dust cloud.

There she is: *Doris.* Clamoring through the dust cloud, her white belly like a bull's-eye. Rick lifts his gun, swearing when he realizes Vin's in range still.

"Get out of the way," he yells, and then he shoots anyway. Vin jerks the wheel of the golf cart, but Rick aims too high. It misses her and sends her scattering back to the volcanic boulders they've claimed as their roost.

God, he's getting too fucking soft, but he didn't want to hit Vin.

"Did you have to shoot at me?" Vinny demands as he pulls up to the steps, turning off the cart and stalking up them.

"You got in my way," Rick says, holding the door open for him. "Fucking Doris."

"She's crazy," Vin agrees, heading to the living room that Rick's turned into his office of sorts. Better view of the birds' roost than the back bedroom he was using.

"News?" Rick asks.

Vinny grins. "Just got the call from my guy at the airport. The PI the Harpers sent to get Chloe must've found her. She just called the service to get the plane ready."

Rick's entire chest feels like a beer can squeezed too hard. It's been so long, trying to get her. Chasing after that dumb bitch who wasn't actually dumb, damn it. "Harper's on her way to the hangar?"

"She should be there in about an hour."

Goddamn, he can barely believe it. After all this time.

He's gonna find out where they are. Everything will be okay. Perfect, even. Big Daddy will finally see: it was Rick all along that should've been leading this family after him. Not Richard. And if he doesn't . . .

Well, Rick will have the leverage to *make* him see. Ten million dollars' worth. No more heroin. No more carving out airstrips in the middle of nowhere.

It'll be cool and easy from here on out.

He just needs to get his hands on Chloe Harper.

"Your guy, you got him the drugs?" Rick asks.

Vinny nods. "It's all taken care of. They're paid off. They'll fake some radio problems over the Cascades and land on the strip. Sean will take them off the plane and wait for you."

"She can't be conscious," Rick says. He learned quickly that Chloe Harper would take advantage of every situation. The only way to win with her was to knock her the fuck out and pray she hadn't had the prescience to build up a tolerance to tranquilizers.

"I know," Vinny says grimly, and Rick supposes he does. He is the one Harper tried to shoot in Montana last year. The fact that she missed surprises him to this day.

"Fuck, if this works, it'll finally be done," Rick says.

"Been a long time," Vinny agrees.

Rick grins, settling back on the couch, closing his eyes. He begins to hum.

We're in the money . . .

12

MEL

The plane's not ready when they get there. Mel tries to hide her annoyance as she deals with the apologetic pilot and Chloe paces circles in the hangar like she can't stand being close to even a handful of strangers.

There's something a little wild about the way her eyes rove around a place the second they get inside. She moves jerkily, like she's used to the wilderness, not paved streets and fluorescent lights. There's a particular sensitivity to sounds. Which makes sense, if she spent most of her time in that cabin alone.

"You okay?" Mel asks, going up to her.

Chloe nods.

"Okay, well, I've got to call Gigi before we take off."

Chloe shoots her a puzzled look. "Wait . . . you're not talking about *my* Gigi?"

"She's *my* Gigi now," Mel says.

"You and Gigi are friends?"

"We work together."

"Gigi's a private investigator?"

"Part-time office manager and researcher," Mel says. "I've been on her to get her license, but she spends most of her time at the paper with her mom."

"I'm . . ." Chloe trails off. "Flabbergasted."

Mel can't stop the harsh laugh. "Yeah, well, getting left behind does things to a person. I'm different, so is Gigi. Honestly, I don't know what I'd do without her. At work or just in life. I know my apartment wouldn't be decorated worth shit."

"You let her decorate? Oh, that must've made her so happy."

"Ecstatic. She was deeply offended by the bookcase I made out of two-by-fours and cinder blocks," Mel says. "I even have those blankets that are just for putting on your lap when you sit on the couch now."

"Luxury," Chloe says, and when Mel's head snaps toward her, she reassures her: "I'm not joking. I'm different, too, you know."

"I know," Mel says. "The girl I knew wouldn't have left without an explanation." She shrugs, trying to shake off the hurt. "That girl would've stayed and fought whatever was coming for her."

"That girl . . . she didn't know what I know," Chloe says simply.

"Gonna stay keeping me in the dark, too?" Mel asks.

Chloe swallows.

"Once we're in the air, you can't get away from the questions."

"After lunch," Chloe promises.

Mel contemplates her, wondering if she means it. "I'll hold you to that."

Something—someone—drove her away from Harper's Bluff and out into the wilds. All she has to do is wait until after lunch to get the answer out of Chloe—and she will get an answer. It's the perfect situation: Chloe trapped with her in a plane for a few hours will help her sort this all out. She won't be able to hold strong for longer than that. Mel will get the truth out of her. Finally.

Cheered by this thought, she goes over to finish her conversation with the pilot and, keeping one eye on Chloe, she gets her phone out and pulls up her recent calls.

Gigi answers on the second ring. "It's about time you called me. I was about to contact the Mounties."

"I guess I dodged that bullet," Mel mutters, thinking of all the Mountie-themed gag gifts she won't have to deal with.

"What?"

"Nothing. I'm at the airport."

"The airport," Gigi repeats. "Did you . . . she showed up, didn't she?"

Mel's silence is the answer. She hates it when her silence is the answer.

"Did she try to stab you or seduce you?" Gigi asks.

A little bit of both?

"Don't be ridiculous," Mel says instead of saying *Yeah, Gigi, you totally nailed it. Ten points.*

"Are you okay? Did you fall apart? Do I need to come up there? I will come up there right now. I've got my bags packed just in case."

"Great to know you trusted me to handle this."

"Is she okay?"

"She's different," Mel says.

"Different how?"

"She's taken rustic to a whole other level," Mel says. "But I got her to agree to come home. We'll be able to close the job and collect our fee in less than twenty-four hours and then we never have to talk about Chloe Harper again."

"It's cute that you think that's the end result of all this," Gigi says. "Tell me what really happened. You're being deliberately vague."

"I'm giving you the CliffsNotes before I get on the plane and don't have service," Mel says patiently. "You can let the Harpers know we're departing within the hour. That'll put us touching down around four. Everything will be in my report when I get back. You can get all the nitty-gritty details then."

"Mel," Gigi protests.

"I've really got to go," Mel says hurriedly as the flight attendant approaches her. "I still need to speak with the crew."

"Ms. Tillman, there's some forms I need you to sign," the attendant says.

"Sure," Mel says, setting her phone down on the little kiosk and following her. It takes a few minutes, and when she gets back, Chloe's holding her phone, looking at it like it's the Muppet version of the Ghost of Christmas Past.

"What are you doing?" Mel asks.

"It was ringing. I answered it."

Mel has to quell her annoyance. She tries to remind herself that Chloe's been living like a wild woman in the woods for years. Manners are not in the forefront of her mind. "Who was it?" She takes her phone and sees Gigi had called back. "Oh shit."

"I didn't—" Chloe starts, but she runs out of steam. She stares up at the ceiling of the airplane hangar. Mel wishes she could search her face to see what she's feeling, but she can also kind of guess here.

"Christ," Chloe says. "This is gonna suck, isn't it?"

"More than anything. Plus the whole mysterious-danger factor you're not letting me in on."

"You said—"

"—I'd leave off until lunch. I am. I am. Consider me chastised."

"You're so sulky when you don't get your way," she mutters.

"Says the woman who answered *my* phone and talked to *my* best friend."

"She was my best friend first."

"Now who's sulky. That was a long time ago."

"Yeah, I know," Chloe says, in such a bitter, lost way that Mel's half tempted to call Gigi and ask what they talked about.

She'll find out when she gets back into town, she's sure. Or she'll touch down to a flurry of texts detailing the entire conversation because Gigi couldn't wait to be face-to-face. Either way, she can wait until then.

"Are you all ready?" she asks as the flight attendant takes the suitcase and Chloe's bag.

"Hey, not that," Chloe says, grabbing the backpack as the flight attendant moves toward it. "That's mine."

"I can't just stow it—?" the attendant starts to say.

"It stays with me," Chloe insists.

"What've you got, the Harper family jewels in there or something?" Mel asks.

"Something like that," Chloe says.

"Fine, come on." Mel waves toward the stairs.

Chloe arches an eyebrow. "I have to go first? Just to make sure I don't bolt, huh?"

"I don't think you'd get very far on the runway," Mel says. "You go first because you're the client," Mel continues maddeningly. "It's the polite thing."

"My father is your client. I'm the lost calf you were sent to fetch."

"More like a runaway calf. And you're lucky I didn't have to rope you down," Mel mutters. "Come on. Stop being so stubborn."

"I hope he paid you a lot," Chloe calls, but she marches up the stairs and disappears into the jet, much to Mel's relief.

"I'm definitely asking for a bonus," Mel says as she follows her.

13

MEL

It starts out as a normal Saturday. She had spent the day hauling junk for one of the ranchers—sweaty, long hours, but the cash he gave her would add nicely to the wad she's got stashed in her tampon box, away from prying eyes. Even her father won't go there.

It's afternoon by the time she gets to the park. She stopped at home to change and shower, which makes it even later than her usual time. She picks up Burger Barn as a treat for him and later it'll haunt her— *What if the line had been longer? What if she'd been too late?*

Mel parks in her normal spot, waving to Mrs. Benson who's doing her normal laps around the trail, but she doesn't stop to talk. She wants to make sure Ted gets his food while it's still somewhat hot.

Someday, they're going to be able to eat at a table that's not a picnic table. One that's in their own place. It's all she wants and she's thinking about how much more money she can add to the tampon box if she does another two months of hauling work. Buying her truck and building the trailer-tow from an old boat trailer and scrap wood was one of the smartest things she's ever done. The junk hauling pays more than she'd get working at Burger Barn.

She takes a left turn off the concrete track that loops around the greenbelt, where the ground bleeds into a narrow trail through the thick river brush. She trudges through the underbrush, thinking that she needs to bring her clippers out to cut back the blackberry bushes again when she hears a sharp, yipping bark. The kind a hurt dog makes.

"Marigold!" Mel picks up the pace, but gets caught in the damn blackberry vines. Fuck that horticulturist guy who got it into his head to plant berry bushes everywhere on the West Coast so they became invasive as hell. She hates that guy, even if she loves blackberries. She's still untangling herself when Marigold comes breaking through the brush and loping toward Mel, the leash trailing behind her.

Ted never lets Marigold off her leash. She yanks herself free of the blackberries, gouging her leg in the process just as Marigold reaches her.

When she crouches down, she can see the dog's panting in distress. Reaching out to calm her, Mel frowns when her hand comes away damp. And then she's up and yelling when she sees her skin's stained red and Marigold's not wounded.

"Ted! Teddy!" She tears down the trail, her feet hitting the smooth dirt gracelessly as she sprints through snagging brambles, punching through them with force to get to his campsite tucked in the hollow by the river. It's a good spot. Close enough to the water to cool the space during the heat of the day, far enough from the trail and the deputy's regular route when they come rousting. It must have not been a good spot today, oh god, what's happened to him?

She crashes into his campsite, yelling his name. She only has seconds to take it in: the broken tent poles, the stuff strewn about, the pan Ted uses to heat food up scattered next to his prone body, shining dark with—

—oh shit, that's her brother's blood. The realization hits her so hard that saliva rushes into her mouth and she has to turn and vomit into the dirt. It only takes a second, mercifully, because she can't focus on being sick.

It's like moving through cement. She knows she's rushing toward him, calling his name, she *knows* she's moving faster than she feels. He's so bloody.

"Ted? Ted, talk to me," she says, trying to see where the blood's coming from. It's his head, right? She thinks it's his head. That's bad. Or maybe not. Maybe it's just a cut.

Her eyes settle on the cast iron pan.

It's not just a cut. Someone beat him.

She takes a deep breath. "Teddy?" She wriggles her hands under his shoulders and lifts him up. That does it. He begins to cough. He coughs *blood*, which is terrifying, but he's breathing. That's what coughing means. Kind of.

"Mellie?" He blinks up at her, bewildered. "No. Get out of here. He'll come back."

"Who?"

"I wasn't using," Ted says. "I promise."

That hadn't occurred to her. Should it have? Her father would be laughing at how naive she is. She's not, though. She's too observant to be. She'd know if he was using. She'd notice, like she did when she was little. There were no signs. No triggers he couldn't deal with. He was doing good. She trusts him because he's given her reason to.

And now he's bleeding all over her, oh god, she's got to get him to the car.

"We've got to get up," she insists. "Get you to the hospital. Come on."

"I wasn't using. I told him I didn't want to buy. I don't know why it made him so angry."

"Who?"

"Guy I used to buy from. Toby someone."

"Toby Dunne?"

"That's him."

She loops her arms under his and lifts him, biting the inside of her cheek to keep from crying out when he yells, a cracked sound of pain that shudders through his skin into hers.

"Come on, just down the trail," she says, looping her arm around him, taking on his weight as they stumble down the path. "Just to the car and then the hospital and then I'm gonna go fuck Toby up."

"You don't want to mess with him," Ted protests. "He works for dangerous people."

Mel could give a fuck, but she doesn't say it as she pants under his weight, focusing on her feet. Her abs burn as they make it to the concrete track loop. She casts a nervous look over her shoulder, but Mrs. Benson has finished her workout, leaving Miller Park quiet for the night. Thank god. Mrs. Benson would definitely call the sheriff.

She gets him and Marigold in the truck. He's bleeding all over the bench seat. She's never driven so fast in her life. The hospital is on the other side of town and he goes quiet—all she has is his ragged breathing to tell her he's still alive.

Screeching into the parking lot, she almost takes out the ambulance parked in the bay, she pulls right up to the sliding doors. An orderly catches sight of her covered in Ted's blood and comes running.

"He's hurt," Mel says as the orderly rushes to him. "Help him. Please."

She keeps standing there, as the orderly shouts and more people stream out. They get Ted on a gurney and push him through the doors and away. Her knees want to buckle, but she can't. She's got to stay steady.

She's got to find that fucker Toby Dunne and kill him.

14

MEL

They get into the air smoothly. The Harper family jet is a time-share with three other families. The things you learn, working for rich people. But it's nice, plush ivory seats and gold carpet and actual dinnerware. On the trip over, the food had been the opposite of airplane dreck.

Mel chews a piece of gum to help her ears pop as the attendant bustles around in the front of the cabin, only visible through a slight gap in the curtain.

Chloe chose the seat across the aisle, so Mel swivels her chair to get a good look at her. Chloe doesn't glance up from the tattered paperback she pulled out of her pack before takeoff, she just says, "You promised: not until after we eat."

Mel tries not to deflate. "I could ask her to serve the food early," she threatens.

Chloe turns a dog-eared page. "You won't," she says. The book's cover is so creased and worn Mel can't make out the image clearly.

"What's the book?" Mel asks, instead.

"Just something silly," Chloe says, putting it away before Mel can get a better look at the spine. "Tell me what's been happening since I was gone."

"Seriously?"

Chloe shrugs. "What else do we have to talk about?"

Mel just lets the silence sit there and Chloe rolls her eyes.

"Fine," Mel says, unable to wait Chloe out. "Burger Barn opened a second location. There's a Starbucks near the 5's on-ramp now. Oh, and Harper Bluff's prodigal daughter disappeared on everyone and didn't come back for six years. Wanna tell me more about that?"

"If anyone is the prodigal daughter, it's Olivia," Chloe says. She chews on her thumbnail, like she's trying to fight the urge, but she ends up asking anyway: "Do you know how she is?"

"Gigi talks about her sometimes. I think they get coffee when Olivia's in town. She works in Chico. I think she's a lawyer. You have a niece."

"I know," Chloe says. "Adrienne. After our grandmother."

"She'll be happy to meet you," Mel says.

"Oh no, I can't—" Chloe starts to say, and then catches herself and Mel understands: if Chloe meets her, she has to leave her. It's better that she doesn't know her.

"Oh, Chloe," Mel says, with so much gentle sympathy it grips her tight.

"When you look at me like that . . ." Chloe stops, tries to wrench herself from Mel's gaze and maybe she fails or maybe she gives up. Mel wonders which is better and then she's giving in to instinct; unbuckling her seat belt, crossing the space between them. She kneels in the aisle so that they're at eye level. Her hand settles on the armrest, just a brush away from Chloe's arm.

She still knows the pattern the scatter of moles up her arm makes. She could trace it with her eyes closed, even now. She could reach out and . . .

. . . then she does. Chloe tenses under the touch, but she doesn't move, she watches the drag of Mel's fingers like it's the most scintillating thing in the world.

"I loved the fuck out of you," Mel says, unable to look at her, only at her arm, at that little snaking constellation those beauty marks make. If she looks at her . . .

Well, she is *not* going to end up joining the Mile High Club, is all she'll say. She has to resist.

"Mel—"

Mel's hand curls around her wrist like a supplicant. "Just. Let me?" she asks, and Chloe falls silent. Mel thinks she might nod, but she can't look at her (not with those eyes, not like that, not if she wants to actually say something important, and there are so many important things to say).

"When you left, it just about killed me. And you know better than anyone, Chlo, that I'm pretty hard to kill."

"You are," Chloe agrees.

"But once I could breathe through it, once it wasn't just about the hurt and me, I started to realize you didn't just do it to *me*. You did it to your parents. Your friends. The niece you've never met." She shakes her head. "You abandoned *all* of us."

"I had to." It comes out small, but it thrills her. The first crack in the wall Chloe's put up.

Mel has to fight with herself to not jump on the confession. She keeps tracing the pattern on Chloe's arm, wondering if it's lulling Chloe as much as it's lulling her.

And then . . . Chloe's hand covers hers. Mel stills, unable to tear away.

"I didn't want to," Chloe continues.

Mel finally looks at her. That cornflower blue in her eyes. She used to take the wildflowers that grew all over the archery range and place them over her eyes. They still couldn't match her blue. It was a color she hadn't seen since and she hadn't realized how much that hurt.

"You had to," Mel echoes, when the silence grows too long. The distinction is important.

Chloe doesn't nod, but she doesn't really need to.

"Chloe, just tell me—" she starts to say, she starts to lean in, too, desperate for more than answers, but the curtain separating the cabin swishes open, causing her to pull up and away, turning back to her own seat.

"Are you ready for lunch?" the attendant asks, oblivious to what she's walked into.

Mel has to count to five before she smiles at the woman. "Of course," she says. "Thank you."

"I'll wash up," Chloe says, getting up and disappearing into the bathroom down the aisle without another word.

When the food arrives, Mel starts to poke at it—some sort of chicken in lemon sauce with asparagus—before Chloe finally comes back.

"You okay?" Mel asks her, because she's pale.

"Yeah," she says, sitting down in front of her own food.

"It's not bad," Mel says.

Chloe nods, taking a bite after she scrapes some of the sauce off. "Will you tell me about Gigi?"

"What about her?"

"You two are friends. How does that work?"

Mel contemplates the asparagus. "You said you knew what happened three years ago. That you kept tabs on us."

"I kept tabs on everyone but you," Chloe says.

Mel has no control over the shaky breath she lets out, that gut-punch sound that escapes before she can protect herself. *Well, fuck you, too, Chloe.* She hates how much it hurts, that she wasn't worth cyber-stalking.

"We became friends after that. Gigi . . ." Mel doesn't know what to say. She finds herself reaching for the acorn charm around her neck.

"It was really fucking hard for Gigi," she says finally. "And it was one of my first cases. It put us together and she didn't really have anyone else. That first year, there were times where I—" She stabs her chicken. She's said too much. It's none of Chloe's business. She knows what Gigi thinks of her.

"She's not the same," she finally says. "Obviously. She lost . . ."

There're no words for what she lost. How it happened. It took years before Mel could close her eyes and not dream of the blood.

"I brought her in to organize the office because I was worried she'd lose herself in the grief instead. And she ended up being amazing at it, of course. But most of the week, she's at the paper with her mom."

"Gigi working at *The Harper's Bluff Gazette*." Chloe shakes her head. "It's like *The Twilight Zone*. She always swore she'd never take over the family business."

"She did what she had to," Mel says. It comes out sharper than she intended and now Chloe's the one shoveling food into her mouth to cover the awkward silence.

Their loyalties have shifted and it couldn't be more apparent. When they were together, Mel didn't have much of an opinion about the twins. She thought they were annoying—Gigi in particular—but she'd been operating with limited information. She wasn't anymore.

She doesn't know what the hell she would've done without Gigi, after everything went down. She hopes Gigi can say the same about her.

"So you two are really close," Chloe says, and Mel kind of hates how puzzled she sounds.

"She's my best friend," Mel says without any hesitation. "And she's been through hell. So I hope you were nice to her on the phone, even if hearing her voice was a shock."

"It was definitely a surprise," Chloe says, taking another bite of chicken and making a face.

"Not as good as your camp-stove cooking?" Mel asks.

"Hey, I had a sweet kitchen setup," Chloe says. "It took me forever to learn how to cook that first—" She stops, staring down at her chicken.

"You're just putting off the inevitable," Mel says, but she doesn't push further. They made a deal.

"I'll be right back," Chloe says, instead of listening to her—story of her fucking life, really, right there.

She stalks off to the bathroom and Mel winces when she hears her retching in there.

"Could we get some ginger ale?" she asks the attendant when the woman pokes her head in to see how they're doing.

"Of course." The woman disappears behind the curtain.

Is it the altitude or is Mel actually making her sick here? Fuck.

She leans her head against the seat, closing her eyes. How many more hours of this?

She wants to tell herself it'll all be over as soon as she delivers her to the ranch. That's what she told Gigi, after all. But Mel knows that's not true. Chloe needs protection, or something. As soon as she thinks this, she almost snorts, because the woman invaded her van with a hunting knife that was well-worn and she'd been more than ready to use it. Plus the lethal booby traps and whatnot.

But that didn't mean she wasn't in danger.

You're not a cop, she reminds herself. Most of the time, that thought brings profound relief. She's never had much of a good opinion regarding law enforcement. But right now, it causes a wrinkle and Mel hates wrinkles in her plans.

She's not a bodyguard, either. She's never run a security job or team, though she has a few friends in the business. She could call them in.

Her eyes try to pop open, but she finds it's a sudden struggle.

What the fuck?

She's been so focused on building a proper security plan and staffing it, she didn't notice the fogginess creeping over her.

Mel blinks, her eyes heavy, her chest slow as she takes in a deep breath. Did they change altitude too fast? Did they—

She glances down at the chicken. Chloe had been sick.

"Chloe?" she calls, going for her seat belt. Her hands fumble. They're much too heavy.

Shit is the last thing she's aware of thinking before she swirls into the fog.

15

CHLOE

THE SWEET SIXTEEN PARTY

Her dad's gone all out for her party. There are at least two hundred people here, milling underneath the tall white tents, talking, drinking, lining up to get tri-tip from the big grills. Woodsmoke scents the air, winding with the pine and hay and manure that's always there when you've got cows around, even when they're wild foraged.

Chloe wears her grandma Adrienne's cowboy boots. She plaits her hair in double braids and ties white ribbons at the ends to match her best sundress. Even her mother tells her how pretty she looks.

Everyone wants to meet her—most of the people here are her father's friends, but she doesn't mind because as the guest list grew, her dad let her invite whoever she wanted. And she basically invited the whole school.

Toby would be sure to come now.

The first hour disappears as her dad takes her all over the party, talking to adult after adult. She is a politician's daughter, though it doesn't come naturally to her the way it does Olivia, and she smiles and accepts happy birthday after happy birthday. Her father leaves for a moment to talk to one of the Thompsons—they own the last remaining lumber mill in town—and she spots Toby across the room.

It's infuriating, watching him stroll around, hands in his pockets, not a care in the world.

How? That's the thing that's circled in her head every hour since that day. Chloe's pretty sure she'll never have a decent night's sleep again. How could he just drive away? How was he not changed? Not haunted?

She completely loses track of the conversation she's in, so when someone says, "Don't you think so, Chloe?" she just nods.

"Absolutely," she says. "I'm so sorry. Can you excuse me?"

"Oh, I don't think—" one of the Thompsons says, but she's not paying attention anymore. The lure of Toby—of confrontation—is too much.

He's by the drinks table. She makes a beeline for him, laser-focused on her goal. Just a few more steps . . .

"There you are!" An arm slings around her shoulder, the scent of peonies wafting over her. Gigi's pink skirt is tiny—it's more of a suggestion, the shiny material so reflective it almost looks plastic.

"Hey," Chloe says, one eye still on Toby, he's talking to Tiffany Parker. "I'll be right back, okay? You look amazing, by the way."

"You should've seen my mother's face." Gigi smirks, but she doesn't let go when Chloe tries to tug away.

"Uh-uh!" Gigi argues, pulling her back. "I've been given a mission by your father! C'mon!"

"Gigi—" Chloe protests, but Gigi's surprisingly strong as she yanks her through the throng and toward the front of the house.

"Gigi, really, I've got to get back," Chloe says as they brush past a brunette who clips her shoulder so hard she lets out a "hey!" but the girl's disappeared before Chloe can spot her.

"Come on! Just a little farther," Gigi says.

"This better not be some sort of prank."

Her boots crunch over the gravel as the porch light comes into view.

"SURPRISE!" someone screams as they turn the corner and she lets out a startled noise, halfway between a laugh and a sob. Her emotions—already strained to the limit—bubble over. It's like she doesn't know which way to go as she stares at the bright red BMW with a silver bow on the hood, her parents standing there beaming along with Whitney and Olivia.

"Oh my god!" she says, and it's like she loses all sense of herself because she bursts into tears.

"Oh, honey!" her dad says while her mother goes, "What in the world, Chloe?"

"I'm sorry," she says, between sobs. "I'm sorry," she says again, trying to catch her breath, shake herself free of the horrible tightness in her chest. "Thank you," she manages to choke out. "Oh wow, thank you guys."

Her father had started to officially teach her to drive a few weeks before she found Jamie on the side of the road. But she'd been driving trucks and Gators and four-wheelers on the property for years.

She hasn't gotten behind the wheel since she witnessed the hit-and-run. She knew her father had noticed. Was this his response? Was this his hint? *Time to toughen up, sweetheart. Get back on the horse.*

"I thought the color was perfect for you," Mom offers, and then she smiles. "My firecracker."

"And I helped her pick the interiors," Whitney adds.

"Well, then, it's the classiest car ever," Chloe says, trying to get control of herself.

"You okay, Chloe Bryce?" he asks her in a low voice, his eyes troubled. She kisses her father on the cheek.

"It's just been such a beautiful day," Chloe says. "I'm gonna go clean up, okay?"

"Here's your keys." He hands them to her. They're attached to a key chain that's fluffy and red. Definitely Gigi's doing. "Your mother and I have the other set. I'll park it in the field tonight, so it's not in the way of everyone coming out, okay, sweetheart?"

"Sounds good."

"And I'll take you out next week on a real drive. You gotta start somewhere."

So he *had* noticed she'd stopped driving. She feels a flash of guilt. Why can't she be strong about this? Why does she have to fall apart?

"Thank you, Daddy."

She hurries into the house and goes straight into the bathroom, trying to breathe around the tightness in her throat. The twins will be knocking on the door any second, she knows it. Chloe braces her hands against the sink, trying to get hold of herself. She has to get away from the twins. Fast. Otherwise they'll stick to her all night and she won't be able to confront him.

And that's how she ends up climbing out the bathroom window onto the roof of the porch. She hears the twins in the kitchen as she drops onto the ground, scraping her knee against one of her mother's blueberry bushes. She keeps herself in a crouch as she passes by the kitchen window, heading straight back to the party. Merle Haggard plays on the speakers because her daddy is a beloved stereotype sometimes and she searches the sea of cowboy hats, trying to find him.

There's only so much time left. She needs to get him alone.

She spots him by the drinks table, his vape dangling from his lips. Her heart knocks against her rib cage like she's a girl beholding her first love.

But it's better than that: she's a girl closing in on her worst enemy.

She can still hear the terrible screech of tires against asphalt. The thud that she didn't recognize at first, but knows now what it was. How Toby just drove away, remorseless.

She just needs to get him alone to confront him. It'll be all over once he knows he's been caught. He'll have to turn himself in.

And then, maybe, the nightmares will stop.

16

CHLOE

THE PLANE CRASH

Chloe comes to as the man holding her climbs out of the plane, hitting the ground with a *thump*. It jostles her into consciousness and she blinks groggily, her curls swinging back and forth as she tries to make sense of the world and the ground four inches from her nose. He's got her in a fireman's carry—everything's upside down.

She's not brilliant like Mel, but she's honed her instincts in a different way, toward recognizing danger of all kinds. Which is why she stays limp instead of tensing up and alerting him that she's awake.

Did they land? Is she home? Where are they?

Her mouth feels like cotton. Was there something in the food or the drinks or the . . . the sauce. The sauce for the chicken. She'd asked for it on the side, but the flight attendant had "forgotten." She licks her lips, chasing the faintly chalky taste. Definitely drugged.

The Dicks have caught up with her. Goddamn it. Where is Mel?

He's moving fast, the man carrying her. One of the pilots, maybe? But she examines what she can see of his outfit: his pants, they don't look like pilot pants. They're Carhartts. Mel would be so proud she actually noticed. God, she fucking missed her and her soft freckled skin and that crinkle of her nose.

Oh yeah, the blood is definitely rushing too hard into her head.

That's when her eyes catch on the bulge near his ankle.

A gun.

Steadying her breathing, she glances to the side as he moves. Fallen branches. Trees. Red dirt. It looks like NorCal. She can't check her watch to see if enough time has passed for them to be home.

She sucks in another breath through her nose, slow and measured so he won't take notice. Pine sap, sharp in the air, followed by the alarming smudge of smoke. She twists her head to the side, not caring this time if he notices.

Oh god. The plane. It didn't *land*.

It *crashed*.

Smoke rises out of the nose, the glass shattered in the front, pine boughs stuck through it like javelins. She tries to get a better look at the plane door—to see if the smoke has spread to the main cabin, but her captor is making good time. They're weaving through the trees at a clip, leaving the jet behind. She has to do something. Attack him, or—

He dumps her on the ground in a way that tells her he's either dumb or absolutely confident the drugs were enough to keep her knocked out for a long time. But she'd scraped a good amount of the sauce off the chicken and then thrown up from nerves in the bathroom. She must've gotten only a light dose of it. But Mel . . . she might've eaten more than Chloe.

She has to get back to her.

Chloe keeps her eyes closed. Not screwed tight, but resting shut, her lips slightly parted, her dry mouth *dying* for a drink of water. When she hears a *thump* a few feet away from her, she chances a look through mostly shut eyes.

He's got their luggage. Her heart leaps. The dumbass grabbed their luggage!

Do not look excited, do not look excited. She keeps breathing slow and steady, all her focus on her backpack. It's two feet to her right. Unfortunately, he's standing right next to it. He steps away from it, pulling something from his pocket. Chloe's so busy contemplating how to reach for the backpack without him noticing that she doesn't notice what he's pulled out until he starts talking. She nearly jumps out of her skin when he growls, "We've got a big problem," and then relaxes in a noodling of her muscles when she realizes he's talking into a sat phone. "The plane crashed." He stops talking to listen. "No! I'm not joking, Vinny! The fucking plane crashed!"

Vinny was Rick's second-in-command. Chloe's come across him twice now. She almost shot him last year in Montana, but he moved at the last second. Pity, really.

"I know that wasn't part of the plan," he mutters into the phone. "But I'm calling you to tell you the plan's fucked. This whole thing's fucked. You told me this was an easy transfer job. Get them from the jet, wait for you to deliver the girls to the estate. This just got a whole lot more complicated. I want a lot more money for this. I had to pull the damn girl out of the flames."

He pauses again.

"I got the blonde out. You told me the blonde was the important one."

Silence.

"What do you mean, you need the brunette, too?"

Chloe was starting to think this guy stuck to simple facts and not much else.

"Fuck this, Vin!" the guy snarls into the phone and then he whirls around to look at Chloe.

She stays still, her breathing even and deep. Vin is Rick's man, not Big Daddy's. Who's running this thing? Rick? Had Big Daddy given up bankrolling him? *That* was an interesting thought, considering the new shell company someone in the Newell family was funneling money through.

She can hear and feel the man shuffle closer to her, which means that she's expecting something, but she's not quite ready for him to *kick* her right in the hip.

Resisting crying out is almost impossible, but her life is on the line, so she manages.

Mel. She needs to get to her. But she can't without alerting her captor to her not-fully-drugged state. Then things would get very messy, very fast.

There's a faint shouting in the distance. The man swears and starts stomping back toward the crash site. Chloe forces herself to stay still longer than she'd like, just to be sure he's out of sight. While she stays frozen, she can hear a voice, getting clearer and stronger. A voice calling *her* name.

Mel.

Chloe springs to life as soon as she's sure it's safe, rolling to the side to grab her backpack. She's got it unzipped in under five seconds—she's practiced enough—and the bow unfolded in fifteen. She's up and on her feet, the soft quiver unwrapped and filled and over her shoulder.

Sometime through the years, carrying a weapon through the forest with the intent to kill had become familiar to her. There's something alien about killing. Something disturbing but rooted deep in her at this point. She holds on to that. That it's not second nature, even though holding the bow is. Even though survival is.

She never wanted this. She just wanted to live long enough to put an end to a war she accidentally stepped into at sixteen.

Still does.

Her head and hands steady as she follows the smoke through the forest, toward the sound of voices—his and Mel's. He didn't take Chloe far, thank goodness.

Peering at them through the trees, she keeps down. He's speaking calmly to Mel, his thumb jerking behind him like he's talking about a location or a landmark. But her body language doesn't scream relieved or rescued. No, she's stiff as a board.

She's not buying whatever story he's trying to sell her. *That's my girl.* That little burst of pride spurs Chloe along as she moves low and balanced, her hands gripping her bow. She raises it, lines up her shot, breathing steady.

"You're gonna be okay," she hears him say to her. "Why don't I—"

He steps toward Mel. Chloe lets the arrow fly. She gets another nocked and releases. It lands clustered tight in his chest, right next to the first.

He drops to his knees, gurgles out blood, and then falls face-first into the ground.

Mel, to her credit, doesn't scream. Chloe strides forward, another arrow ready as she does a circle of the area. Are there more? Rick would never just leave one guy out here.

"You good?" she asks, her eyes sweeping down. Alarm lances through her. "You're bleeding."

"The plane crashed," Mel says. "I woke up with a steak knife in my leg. I'm pretty sure there was something in that chicken they gave us. And you just shot some dude. So no, I'm not *good*, Chloe."

Oh shit, she's mad. Mel's temper is the slow-burn kind, but when it explodes, watch the fuck out. See: Toby Dunne.

Still, Chloe wants to trace Mel's bloody face with her eyes and her hands and her lips because there's wreckage burning behind them and a body between them and jet fuel in the air and yet they're somehow alive.

She's always loved this woman, she's always surviving with this woman. Nothing ever changes.

That's good and monumentally terrible sometimes.

"He dragged me out of the plane. He wasn't here to rescue us," Chloe says, because she's going to have to explain now. *Christ.* She's going to have to explain. She can't let Mel run away from people in the woods for the *second* time without letting her in on the whole thing.

Damn it all, that's the last thing she wants to do.

She distracts herself by pulling her arrows out of the guy. She's only got so many and she'll need them all. Maybe Mel will cool down if she gives her a few seconds. She can't really give her minutes. There's got to be more guys in the woods. This one said something about a strip—a Newell landing strip, she'd bet. She's suspected for over a year that Rick had moved his operation. She'd been trying to find which private landing strip he trafficked out of for almost as long. The thought that she might've found it—quite literally crashed near it—fills her with such giddiness she almost giggles.

The problem is, that would mean the only way in and out of here is a plane. So be it. But it does make things tricky, considering she doesn't know how to fly one. That means kidnapping and control of a hostage. They'd need to get their hands on a gun or a knife. A bow and arrow meant shit at close range.

"We need to move," Chloe says, kicking the guy over and searching his pockets. When she finds the gun, she tries to hand it to Mel. "Melanie. Take it."

She holds out the gun and for a second, she's worried Mel won't. She has to take it. Guns have never been Chloe's thing.

A bow is an elegant weapon. It requires strength. Strategy. Focus. But it's a distance weapon unless she snaps an arrow tip and gouges someone's eye out. It's not like she hasn't thought of it.

A gun is a blunt weapon. And Mel is nothing but that. Too tall, too tough, and just a little too smart to be anything but a threat.

At sixteen, Chloe's heart beat for her. She would've done anything for her.

At eighteen, she was forced into proving just how true that was.

Chloe's hand trembles as she waits, that damn heart that's all Mel's in her throat.

But Mel doesn't take the gun. Mel just *loses* it and starts ranting about booby traps and Jodie Foster, and only stops when Chloe hears something. They have to get out of here. The only way Mel's moving is if she gives her what she wants: answers.

But they don't have the time, so she gives her the best she can: a promise. She offers the gun again, her blood thumping terribly, because what the hell is she going to do if Mel refuses?

"Mel," she says quietly. "I need you to trust me. Like I trusted you when I got on the plane."

She holds out the gun.

Take it. Choose me. Choose yourself. Choose us.

We'll die otherwise.

She doesn't take it. Panic starts to claw in Chloe's throat.

"I am the same person I have always been," Chloe says, a final bid for mercy—for both of them.

She is the same. That's what the years have taught her.

She was *always* capable of this. She just didn't know it until she did.

Brand-new nightmare.

Mel takes the gun.

Same old girls.

17

MEL

THE SWEET SIXTEEN PARTY

Mel's knuckles are still bleeding as she spots an enormous bouquet of pastel balloons tied around a simple mailbox at the end of a long drive. She makes a hard right, spraying gravel everywhere as she speeds toward the Harper family ranch.

She'd made a stop at her place to drop off Marigold and pick up what she needed. Then she went straight to Toby's. He hadn't been at his house. Her next try was his best friend's place. Toby wasn't there, either, but Jayden was.

Jayden hadn't given up Toby's location easily. But Mel could be convincing. She hisses through her teeth as she flexes her split knuckles around the wheel. She should've used the bat instead of her fist. She won't make that same mistake with Toby.

There are a few guys guiding cars into a field being used for parking and Mel follows one's waving, parking her truck and stalking toward the music and tents set up behind the sprawling ranch house.

There're more people than she expects—hundreds, if she was gonna ballpark it—but as she weaves through the crowd, she doesn't see him anywhere. It's mostly adults. Mayor Harper must be gearing up for another reelection campaign or something.

She plants herself at the end of the farthest drinks table, festooned with paper puffs and burlap garlands, where she has a good view of everyone. She scoops a ladle of pink punch from a bowl for something to do and takes a sip and then makes a face. It's spiked with vodka. She sets it to the side. The last thing she wants is to be drunk.

"Mel!" Tiffany Parker's squeaky voice is so distinctive, Mel doesn't even need to turn around to know it's her.

"Hey, Tiffany," Mel says.

"I can't believe you came."

"I'm actually looking for Toby," Mel says. "Have you seen him around?"

"Oh," Tiffany says, sudden understanding passing over her face. "You must be jonesing. Yeah, I was wondering. This is *not* your scene. Like do you even know Chloe? But yeah, he's here. I saw him earlier. Why?"

"Can you just tell me where he is?" Mel asks, not wanting to deal with Tiffany's not-so-veiled implications.

"I dunno. Last time I saw him, he was out by the grills."

"Great. Thanks."

"Hope you get what you need."

Mel rolls her eyes, moving single-mindedly through the throng of people under the tent, heading toward the one set farthest down the field, near where three large grills—the kind you tow with a truck—are going.

Finally, she finds Toby lurking on the edges of the grill tent, talking to an older man. Mel watches as Toby passes the man something, a quick exchange that can almost be passed off as a handshake. *Almost.*

Pretty fucking brazen, selling drugs at the same party the sheriff's attending. What the fuck is up with this guy? Until today, Mel hadn't given Toby Dunne a second thought. And now?

Now she wants to teach him a lesson he'll never forget.

Mel doesn't go up to him. Not with all these people around. She's a patient girl. She knows how to draw a target out.

Getting Toby alone shouldn't be too tricky. He's made that one sale and now floats toward the buckets full of drinks. He talks to another guy, then tries to flirt with a girl. But he doesn't make a move to get anyone alone.

He walks toward the dance floor, and that's when a flicker of white—the same flicker that's been in the corner of her eye since she started tracking Toby—moves, too.

Toby's got a shadow, Mel realizes with a jolt. Everywhere he goes, the birthday girl is close behind. Everyone wants to talk to her, so she doesn't go anywhere without being drawn into a conversation, but it's subtle, unless you're tracking Toby. Which Mel is.

But so is Chloe Harper.

What does Chloe Harper want with Toby? Surely she has better sense than to be interested in *him*. It's hard to think of a girl like Chloe developing a drug problem, but wilder things have happened. Is Chloe *jonesing*, as Tiffany had put it?

Mel hangs back, watching both of them now, blood rushing in her ears as her fingers tap against her thigh.

Even if she wasn't the birthday girl, Chloe stands out like a beacon in her sweet white sundress, ribbons in her hair. She looks like a Sunday morning full of possibility . . . and then you get to her feet. Cowboy boots, and not the kind that are for show. The kind that are for use. Beat up and scarred, those boots have history. Mel's attention snags on the boots for some reason, she can't quite figure out why, and before she can puzzle it out, Chloe's feet move away . . . with Toby Dunne following at her boot heels.

As the two of them head toward the field-turned-parking-lot, Mel follows them at a distance. She loses them in the tangle of cars and trucks for a minute when Chloe makes a right turn. Mel makes the same one seconds later, but they're gone.

There's voices. Mel weaves through the maze of vehicles, trying to pinpoint their location. It's hard. Sound bounces and everyone owns giant trucks, whether they need them or not. Chloe's short. You can't see her over the top of a car, let alone a truck.

"I don't know what you're talking about!" Mel hears Toby yell.

Mel whirls. In her jacket pocket, the gun thunks against her leg.

"Stop it!" Chloe's voice pitches high and upset. "For once in your miserable life, stop *lying*. I know everything. I know you hit him. I know you drove away without even getting out of your truck."

Hit who? Another beating like Ted's?

No. Not if he was driving.

"You're being crazy, Chloe," he says.

"*No.*" It comes out so viscerally it has Mel stumbling. It's like it's been ripped from Chloe's throat, a declaration of war. "I was there. I've got it on video. I have proof."

Everything sharpens on that one word.

"What?"

Something trickles down Mel's spine. Warning. She knows that voice in a man. It comes right before rage. And what comes after rage is violence.

Move your goddamn feet, Tillman. She almost clips her shoulder against a mirror in her haste, but she's gotta find them. She has to stop him before—

"I've got it all on camera," Chloe says. "There was a girl van-camping in the Joneses' hayfield. She had her dashcam on, and it was pointed toward the road. I found her. I have the footage of you hitting Jamie. So you're gonna turn yourself in. The sheriff is here. We're gonna go to him, right now, and you'll confess. You'll do your time. Jamie will get the justice he deserved. The Hendersons can finally get some peace with his killer behind bars."

Jamie? The fuzzy picture's starting to form. Everyone had heard about it last year: Chloe Harper had found a little boy on the side of the road, hit by a car and left for dead. It was hushed-voice terrible, the kind of news you didn't speak too loudly. Chloe had been holding him as he died. They said she refused to let go when they found her. Even when it was clear he was gone.

She hadn't wanted to leave him alone, they whispered.

Chloe had been out of school for a week and when she came back, she dressed the same, she acted the same, but there was something in her eyes now. It cut when you got too close.

Mel never knew a good world, so she never had the idea of one shatter. But she thinks Chloe might've thought the world was good and now she knows it's not, and what a horrible way to learn.

But is there a good way to learn? She doesn't think so.

Toby pulling a hit-and-run is disgusting, but not surprising when Mel thinks it through. When you live with a monster, you get to know the signs of a burgeoning one. But Chloe going on some sort of righteous crusade in her sundress and cowboy boots makes things complicated. Does she even have a weapon? A plan? Did she tell anyone she was coming out here with him? She thinks she's just gonna march him over to the sheriff and it'll all work out? Fuck, is Mel gonna have to save her?

Mel creeps forward, the voices getting louder.

They're right there, in front of a bright red BMW with a big silver bow still tied to the hood. She crouches down near a dusty F-150, watching. Toby's back is to her and Mel can only see Chloe's face because she's standing slightly to his left. She's practically trembling with fury.

Mel had never thought of Chloe Harper as naive, but holy shit, if she doesn't have a knife or something tucked in those boots, this girl is gonna die. You don't just tell someone like Toby Dunne to walk over to the sheriff and turn himself in. What the hell is she thinking? You come up behind Toby Dunne with a gun and scare him shitless, tie him up, and *then* you anonymously call the sheriff.

She doesn't think Chloe and her sense of justice and good-girl tendencies got that memo. Fuck.

"What dashcam?" Toby demands.

"It doesn't matter."

"*What dashcam?*" he roars, and he moves so fast, Chloe doesn't have time to react. His hands wrap around her throat. She lets out a pained squeak and then she can't make any more sound. He's crushing it out of her.

Mel's moving. No thought. Well, one thought.

"Hey, asshole!" she yells, bending down and picking up a handful of dirt and little rocks, chucking it at Toby. The rocks pepper his shoulders and head. His hands drop and so does Chloe, right onto the ground, gasping and bloodshot.

He turns to charge at her, but she's got the gun pointed right at him.

He freezes. He's not entirely a dumbass.

"Get away from her," she orders, stepping forward slowly. She can barely hear herself above the blood pounding in her ears.

"This isn't—it's just a little disagreement, Mel."

"Disagreements don't start with your hands wrapped around a girl's throat, Toby," she says. "Get the fuck away from her."

"Put the gun down," he counters.

Mel lowers the gun, just enough to shoot three inches right of his foot. Dirt scatters over his shoe as he yelps, jumping to the side . . . away from Chloe.

Mel steps into the space he's made, putting herself between them.

Gun's right back on his chest by the time he straightens.

She feels a little crazy. She's never pointed a gun at a person before. She has, in fact, had it drilled into her mind by Miss Bev to *never* pull a gun on a person.

Not unless she's ready to kill them.

Is she ready for that? She doesn't know. But she's aiming the gun at him all the same.

The first time Mel went out hunting, she was seven. It wasn't about bonding or learning a skill. It was about hunger. Bob had spent the grocery money on beer. The only thing she could do was sneak the rifle out from under his bed and go over to Miss Bev's trailer, because Miss Bev cooked venison on her charcoal grill in the summers and she had to get it from somewhere.

Miss Bev had taught her everything she knew. And when your motivation is hunger, you get really good at shooting things.

"You okay, Chloe?" Mel asks, keeping her eyes on Toby. "You need help up?"

"I'm okay," she chokes out. Mel can feel her right behind her. She shifts slightly, so she's blocking Chloe with her body.

"You hurt my brother," she says to Toby.

"Your broth—"

"Ted." She jumps on his confusion, trying to stamp down the anger at it and failing. Has he forgotten he almost beat a man to death just a few hours ago? Fucking psychopath. "You *fucked* with my *brother.*" She steps forward. "You shouldn't have done that."

"Listen, Mel," he says. "I don't want to mess with you. I didn't—I didn't know he was your brother, okay? This is just a big misunderstanding. I'm sorry, okay?"

"You beat homeless people up a lot for not buying your shit when you want them to?"

"I just—I needed cash. He used to buy regular from me. I thought—"

"You thought wrong, motherfucker."

"I see that now," he says hastily. "Why don't you just put the gun down, okay? You could do something you really regret."

"Like killing a little boy in a hit-and-run?" Mel asks, watching his face closely.

She has no reason to doubt Chloe's story, but if she had, the shuttered look that snaps over his face would've convinced her. He absolutely did that shit.

"We're going to go talk to the sheriff now," Mel says. It's a terrible idea still, but it's the only choice because of Chloe going off and accusing him without a weapon. Mel can't just beat the shit out of him like she planned. And she can't shoot him a field away from the sheriff *and* the mayor, even though there's a part of her that wants to.

"Yeah, that's gonna work," Toby says. "You're gonna march me into that party at gunpoint?"

"This is my family's land." Chloe slowly gets to her feet, her knees bloody from the ground. Her voice rings out with the righteousness of a girl who has had everything always go her way. Fuck, she is going to get Mel killed. Or make Mel have to pull the damn trigger.

"This isn't the olden days, Chloe." Toby lets out a nervous laugh. "You aren't queen of the ranch, laying down the law."

"My father will listen to me. And the sheriff will listen to him."

And that? Well, that is the undeniable truth.

It's also the exact wrong thing to say to a boy who's already on edge.

"Where is it?" He lunges forward, his arms grasping toward Mel with a too-long arc. She underestimates his reach—she doesn't jerk back far enough and his hand swats at the gun in her hand. It falls to the ground and she lunges for it, but she's not fast enough. She's halfway into her movement when she sees his hand close around the barrel of all things, instead of the hilt.

He's got fifty pounds on you, Tillman, You can't fight him for it. Rethink. Reverse.

She jumps up, grabbing Chloe's hand.

Yank.

She pulls Chloe to her, their hips and chests colliding. There's a painful, unguarded *clack* of Chloe's teeth as she's jarred into the movement.

Dive.

She pushes Chloe in front of her, diving behind the BMW just as the first bullet cracks out. Glass shatters to her right. It slightly reassures her that Toby's a shit shot.

"Two," Mel mutters to herself. There's four more bullets. Can they just wait him out and then try to run? But he doesn't shoot again. Has he realized how limited the ammo is?

"Do you have the keys to this?" Mel asks Chloe, banging her fist on the BMW's bumper.

Chloe nods, pulling them out of her boot. Her face is pale but she presses the button, the *click* of the doors unlocking the sweetest sound Mel's ever heard.

"Okay, good. You drive—"

"No!" She presses the keys into Mel's hands. "I can't. Please. Don't—"

Another bullet cracks. This time, he hits the BMW, the glass shattering over their heads. Chloe flinches away, a piece striking her cheek.

"No time." Mel snatches the keys from her. "You go left." She veers to the right, scrambling for the driver's-side door as Chloe does the same on the passenger side. The key slides into the ignition like the universe knows she needs a win.

"Stay down!" she shouts as the engine purrs to life and she throws the car into drive. But when she flicks the headlights on, *fuck*, there he is. Standing in the beams like a killer in a bad horror movie, gun pointed straight at her.

It's a split-second decision. It'll haunt her for years. Should she have mowed that fucker down then and there?

She'll never know how life would've been different. Because she pushes into reverse and slams on the gas, speeding backward as he shoots at them. The bullets ping against the hood and shatter the windshield, but they don't hit them—and that's one bullet left now.

Mel grips the wheel tight as she comes to the end of the row of parked cars. She spins and she turns right instead of left because all she can think of is *bullet* and *drive, you useless girl, drive*.

She drives, speeding *away* from the bullets, yes, but also away from the house, away from the sheriff and the power and protection of Chloe's father. She hits the highway at full speed, going ninety down a two-lane road, running entirely on fear and no thought but *get away from him*.

It is a mistake that seals their fate.

Because just as soon as she thinks she's succeeded in getting them away, high beams fill her rearview, closing in on them fast. Mel pushes the gas, tries to leap ahead, but it's not enough, it's *not*, and Chloe lets out a scream just before his truck collides with the bumper of the beamer.

18

GIGI

Gigi's awake by five every morning. She's up before the gentle glow of her sunrise alarm reaches full brightness, as usual. She typically doesn't touch her phone for the first hour of the day—she knows how to practice good tech hygiene—but she makes the exception just this once because Mel's up in Canada.

But there's nothing.

She does thirty minutes of kettlebells and another thirty of cardio before she showers. And as she dries her hair, she tells herself she's not waiting to hear the *ping* telling her she's got a text from Mel.

She shuts off her hair dryer and faces the mirror. The Post-it notes surrounding the edges are a mix of new ones, fresh stickiness and bright paper, and old ones, curled at the edges, taped-on in places, water-spattered, but still important.

She reads them counterclockwise, like she always does.

> *Dwell in your truth.*
> *Focus on the goal.*
> *You know what you feel.*
> *She's coming back.*

Her fingers linger on the last Post-it. It's the oldest one. The first she wrote, the day after she realized everyone was giving up but her.

Layers of tape hold it up to the mirror. The ink's starting to fade. But she can't take it down.

She knows everyone thinks she's in denial. She knows the looks she gets.

She doesn't care.

Deep, cleansing breath. In and out.

She determinedly smiles in the mirror. Makes sure her lip liner is even. Fills in the rest of her lips.

Perfect.

Her phone rings from the other room, startling her, because she was expecting a text, not a call. Her mascara goes tumbling into the sink as she hurries into her bedroom.

And then Mel starts talking and god, they are so fucked. Her *voice*. The thread of hope in it. She should never have let Mel go by herself. She's going to lead with her heart and that heart basically beats for Chloe Harper, even after all these years.

This is why Gigi should've insisted on going along. She'd let the fact that Mel was grieving Nat sway her. She'd told herself it was doubtful she would even find Chloe, but she shouldn't have under-estimated the pull those two had. You put them even remotely close enough, they'll swing toward each other like magnets.

Mel says something about Chloe being different and rustic and that they'll be closing the job soon and Gigi nearly snorts, it's so ri-diculous, like, yes, Mel's just going to drop Chloe off at the ranch and never see her again. That's totally a reality that will unfold.

And then! Then! Mel hangs up on her after saying there are flight crew things she needs to do.

Gigi's so mad that she's been shrugged off with such an excuse, she throws the phone at her bed. And immediately regrets it, because it bounces between her mattress and her headboard, falling under the bed.

"Oh for heaven's sake," she mutters, flattening herself onto the ground, noting that she really needed to dust better under here before grabbing her phone. "You're not going to get away from me that fast," she says to the phone in place of Mel as she emerges, a little grimier than before. She jabs Mel's name on her recent calls triumphantly and puts it on speaker for good measure. Not even waiting for Mel to draw a breath when she answers, she says, "We need to discuss how to combat your giant *I'm still in love with Chloe Harper* problem."

There's a distinct, long silence and then, a voice—not Mel's voice—a voice roughened by time but oh so familiar. "Gigi?"

Gigi's mouth goes dry so fast she's sure her lips crack at the same time. She can taste blood in that stinging little corner or maybe she bit down on it, because she didn't expect . . .

Her voice is so familiar. Gigi heard it every day for years.

"Yes, it's Georgia," she says, feeling like she's about to jolt out of her body and go pelting down the road just to get away from this conversation. She's not prepared. She thought she'd have time. She would've made notes and color coded them with specific Post-its.

But now she's here. She's finally here and totally unprepared, and *shame on her.* She knows better. She's been waiting all this time.

"Hi," Chloe says.

"Hi," Gigi says, not because Chloe deserves her greeting, but because she needs to buy time. She paces into the bathroom, trying to focus on the Post-its, but her eyes keep blurring. Why do her eyes keep blurring? She shouldn't be crying, but she's on the edge of it. Damn her. Damn this!

"Mel mentioned you two were . . ." Chloe trails off like she can't even find the words.

"Is she there?" Gigi asks.

"She's dealing with the pilot. I can . . . I can tell her you called back."

"You're well?" Gigi asks, suddenly desperate to keep Chloe on the line. God, it's been *so long.* She has so many questions. She needs so many answers.

"I'm—yeah," Chloe says.

"Your father looked frail from the chemo last time I saw him, but he was still doing his walks. That was about a month ago. I'm due for another visit out there with my momma."

"Thank you," Chloe says. "That's kind of you."

"Your parents were very kind to us when—" Gigi stops. She lets out a breath, and on the line, she hears Chloe take one, like she knows. She has to know, doesn't she? What's about to come?

"I'm going to ask you a question, Chloe," Gigi says. "And I want you to keep in mind that I've known you since you were in diapers. I can tell when you're full of literal or figurative crap, even over the phone."

A pause. "Okay."

Deep breath. In and out.

Gigi's eyes focus on the most-frayed Post-it note at the bottom of the mirror.

She's coming back.

"What the hell happened to my sister, Chloe? What kind of shit did you get Whitney involved in? *Where is she?*"

Part III

THE PROBLEM

19

RICK

AFTER THE PLANE CRASH

One of these days, Rick is gonna get Doris.

He fixes his binoculars on the cluster of volcanic boulders. It's where he last spotted the evil bitch. Right before she sent her crew over the ridge to attack.

But there's no movement on the rock or near it. The peacocks have faded back into the foothills, waiting for another opportunity to strike.

"You spot them?" Vinny asks from the doorway.

Rick shakes his head, lowering his binoculars. When he looks up at Vinny, his eyes narrow. The man looks like a cow's kicked his nuts all the way into his throat.

"What the fuck's wrong with you?"

"Just got a call," Vinny says, and when he doesn't say anything else, Rick gets downright annoyed.

"Spit it out."

"The plane," he says. "It didn't go down where it was supposed to."

Rick tells himself he heard him wrong, but there's never been anything wrong with his hearing. Just his judgment in teenage dealers, which is what got him in this fucking mess in the first place.

"What are you talking about? Did they not get on it? We had a plan, Vin!"

"They got on. The pilot was supposed to land it on our strip . . . but he didn't."

"What happened?" Rick demands.

"Engine crapped out or something. Plane went down maybe five, six miles from where it was supposed to," Vinny says. "Jake was closest to the crash site. He headed out, Sean stayed to guard the strip."

Rick hates this feeling: dread, creeping over him. He's mighty familiar with it. "And what did he find? Are they all dead?"

"No, but Jake is," Vinny says.

"Fuck," Rick says. "Let me guess: arrow to the chest."

"Arrow to the chest," Vinny confirms.

"That fucking girl, she's like a cockroach," Rick says. "She survived a goddamn plane crash?"

"Got a titanium pussy, that one," Vinny agrees.

Rick snorts. "That doesn't even make sense, Vin." But then again, Vinny rarely does. His talent lies in other pursuits. "What do we know?"

"Sean spotted two sets of prints heading out," Vinny continues. "I think they both survived. Sean came back to the strip to report and get orders. Do you want him to follow them? Take them out?"

"Tell him to stay where he is," Rick says. "He'll get an arrow in the chest otherwise. Can't get a goddamn thing done right unless I do it myself. What's the fucking point of being the boss?"

Vinny wisely says nothing as Rick gets to his feet.

He looks over his shoulder, back at the boulder, his fingers itching for his gun.

"C'mon, Vin, we gotta go out to the Trinities. See the family."

"I hate those guys," Vinny mutters.

"Yeah, well, the feeling's mutual," Rick says, grabbing his shotgun, just in case he comes across the little bird bitch and her gang on the way out. He wishes he could shoot Richard, too, because his cousin's gonna give him hell about this, but he knows better than that. He'll have to leave the shotgun in the truck when he gets there.

"Women of all species are gonna be the fucking end of me," he mutters.

———

Big Daddy Newell lived on a hundred-acre spread, the only land that was left from the family's original six-hundred-acre homestead before they moved into town and started ruling it through politics and business and whatnot. This, of course, was before Rick's time. It was some gold-rush shit, really. But it was important to Big Daddy. History or whatever.

Rick had learned a long time ago to pay attention to what was important to Big Daddy. He'd spent his life ten steps behind his cousins already. He wasn't gonna let them get any more headway. It's not his fucking fault his father died and his momma didn't want anything to do with Big Daddy when Rick was a kid.

His cousins got all the attention and focus. And Rick got to grow up in a shitty little mobile home on the river with a momma who was too proud to take anything from the Newells.

They're bad business, baby, she used to tell him.

Well, Rick grew up to be even badder business. He's sure his mother has regrets. Or she would, if she wasn't six feet under like his daddy.

He didn't put her there. Not that he wasn't tempted from time to time. That woman was a little too saintly for his liking, but he loved her as best he could. Got her a marble headstone with gold lettering just like she wanted. He doesn't visit it as often as he knows she probably would like, sitting on her perch in heaven, judging away, but he brings flowers on her birthday.

That's the theme of his life, isn't it? Rick *tries.* His cousins have the same goddamn name as him and silver spoons stuck in their mouths and their asses and Rick is still *trying.*

Life isn't fair, baby, his momma would say.

Maybe once Rick would've settled for fair. But you can ostracize a man only so much. This land he was driving on was a great example. All the Newells lived here. All of them but him.

He doesn't turn toward the big house, he takes the road past it, to the lodge where his cousin Richard lives with his wife.

You don't cross Big Daddy's threshold without an explicit invitation—otherwise you'll be tweezing buckshot out of your ass for a week.

"What do you think he's gonna say?" Vinny asks as the lodge comes into sight, set in a clearing, redwoods and pine trees looming over it.

"Fuck if I know," Rick says. "Stay in here," he says as he parks in front of Hill's Tesla, the pink *Girls with Guns* logo stuck to the back windshield. Of course Richard's wife's got one of those pieces of techy shit. He supposes he can't hope it'll lock her inside and spontaneously combust or something. Pain in the ass, that woman. Always lurking in the background, trying to listen in. Richard doesn't seem to be able or willing to put her in her place. You should never hand over your balls to your woman like that. But he didn't expect much else from good ol' Richard or his progeny. Weak-ass spirits to match their weak-ass chins. No wonder Hill runs all over him. Shit, she's probably a better shot than Richard—woman spends enough time at the range.

"If you hear shooting, come on in," Rick says, half serious as he gets out.

"You really think it's gonna end up that way?" Vinny asks.

Rick shrugs, trying to keep it cool. But they're fucked and Vinny's too dumb to know it, which is good because otherwise he'd run for the hills.

He shuts the truck door, leaving Vinny behind. Bringing Vin in with him will just escalate things faster. The only chance of this working is to slow roll it as much as possible.

The lodge is enormous, much too big for three people, but that's Richard for you. Always compensating and still living on Granddaddy's property.

One of the finest moments of Rick's life was the night Big Daddy got shit-faced on sixty-year-old whiskey and went on and on about how Rick was the only one of his grandchildren who actually owned the land he called home. Richard had left the room after that. He always could handle his shit with everyone but Big Daddy.

Rick had half a mind to call up the man himself, but he knew he was on shaky ground with Big Daddy these days. It'd taken a long time to convince any of them he hadn't been in on it. That the Dunne kid had robbed him. You'd have to have shit for brains to steal from Big Daddy, but apparently everyone in the family thought Rick was just that stupid once upon a time.

He hadn't exactly forgiven them of that, either.

He knocks on the door because Hill's got the bell rigged with this music that goes on and on, and he can never get it out of his head once he hears those first obnoxious chimes. He'd rather do this with a clear head. Because Richard and Junior will blow once they hear Chloe's loose.

Junior answers the door after a minute, a jerky stick dangling from his mouth. "Thought you were gonna meet the plane."

"Change of plans," is all Rick says.

Rick steps inside the lodge, taking off his cap because the last time Hill caught him wearing it inside she'd glared. You never want to earn the glare of a woman like that. She's scarier than Big Daddy—a Calabama Jackie who saw her way into a political dynasty and grabbed it. He's watched her take down and field-dress a buck without getting a drop of blood on her. If he ever needed to get rid of a body for good, Hill would be second on his list of recruits, right behind Chloe Harper, because he's starting to think women are just better at killing. He's already fairly certain they're better at body disposal, given the last six years.

But Hill married into this crazy and got everything she wanted and then some. You've got to be a little unhinged to choose this kind of life. To choose a family like theirs. But choose it she did.

She had a thing about hats in the house. And taking the Lord's name in vain, which was pretty rich considering what her husband really did under that assemblyman cover of his.

"Your daddy home?" he asks, because Junior's brains can fill one of those thimbles Rick's momma used to collect and leave plenty of space. You can't make up for so many defects with handsomeness, but Junior certainly tries. *He looks good on a poster, at least,* is all Big Daddy will say.

"He's on a call, you'll have to wait," Junior says.

"Junior, who is that?" calls a voice from down the hall. Hill comes into view, silver and turquoise around her wrists, long skirt sweeping down to the cowboy boots clicking across the expensive floors. *White oak from England*, Richard had told him once, like it was supposed to impress him. "Oh, Rick," she says, making it sound like she's handing down a death sentence with the greatest pleasure. "You're here."

"Hello, cousin," he says, because he knows it annoys her to be reminded: she married into the *whole* family, him included.

"Do you need a drink?" she asks, already moving past him toward the kitchen.

"You know I love your sweet tea." He follows her, because Richard's either really on a call or he's on a power trip and told Junior to say that. Either way, it's gonna be a while.

"What plans changed?" Junior asks, lowering his voice like he thinks his mother can't hear. This close, Rick almost chokes on the cloying scent of Junior's aftershave.

"Later," Rick says.

"I get five minutes with Harper. Dad promised, after what she did."

It's like the kid's never been stabbed before. That was something like three years ago and he's still whining?

"Shut up," Rick says, as they walk into the kitchen dominated by charcoal-streaked marble and gold cabinet knobs.

"I'm gonna get my piece of her," Junior says, like the overdramatic little fucker he's always been.

"I will cut your tongue out if you keep talking around your mother," Rick says in an undertone, one eye on Hill, who's half inside that giant fridge of hers. You could store at least two bodies in there if need be. Three, if you chop them carefully. "You need help, Hill?" he asks.

"I've got it," she says, bringing out the pitcher. "Honey, get me the glasses, will you?"

Junior sighs like it's the greatest ask since God asked Abraham to sacrifice Isaac.

"How's tricks, Hill?" Rick asks, sitting down at the counter on one of the stools made out of tractor seats. Richard was big on making himself look salt of the earth, but closest thing his cousin ever got to riding a tractor was sitting in these ugly, eight-hundred-dollar-a-pop seats, making his ass ache for no good reason except *aesthetics*.

"Things are fine, Rick," she says, stressing *things*. She brings a pitcher of tea over to the counter, where Junior's slammed two glasses down and flung himself on the nearest stool.

"Your girl group doing good?"

"My concealed-carry classes for women continue to be a success," she says. "We've added three more workshops for the summer."

"Gonna get one of us fine men killed by a jealous woman one of these days if you keep teaching them how to shoot so sharp."

"One can hope," Hill says, much too serenely.

Junior snickers and then looks concerned, as if it's suddenly occurred to him that one of those women might shoot him. Considering his history in getting stabbed by an angry woman, Rick can't exactly blame him. But it's been years since a woman's shot at Rick. Ah, memories.

"Cousin!" The bellow comes down the hall, a summoning of Rick, in a voice just a tad too similar to his own to ignore. They all look alike, sound alike, *like I cloned you*, Big Daddy likes to joke.

"What?" Rick yells back, just to antagonize him. Hill shoots him a look, her pink mouth flattening in disapproval.

"Modulate your voice, please," she says.

"Tell that to your husband." Rick gets up, taking his sweet tea with him, ignoring her when she says, "Take a coaster," like he's a child. If Richard objects to water rings on that fancy desk of his, he can take it up with Rick himself.

Junior follows him as he makes his way down the hall, still a little too close.

Rick doesn't knock on Richard's door, he just pushes inside. Books cover the main wall—he can guarantee you Richard's read maybe three of them. Just like the buck heads mounted on the opposite wall aren't ones he shot. Rick shot those. Richard bought them off him.

But that's kind of the way of it and always has been.

His cousin has done well for himself. He's done what no other Newell has—taken the political reach beyond the county and down to the capital.

And Rick . . . well, Rick has done well for himself, too. But he isn't a state assemblyman.

"What are you doing here?" Richard asks.

"Thought I'd pay a visit." Rick sets the sweet tea glass on the desk, then sets himself down in the leather chair, propping his boots up on the edge.

Richard slaps them off, knocking the glass to the ground in the process. Rick lets him, he gives him that, just grinning as his feet and the glass hit the floor. It shatters, spilling tea everywhere.

"Hill's gonna be mad at you," Rick says. "Isn't that rug expensive?"

Richard just glares at him.

"You're supposed to be at the meet-up point," Junior says. "It's nearly three."

"I'm glad he's graduated to finally being able to tell time," Rick tells Richard.

"Stop playing games, Rick," Richard says. "What's going on? Why are you here?"

"Plane crashed," Rick says. "About five or six miles from the strip. Something went wrong with the engine."

"What?" Junior barks. "No fucking way! So she's already dead?"

"She survived long enough to shoot my guy, so I'd say she's fine. Sounds like the other one survived and is with her, too. My guy Sean, he saw two sets of tracks heading north."

"Right toward the strip," Richard says, sitting up straighter. "Has the forestry moved in? Cal Fire?" He pulls up his phone, tapping open a fire scanner app, flicking through the channels. "Why are you still here?" He doesn't even look at Rick, the motherfucker.

"I'm still here because we need to make a plan."

"You need to go out there and get her," Richard says. "What more of a plan do you need? We finally know where she is. *Go get her.*"

"She killed my guy. She's armed, and she's dangerous."

"I still want my hour with her," Junior gripes.

"Shut up," Richard says, holding out his hand as he tilts his head toward the phone. The scanner app crackles, a voice breaking through: "Eagle's Nest 8 to HQ. Smoke spotted. Isolated black plume. Any small aircraft scheduled to go over the north quadrant? Near Ellis Peak. Over."

"That's it," Rick says.

"Then *go*," Richard tells him. "Find her. Knock her out, hog-tie her if you have to, but you bring her back. Both of them."

"You keep talking to me like I'm one of your little aides and we're gonna have a problem," Rick warns.

"I'm more interested in paying attention to the *real* problem than your ego, cousin," Richard says. "You lost her. Go get her. Because if she dies without telling you where they are, you know what'll happen. Big Daddy'll feed you to the pigs."

"He'll feed you to them, too! This is on you as much as it's on me," Rick says. "You're the one who gave me the money to blackmail the pilot. Clearly he fucked up."

"You're the one who thought you could scare Chloe Harper into telling you where she buried that boy all those years ago and started this. Big Daddy will not forget that."

"Maybe we should go to him and see what he says we should do," Rick says. It's a gamble, but he wants to see how Richard reacts.

He's played poker enough with his cousin, he knows his tells. He's resisted using this knowledge time and time again, because there's value in a powerful motherfucker like Richard thinking you're an idiot. Men who stay powerful motherfuckers don't walk into traps often. You've got to be patient.

Rick's been a patient man. He's had to be.

"Big Daddy's not seeing anyone right now," Richard says, like there's no discussion to be had around it.

"Maybe I'll go up to the big house and see if he wants to chat—" Rick starts to say.

"Was that glass breaking?" comes a voice from the doorway. Hill glides in without another word, dustpan and broom in hand. "Honestly, Rick, I told you to use a coaster."

"Coaster's not gonna keep the glass from falling," Rick points out.

"Rick was just leaving," Richard says.

"No, Rick was just talking about going to visit Big Daddy," Rick says. "It's been a while since I've seen him."

"He's been on a tear, the old dear," Hill says, tutting when she sees the stain on the carpet. "Didn't Richard tell you?"

"Like that scares me," Rick says.

"It should, he's very upset with you for some reason," Hill says. "I wish you boys'd stop messing about like you do. It stresses your grandfather out and he doesn't need that at his age. Especially in an election year."

"I'll go and apologize." Rick gets up, but Hill plants herself, the dustpan full of broken glass vibrating between them.

"You will not go and antagonize him," she says. "Do you want to give him another heart attack?"

"I didn't give him the first one!" Rick protests.

"Didn't you?" she asks. "Don't bother him. You've got a message for him, I'll give it to him."

"Rick's got business to attend to, anyway," Richard says meaningfully. "You're running out of daylight, cousin."

Rick glares at him, but he can't exactly get into an argument with Hill in the room. And he does need to get out to Ellis Peak before it gets dark. Plus, Vin's got to be sweating his balls off out there in the truck. Rick should've cracked a window or left the keys or something.

"Maybe Junior wants to come with me," Rick suggests.

"Hell yeah." Junior leaps up.

"Absolutely not," Hill says, before Richard can even open his mouth. Rick raises an eyebrow.

"You don't even know where we're going."

"I don't need to. Dick Junior is leading in all the polls. Neither of my boys are gonna be seen near you in public, Rick. Those are Big Daddy's rules."

He doesn't say anything. He thinks a few choice words toward her, instead.

"You stay out of sight," Hill reminds him. "You may be family, but your place is in the shadows."

"You're a bitch," he says as Richard jerks to his feet in response, and Junior gives a half-hearted "Hey!" But a woman like Hill, she doesn't need protection. She's the kind of woman a man needs protection from.

"It takes one to know one, Rick," she says. "You can see yourself out."

She swishes through the door, skirt floating around her like a wayward wind.

"You heard her," Richard says. "Go and solve this. Because if Big Daddy finds out you've ruined our one chance at getting Chloe Harper..."

"You're toast, dude," Junior adds, because he's never learned the effect of a trailed-off threat.

"You sure you don't want to come?" Rick asks, thinking he could lose Junior down a ravine and solve a huge pain in the ass, for himself and for the entire town. Because if he becomes mayor, the town's gonna go bankrupt in about six months.

"Mom said I couldn't," Junior says, like he's not thirty fucking years old.

"You're the most useless shit stain I've ever met," Rick says, pulling his cap on, because fuck Hill. She can pepper his ass with buckshot for doing it if she wants.

"Find her. Don't kill her. And get the goddamn location out of her," Richard says. "Or so help me god, Rick, I won't wait for Big Daddy to deal with you. I'll end you myself."

20

MEL

AFTER THE PLANE CRASH

Mel can't think of many things worse than having to hike through the wilderness after surviving a plane crash. Plus dodging whoever's trying to kill them—both by air and by land. If there's a sea somewhere, they'll probably be trying to use that, too. Persistent fuckers, whoever they are.

But there isn't a sea, mercifully. At least, she's pretty sure there isn't. Her watch is still going and it's almost five. They took off just after noon, and lunch was served around two. That means they might have been in the air for most of the four-hour trip. The trees are too tall for her to see any mountains to track where they actually are. But the terrain, the trees, the volcanic-rock formations they passed by a few minutes ago . . . it all tells her that they might be close to home.

She follows Chloe, gun in hand. What else is she supposed to do? Her head throbs and her legs ache, but it'll be dark soon. Even if Chloe wasn't the job, she can't exactly abandon her. She isn't sure she'd want to.

So she follows, her senses jangling like loose change in a too-big pocket. It has to be sabotage, right? That's why the plane crashed? Will the smoke be enough for someone to find them? Will there be enough time? Has Chloe pissed off someone powerful enough—and crazy enough—to try to kill her via *plane crash*?

What the fuck did she do?

"Your bag's up here," Chloe says, striding toward where the pine trees thicken. "He had a sat phone, the guy who grabbed me. He set it down over here." She scrabbles around in the underbrush near the base of one of the trees, her fingers hitting the plastic. She pulls it out and Mel's heart leaps. Maybe they can call out. If someone's able to get their coordinates then this could be over before nightfall. Thank god.

"Shit," Chloe says, after the phone powers up. She tilts the screen toward Mel.

ENTER PASSWORD

"Fucker," Mel spits, taking the phone from her and mashing the useless buttons. She can't even call 911. It just keeps asking for the password.

"What about your phone?" Chloe asks.

"Still on the plane," Mel says.

"And your bag?" Chloe asks. "Anything good in there?"

Mel unzips the suitcase, pulling out her foldable water bottle and a pair of clean socks, a spare change of clothes, her pocketknife, her fleece, the stash of emergency protein bars, her toiletry bag, and Nat's file on Chloe. Mel grabs the laundry bag last, stuffing everything inside it. There's not much else in her suitcase—mostly pajamas and more clothes—that'll be worth taking.

Chloe never stops moving, making a slow circle around Mel.

"You're welcome to look," Mel says, standing up. "If there's anything you think might be useful." She gestures down to the open suitcase.

Chloe crouches, rooting around in her bag. She grabs a pair of leggings and then her hands brush up against a piece of paper that had fallen out of Nat's file on her. Mel's stomach dips dangerously when she flips it over and Nat's familiar scrawl is there.

"How did you end up working for Nat Parker?" Chloe mutters, handing her the paper with more than a little disgust.

Mel glances down. Of course it's the page where Nat's written out all of Chloe's known traits. The good ones and the bad ones. Plus several theories. Nat was nothing if not thorough.

"I asked her to find you," Mel says.

"You did not."

"What was I supposed to do? I was eighteen and dumb and heart-broken. It's a terrible combination."

"I didn't think you were *that* dumb. What did she say?" Chloe asks, sounding too curious to resist.

"She told me that she'd find you if I told her what happened the night of your party," Mel says.

Chloe flips the suitcase closed. "And did you?"

"Of course I didn't," Mel snaps, unable to take the look she's giving her. "I kept your secret, Chloe. You don't have to worry. Instead, my stupid teenaged ass burst into tears and Nat brought me inside the house and made me tea and then she made me actually drink it. She loved that bitter-as-hell black stuff. I could never get her to drink anything else. I swear, Lipton's was tastier than that shit. I even bought her this fancy set from England for Christmas this year, all early so I was prepared, and she ups and dies on me before we even get through summer, so now she can't even taste it and bitch at me about how the dollar-store stuff is perfectly fine."

"She's—she's gone?" Chloe asks, startled.

"She met your dad in chemo. That's how she got involved in the first place. Though the damn woman was so nosy, if she had heard he was looking for a PI to find you, she would've been on it in a second. She always wanted to know what happened the night of your party."

"You never told her? After working with her for years?"

"She made me a deal that night I showed up and she made me drink that shitty tea for the first but definitely not last time," Mel says. "She told me if I wanted to have any kind of life, I had to leave you behind. And then she turned around and gave me a life. She taught me everything. Paid for my license. Had me and Ted over for Thanks-giving. She saved me.

"And now she's dead and she tried to fuck with me in the end, she tried to get me to tell her what happened right there as they got ready to take her off to hospice. She was still curious. She couldn't rest, knowing there were missing pieces she couldn't find to make Toby's disappearance fit, and that old coot, she loved it when things fit. And I couldn't do it. Even after all those years—I knew her way longer than I knew you—but still—" Mel shakes her head. "You got in me so deep, so fast, and so early. We were so fucking young. I may have left it, when it came to looking for you, but I never was able to let go of you."

"Mel."

Mel shakes her head. Eyes on the ground. Heart in a box, dead and buried long ago.

"We need to move," she says. "Find some tracks. It'll be dark by eight, we need to make good time. That asshole with the gun had to come from somewhere."

"Mel," Chloe says again, even quieter.

"I'm not looking for your pity," Mel says. "And you certainly don't deserve my loyalty. But you've had it all this time. So let's go before more guys show up for you to shoot. I'd rather not have too much blood on my hands by the time we get out of here."

Chloe's lips press together, holding back whatever she wants to say. But her survival instinct wins out—it *always* wins out. That's the thing that Mel needs to cling to.

They know how to survive together.

Mel slings her laundry bag over her shoulders, grateful she chose the backpack kind. Makes carrying it through the wilderness a little easier.

"Let's go," Chloe says.

21

MEL

Ted's been back at Miller Park for a month now. Two weeks in the hospital, two weeks in a shitty motel that sucked Mel's savings dry all the same, and then back on the streets.

She doesn't bother to ask Bob if Ted can stay in the trailer. She's managed to keep Ted's presence in town secret for a whole year and she's not going to mess that up now.

Instead of doing his normal route with Marigold from the gas station to the bridge and back, Ted sleeps a lot these days. It makes her nervous, the thought that someone might hurt him again. So she spends most of her free time with him and when she gets on his nerves—because she does, she's his little sister—she goes to sit at the picnic tables, doing her homework.

It's dark by the time he gets settled for the night and Mel walks back to the tables. The one she thinks of as hers is on the far right. It's just under the streetlight on the path so she can do her homework even when it gets dark.

Mel frowns when she sees the car parked under the streetlight, because it's not one of the regulars. Mrs. Baylor walks her pugs in the mornings because it gets too hot for them in the afternoons. Mrs. Benson works out in the evenings, and James Epperson bikes on his lunch break. She knows everyone who comes in and out of this park—the unhoused people who live in the greenbelt and the housed ones who use the park.

She goes over to her own car to get her backpack out and that's when she sees it: a white card tucked under her windshield wiper.

Nat Parker
Private Investigator
530-555-0131

She flips it over.

I'd like to talk to you about your brother.

Mel looks over her shoulder. There's someone in that car. She can see their outline because they've got their ceiling light on.

If Mel thought it through, she probably would've stopped herself. But she doesn't think it through. She stalks right over to that car and slaps the card against the windshield.

"What the hell is this?" Mel demands through the glass.

The woman slowly gets out of the car, shutting the door carefully, totally unfazed. Mel can't help but notice: she puts her back against the car, just in case.

She focuses on the woman. Forties. Prematurely gray and accepting it, it seems like. Her hair is cut close to her scalp and it suits her. Her hands are sun-spotted. Her boots—steel-toed. Her jacket—much too warm for this weather, but it does a good job at hiding that concealed carry Mel knows she's packing.

"I thought it was clear," the woman says, her blue eyes turning on Mel. It's like a spotlight on you. Her skin crawls under the scrutiny. "I'd like to talk to you about your brother."

"Teddy hasn't done anything," Mel says instantly. "He's been clean over a year. He's got a sponsor and everything."

"I wasn't accusing him of anything," Nat says. "I understand he had an accident that required hospitalization recently? He told nurses that he"—she looks down at her notebook—"fell out of a tree."

Oh god, Teddy, that was a stupid excuse.

"That's right," Mel says. "It was a, uh, tall tree. He hurt himself pretty bad."

"The ER receptionist said a young woman dropped him off and then left just as quickly. Was that you?"

"Yeah," Mel says.

"Why didn't you stay?"

"I'm not a doctor or a nurse. I wasn't very useful sitting in the lobby. And I had to tell my dad he was hurt."

"You ended up in the hospital a short time after that, didn't you?" Nat asks, shifting to casual so smoothly that it's spooky. "The next day, in fact?" Mel had never met anyone she'd describe as *slick* until this moment. It sends her skin crawling like she's found a tick on her.

"I was in a car accident," Mel says. "It didn't have anything to do with Ted's fall."

"Unlucky streak for your family," Nat says.

"That's how it goes sometimes."

"And how do you know Jayden Tucker?"

Her heart skips a beat, but a lie comes to her lips like it's second nature. "Jayden and I hook up sometimes," she says, trying not to sound as revulsed as she is at the idea of fucking Jayden. "Oh my god, is this what this is about? Did Jayden send you after me because I slapped him a little when I found him with that other girl?"

"Is that what you call what you did to Jayden? Slapping him a little?"

Mel remembers the crunch of cartilage under her knuckles. She'd at least broken his nose before he'd given up Toby's location.

"He broke my heart! He slept with one of the cheerleaders. I caught them *in the act*," she says, widening her eyes and trying to sound absolutely heartbroken.

Nat smiles. That slick, knowing smile of a player who recognizes their fellow.

"It was good to meet you, Melanie. Keep my card. I have a feeling you're going to need it."

She gets back into her car and turns it on—she doesn't even look back to make sure Mel's out of the way, she just pulls out like a big ol' princess bitch, expecting the world to move for her.

"Shit," Mel says aloud, just to clinch it.

Nat Parker starts showing up everywhere. At the park. Near the school on her way home. Mel's even pretty sure she tailed her in a silver Honda on one of her trash-hauling jobs.

When she spots the woman lurking near the trailer after a full week of not-so-discreetly following her, Mel's heart drops down to her shitty boots. She strides toward her, trying to project confidence even though she knows: this woman sees through her.

This woman sees all.

There's no proof, she keeps telling herself. *She's just chasing threads.*

"Stalking is illegal," Mel tells Nat, grabbing her keys out of her pocket and measuring the distance with her eyes, wondering if she could just push past her to get inside.

Nat's positioned herself perfectly: Mel has to walk to even get to her, and then she can just follow her straight to the rusty trailer steps where the bottom one is bent at the edge and makes you trip. Mel's bit it on that stair at least six times in her life. She should probably get another tetanus shot before it happens again.

She's managed to avoid a Mount Bob eruption for eight months and twelve days. It's a record.

This woman is gonna ruin her streak. Mel can feel it.

"We need to talk," Nat says.

"Last time I checked, you're not a cop," Mel says.

"I've been hired by the Dunne family to look into their son's disappearance."

"Not sure what that has to do with me."

"Why wouldn't you want to talk to me, if you're not involved?"

Mel starts to move at a clip. If she's just fast enough—

"My daughter mentioned you were mighty interested in getting Toby Dunne alone at Chloe Harper's birthday party," Nat says.

Mel stops. "Your daughter?" she's startled into asking.

"Tiffany," Nat says.

Well, that's another explanation why she doesn't like Nat, if Tiffany sprang from her loins. Christ.

"Tiffany is a pretty unreliable narrator, if you haven't noticed," Mel says, and there's a little twitch to Nat's left eye that tells her she's well aware of her daughter's . . . deficiencies.

It's not like Tiffany was born terrible. Probably. But she seems determined to choose the meanest, easiest path to all the things she wants.

"Then why don't you tell me your side of it . . . as the reliable narrator," Nat says. "I can even come inside." She jerks her head toward the trailer.

"No," Mel says.

She makes a split-second decision, because Tiffany Parker has messed with her and she is gonna fuck that girl up later for it, but she can't right now without clueing in her mom, which really pisses her off.

Mel moves forward, until she's right up in front of Nat. Nat's a tall woman, tall like Mel, so they're eye to eye. But Mel's shoulders are

broader. She's bigger. *Husky*, Bob likes to say when he's being gener-
ous. When he's not, he gets cruel. Mel's learned the dangerous way
there's value in being powerfully built.

"You're not coming into my home," Mel continues. "You're gonna
leave. And you're gonna stay out of my garbage, because I know nasty
PIs like you love to dig in the trash. And you're gonna stay the fuck
away from my father, you hear me?"

Nat's eyes glitter as she takes her in. "So you're protective of your
father, too. Is he the one who helped you?"

God, what does she know? What does she *think* she knows? Because she can't *actually* know. But if what she thinks she knows is
close enough . . .

There's no body, she reminds herself. *Even if they find his truck,
they can't do anything without a body.*

"Stay away from my family," Mel says firmly.

And of course, just as she says it, because she's cursed with terrible
timing—always with the terrible timing—the trailer door behind her
bangs open.

Bob steps out, storm on his face already. He hates when there's
noise outside, which is fucking rich, living in a trailer park, especially
across from the Baker boys, who are absolutely growing weed in their
double-wide and blare music from Friday afternoon through Saturday night.

But that's Bob: in a perpetual shit fit.

"What is this?" he asks, his eyes skating right over Mel and onto
Nat Parker instead, which is a relief.

"She's fucking crazy and keeps bothering me," Mel says. She will
throw her under the Bob bus to get inside.

"Bothering you?" His eyes narrow.

"Mr. Tillman, I assume?" Nat asks. "My name is Nat Parker. I'm
an investigator."

"A cop?"

"A PI," she says.

"So she's not under arrest?"

"No," Nat says, and she says it in a way that seems to imply *not yet.*
A prickle of fear zips down Mel's back.

"Mr. Tillman, did you happen to hear about the Dunne boy?" Nat
continues. "It was the big story in the papers a few months ago? He

went missing in June, somewhere between here and Grants Pass in Oregon."

Now Bob's focus is on her instead of Nat. Shit.

"Yeah, I heard," he says. "What about it?"

"I have reason to believe your daughter was one of the last people to see the boy before he went missing."

"You have something to do with that?" he demands.

"I told you, she's crazy," Mel says.

"Are you Ted's father, as well?" Nat asks.

Bob's eyes burn against her skin. "Why the fuck is she talking about Teddy? Is he back in town?"

"It's nothing," Mel says quickly.

Damn it, if she had managed to keep Ted being back in town a secret for another six months, she might've had enough saved back up for a deposit on an apartment.

Oh, who was she kidding. She spent all her savings—all the apartment down-payment money—to take care of Ted after the hospital. It'd take another year of junk hauling to get the money now. Another year of him sleeping rough. Another year of worrying. Another year of wondering if he was gonna leave her again.

Stability was important for recovery and Ted didn't have as much as he deserved. She kept trying. She really did. But she was sixteen still. She needed to be older. Better.

"Ted was the victim of an attack last month. He was at the Harper's Bluff Hospital for almost two weeks. Did you not know?"

"I don't deal with tweakers who steal from me, even if they are my blood," Bob says.

"I see," Nat says, and Mel hates those words more than any other, because this woman? This woman *does* see. She sees everything. Mel's exposed, flayed freely, and she walked right into it.

Bob looks at her. "Did you know he was hurt? You helping him again?"

"I'm not talking about family business in front of her," Mel says.

"You'll do what I say."

She shifts from foot to foot, preparing herself. You don't want to tense into a blow. Bob broke a few of her teeth before she learned that.

"Maybe I should—" Nat starts to say.

"You're the one coming around, asking questions," Bob tells her. "I'm getting you answers. That's what you want, innit?" He sucks at the wad stuck in his cheek and spits out a stream of brown . . . right at her feet.

She doesn't even look down or flinch in disgust. Nat Parker keeps her eyes right on Mel, who can barely look at her. She's not even something like a deer caught in headlights. She can't even be graceful.

No, she's a starved raccoon in the middle of the road, scarfing down roadkill as the car careens toward killing her.

"I don't believe it was your daughter who dropped Ted off at the hospital," Nat says, before Mel can say anything. "She was at a birthday party for a friend at the time. That's why I wanted to talk to her. Last time anyone saw Toby Dunne was at the party."

"So you're just talking to all the guests?"

"Of course," Nat says. "I'll get out of your hair. Melanie—" She nods at Mel, a warning in her eyes.

Mel watches her go, baffled at the shift. She saved her ass. Kind of.

"You talking to Teddy?" Bob demands as soon as she's out of earshot.

Mel doesn't even flinch when he raises his hand . . . or when the trailer door down the way bangs open and Miss Bev steps out, hands on her hips.

"You're not getting into trouble over there, are you, Bob?" she calls. "I don't want to have to call the sheriff again."

"Get inside," Bob says, jerking her arm and entire body around so she's facing the trailer door. Mel contemplates fighting it, but she knows it's no use.

She goes inside.

She doesn't make a sound.

She knows better.

22

CHLOE

She has to tell Mel. Chloe doesn't even know where to start, so she focuses on tracking instead. She never had her father's skill for this, but the man she shot, he hadn't bothered to move through the forest with care. He was about as subtle as a wayward calf and *those* she has experience tracking down.

She spots indentations of boot prints in the still-soft ground.

"He came from the north," she says, pointing. "This might be easier than we thought."

"Oh yes, easy," Mel says. "A nice stroll through the wilderness after a plane crash is just the thing. Positively bracing in the best way. It'll be the new extreme sport."

"Better than trashing Everest with bodies and junk," Chloe says, ignoring the sarcasm even though it'll annoy her further. Mel rolls her eyes and they walk in silence for a good half hour. Their entire focus on the terrain, on any possible threats ahead or around them.

Chloe's head still aches from the smoke and whatever drugs she didn't vomit up, but she's not injured like Mel. "Your leg okay?" she asks as she spots another boot print.

"It'll be fine," Mel says.

"You gotta tell me if it's not."

"I won't slow you down."

"I'm not worried about—" Chloe stops, taking a deep breath. "I'd carry you, if I had to," she says finally.

"Big promise for such a little woman," Mel says.

"I could bench-press you," Chloe snaps, offended.

"I have no doubt of your ability," Mel says. "But your resolve to not leave me behind? Another story."

"You're really gonna act like this now of all times?' Chloe asks, spotting another footprint about three feet ahead. He definitely came from the north. Her hand tightens around her bow. If she knows the Dicks—and she does, very unfortunately, after six years of this shit— there's at least another one out there. Maybe more.

"Shit," she says suddenly.

"What?" Mel asks.

"Nothing, I just twisted wrong," Chloe says. She's no Mel, brain-power wise, especially after a plane crash, but how did she not think of it before? If the Dicks put guys out here in the forest, that meant one thing.

Something went wrong. They weren't supposed to crash. They were supposed to have landed on the strip.

That meant it wasn't too far. She had the advantage. She just needed to survive.

Water. Shelter. Warmth. Her father's voice echoes in her ears. *Weapons. Food. In that order, Chloe.*

Mel's got her stuff. Chloe's got a bow and arrows, twenty-four waterproof matches, a few pouches of tuna, and half a dozen protein bars. So water and shelter are the only things left on the list.

And, you know, safety. Not that they're going to get anywhere close to that.

She needs to tell her. Soon. It's dangerous, Mel walking into this with no knowledge. But if she starts telling her now, she's gonna get mad and then she'll probably start yelling about the Oregon Trail again or list the exact way you make heroin from poppies, because of course she knows how. She knows *everything*. She's Wikipedia on steroids.

But she doesn't know this.

Her foot squelches in mud as the forest thickens around them. The ground is at a decline, steepening with each step. Downhill is good, Rick would need flat land for a landing strip.

She hears before she sees it—the burble and rush of water. "Look," she says, pointing ahead when the stream comes into sight. "We should fill up."

Mel nods and they scramble down the bank. Mel pulls out her collapsible water bottle, dipping it into the stream. "Let's hope we don't get dysentery."

"Again with the Oregon Trail," Chloe says.

Mel shrugs. "Not all of us had brand-new computers as a kid. You know where we're going?"

Chloe starts at the abrupt change of subject. Mel slants a look at her from her crouch by the water.

"You told me you'd explain after lunch," Mel says. "It's after lunch."

"You cannot hold me to that when we've suffered a *plane crash*," Chloe says.

"Can't I?" Mel asks. "Because you killed a dude."

"So did you," Chloe shoots back, entirely childishly.

"Yeah, but you know why I did that, and it was eight years go. This was maybe forty-five minutes ago and you haven't told me why."

"I told you he wasn't here to help us."

"You know that's—" Mel cuts off completely, straightening in one smooth movement, the bottle of water dropping to the ground as her hand goes for her waistband where the gun's tucked. "Get behind me."

"No way," Chloe says, arrow in hand.

"Don't argue," Mel says. "Get down!"

She tugs her toward a group of manzanita bushes, ducking behind them. Chloe kneels down next to her, watching through the branches.

The movement is subtle—this guy, he *does* know how to move through the forest. Not Rick's man Vinny, then. He's a bumbler. Or Dick Junior, not that she expected Mr. Precious to sweat out here in the forest. But Rick has trust issues with his underlings, especially after what Toby pulled.

Did he hire out this time? That would be risky and pricey, for this level of silence, but maybe Big Daddy splurged once he got news Chloe was coming back.

God, if Mel had just left her alone for a few more months, maybe she would've been able to track the shell company and use it to her advantage.

But by then, her father might be dead.

Chloe can't blame or fault Mel. If she gets out of this forest alive and back to her father to say goodbye, that means everything.

Key word here: *if.*

More quiet rustling along the trees across the creek. He's staying in the cover and Chloe can't tell if it's because he spotted them or because he's just scoping the area. It's smart to stake out the water source. There might not be another for miles.

But the smoke from the crash could have drawn Cal Fire out. Cal Fire had those firefighters who jumped out of planes for this exact reason: you can't drag firefighting equipment across these mountain ranges. Half of the ways in are roads that had long fallen off maps.

Mel watches as the movement in the trees—too consistent to be the wind—rustles to a stop across the creek from them.

"Shit," she hisses, spotting it right before he does: Mel's water bottle, glinting silver as the sun hits it.

Next to her, Mel tenses as she comes to the same realization as Chloe. They're screwed.

A barrel-chested man with a black beard creeps out of the trees. Chloe's never been a gun person, but she knows the one he's carrying is serious shit just by the size. She knew Rick had majorly upped his game over the past four years, but this kind of weaponry? For her?

She really had driven him off the ledge of reason. She didn't mean to. But he was just so frustrating. He never gave up. But then, neither did she.

She had managed to keep hold of her sanity. A little. Maybe. That was exactly what someone driven mad by being hunted by a crazed drug lord might say, come to think of it.

Focus, you idiot. Mel's not shaking next to her, she's gone still and silent, her entire body alert, her hands clutching the gun.

Don't shoot, Chloe mouths at her. She taps the bow. *Better.*

Superior, really.

The man's on the opposite bank now. The creek's not deep, not like the one Chloe built her rope bridge over. He'll just splash across and when he spots them . . .

"Twenty seconds," Mel whispers, nodding to the boulder about twenty feet to their right. "I'll dive for the boulder and draw his fire. You pop up and shoot him before he shoots me."

"Shitty idea," Chloe counters.

"You got any better ones?"

Splash.

He's in the water. No time to lose.

"Nope," Chloe says, and it's like she's just been waiting for any sound from her, because Mel rises before she's even finished popping her *p*.

Mel runs. He swings the gun toward her and then his entire body as her momentum builds and she dives toward the boulder as the first bullet hits it. It's all Chloe needs, she's up, her arrow nocked. She pulls back, her arm aching from the crash, letting it fly.

It punches through his arm instead of his chest.

"Shit!"

She reaches up to nock another arrow, but before she can even grasp it, a shot rings out and the man jerks like a puppet with cut-off strings. A terrible, full-body movement, his head pops up to the sky with the momentum as the back of his skull explodes.

Chloe bends over and gags at the sight. *Christ.* There's a reason she shoots people with arrows instead.

Mel stands behind the boulder, both hands clutching the gun so tight Chloe's a little afraid she can't let go.

"Mel," she says slowly, wiping her mouth with the back of her hand. She straightens, trying not to look at the man now floating in the creek, bouncing gently back and forth as his brain matter leaks into the water. The bears around here are going to have an interesting palate after today.

"It's okay," Mel says. "I'm okay."

"You really don't look okay," Chloe says, stepping toward her in concern.

"Well, I've never shot anyone before," Mel says, staring down at the man. "I just . . . I didn't want to miss. If I missed, we would be really screwed. So I didn't miss."

"That's good, 'cause he was going to kill you if you missed," Chloe says. "And then me."

"Agreed," Mel says. "I just—" She stares down at the man and then back at Chloe. "Are you going to tell me why I've just killed a man? Because I'd really like to justify this in my head and fast before I have to possibly kill more people to get out of here. Are there more people, Chloe? More coming for us? For you?"

Chloe takes a deep breath. It's now or never.

Mel has been in the dark about what really happened, this whole time. Chloe chose that for her when they were eighteen, and she hasn't regretted it, but it's nearly killed her.

"Yes," Chloe says. "More people are coming. The whole lot of them are coming. Probably to kill us."

"Tell me what is going on," Mel demands.

There is no choice. No avoidance. No dancing around it. Not when the love of your life has killed not once, but *twice*, for you.

Chloe's kept it in for so long—has been on the run for *so long*—that it's hard to know where to start. She'd been so sure, the first year, that Mel would find a way to track her down. She used to dream about it so much it almost felt like it happened.

But she'd long ago abandoned rehearsing speeches for the day that Mel came for her. Because after a few years, she realized Mel wasn't coming.

The only people coming were Rick and the rest of the Dicks.

The only place to really start is at the beginning.

"Do you remember Toby Dunne?" she asks.

"Do I remember Toby?" Mel repeats incredulously. "Do I remember the boy who chased us into the woods and tried to kill us because you were about to expose him for running over a child? Do I *remember* him?"

Chloe doesn't even bother to interrupt her. She just lets her go. She's missed it so much.

"No, of course not," Mel drawls. "Of course I don't remember Toby. I don't remember fighting for my life against his linebacker ass. I don't remember you pushing him off that goddamn cliff. I don't remember having to *stomp* on his fingers so he'd let go. I don't remember the six hours it took to *bury him*. Nope. Not at all. Toby who?"

"This is unnecessary," Chloe says, trying to sound prim and failing miserably.

"What does Toby have to do with this? That was years ago. We were kids."

"Toby has everything to do with this," Chloe says.

"Tell me," Mel says, all that keen focus on Chloe and she hadn't forgotten what it was like, more like she'd been haunted by it. All that intelligence, focused right on her. It was intimidating. Exhilarating. Way too revealing.

God, Mel must be the best PI. She already knows half of what you're going to tell her by looking at you.

Chloe takes a deep breath. Here it is. The moment she really should've practiced for. Mel would've practiced. Mel wouldn't have run in the first place. She's a fighter, Mel is.

And Chloe's a runner.

That's the difference between them. The thing that's defined all their moments, even the first. It's why Mel brought a gun to confront Toby while Chloe confronted Toby in her best sundress with nothing but her naive sense of justice and foolish sense of security from being on her father's land.

She can't run anymore.

Mel has stopped her in her tracks. Like always.

"Nat Parker suspected you," Chloe says. "But someone else suspected me."

23

CHLOE

TWO YEARS AFTER CHLOE'S SWEET SIXTEEN PARTY

There's a truck trailing her. Considering her experience with trucks and this road, it puts her on edge. Chloe tucks herself farther into the shoulder as she runs, so she's made space for them to drive past.

But they don't. More than sweat trickles down her spine as the truck slows, scattering gravel all over as the driver pulls half off the shoulder and matches her pace.

She doesn't stop—not immediately—she's not gonna get yanked into some asshole's truck where no one can see her. She pushes ahead, he's not ready for her unexpected burst of speed. She cuts in front of the truck and dashes into the middle of the empty road, giving her a good look into the driver's side and causing him to have to shudder to a halt with a curse.

Blood pounds in her head as she stares at the man. She recognizes him, though she's never met him. Olivia pointed him out to her once, at one of the rallies when Dad was running for mayor the second time after losing to Richard Newell the first time.

If Daddy fought dirty, he'd just go after that guy, Olivia had told her. *He's the mayor's cousin, the drug dealer. Rick.*

"You stay away from me," she says. "I know you know who my daddy is."

Rick grins at her. "I remember seeing you up on that stage, election night. You were wearing a dress with sunflowers. Crooked braids. You were so sweet. Did you grow up sour, Chloe Bryce?"

She flinches at the casual use of the name only her family calls her. How did he know?

"I always thought your big sister would be the firecracker of the family," Rick continues. "She being the athlete and everything. But look at you. You proved me wrong. You've got a beast inside you."

She's not sticking around to figure out his riddles. He's probably high off his own product. "Leave me alone," she says, putting one of her earbuds back in her ear and starting to turn.

"Can't do that," he says. "I've got something to ask you."

"Well, I've got no answers. Get out of here."

"You're gonna get in the truck, Chloe Bryce," he singsongs.

More fear snakes its way down her spine. A memory that's not a ghost, but still solid in its newness. She knows what it feels like to be one breath away from the *be killed* part of *kill or be killed*.

It's the same feeling rushing through her right now.

She wasn't prepared that night with Toby. Never again. She's got a Taser tucked in her hip pack. Her hand goes to her lower back where it's shifted during her run, unzipping it, fingers closing around it.

"You're gonna get out of here," she says, pulling the Taser out and flipping the switch. It sparks angry and sharp between them, the electric hiss and pop sizzling in the air. "Or you're gonna get this shoved in your crotch."

"Did you zap Toby Dunne with that before you killed him?"

She does *not* drop the Taser. But her hand spasms so hard around it her thumb sparks it live again, the sound crackling to meet his rising laughter.

"Aw, baby girl, you've got no poker face. How did you get away with murderous shit so long if *this* is how you react?" He clucks his tongue at her as he gets out of the truck, strolling into the middle of the empty road like he's got no care in the world. Chloe needs to run. But he'll grab her. Why isn't there a car coming? Why isn't anyone coming? Why did she run on the road today instead of through the fields?

He was waiting for you, he would've found you, he knows, run, you can't, but he knows, so you have to. Stuck, you're completely stuck.

"Get in the truck, Chloe Bryce."

"*Stop calling me that,*" she snaps, unable to stop herself.

"Aw." He clucks his tongue again. "I feel like I know you now, the time I've had to spend figuring out what you did. Like I said, I thought your sister would be the firecracker. Unless . . . is she the one who helped you?"

Her eyes widen. "If you say another word about my sister—"

"God, that lack of poker face." He kisses his fingers and bursts them to the sky. "You really are sweet as a peach, but you're rotten underneath that pretty fuzz. I love that in a girl. Are you really gonna try to jab me with that?" He flicks his hand up to his hip, pulling his jean jacket with the chewing tin outline worn into the front pocket back to expose the gun at his hip. "Wouldn't be the first time. Feels kinda nice after a while. The vibrations, you know."

Her face goes hot, her ears tinny as she keeps her grip on the Taser and the distance between them. Could she run into the field? Try to make it for the tree line what . . . three, four acres away? Could she outrun him? Her eyes sweep down. He's wearing cowboy boots. He might slip if she gets to ground with pine needles, but he might not.

"Get in," he says again.

"Or what, you'll shoot me?" she asks shakily, trying to buy time. Can she run? Will he try to mow her down if she tries?

He pulls out his phone and holds it out. On the screen is her sister, sitting outside a coffee shop somewhere in Palo Alto.

"My friend who's watching her sent it to me a few minutes ago," Rick says. "It'll take less than thirty seconds for him to grab her."

"She's not part of this. She didn't—" She stops, she can't admit it. But does it even matter?

He knows.

"Fine. She didn't help you. Then that means she can stay out of this if you come with me."

"What do you want?" she asks.

"I want you to tell me what the fuck you did to Toby Dunne," he says. "He has something of mine. Something he stole." His gaze sharpens on Chloe, assessing her as the blood drains out of her face. "Did you find it?" he asks suddenly. "Did you find them?"

"Find what?" she asks shakily, in genuine confusion.

He sighs. "Oh, sweetheart, I was hoping you had them. It would've been better for you. But you can't lie for shit about this, can you?"

"I don't know—what . . . what did Toby take from you?"

"Diamonds, baby girl. A fuck-load of them. And if that cute little face of yours is telling the truth and you don't have them, that means he's still got 'em. So."

He gestures to the open truck door with a flourish.

"Get in," he says. "And take me to where you killed that boy."

24

MEL

"Diamonds," Mel says slowly, staring at her as Chloe finishes. "Toby stole *diamonds* from a drug dealer."

Chloe nods.

"This all started because of a fucking treasure hunt?" Mel demands.

"It's not a treasure hunt. I mean, kind of. But also no. This started with a robbery that neither of us knew about. Toby took the diamonds from Rick—I think probably the day of my birthday."

"That motherfucker. Who steals a drug dealer's diamonds? Did he have a death wish or something? The only thing worse you could do is steal their product."

"They're not even Rick's, is the thing. The diamonds belong to the family."

Mel's eyes widen. "So Toby stole the Newell family jewels? Fuck. That's . . ."

"Stupid. Dangerous. And it would've gotten him killed, but . . ."

". . . we got there first."

"Yep."

"We have the worst fucking timing," Mel says.

"And we continue to," Chloe says. "Come on, we have to keep moving." She eyes the dead guy in the stream. He's currently half wedged between two stones, rocking not-so-gently between them, the water rusting around him. "Do you want to take his gun?"

"Fuck no," Mel says. "First, it's all wet. Second, it'd probably knock me off my feet. I'm good with the handgun."

"If he came from that way"—Chloe points—"that means they both came from the north. I'm pretty sure if we walk long enough, we're gonna hit an airstrip that Rick Newell uses to fly product under the radar."

"You want to head *toward* the drug dealer who wants to kill you?"

"They've got to have a plane that can get us out of here," Chloe says.

"Did you pick up pilot skills while you were gone?"

"I wish. But holding whoever's left hostage to fly us is the only plan I've got. I don't think we're near a road . . . Rick wouldn't exactly build his drug-trafficking hot spot somewhere just anyone can access."

Mel swears under her breath. "Okay, let's go. And keep explaining."

They cross the creek upstream, so they're not wading through blood and gore downstream. Mel studiously avoids looking at the man, like she doesn't want to commit the sight to the photographic part of her memory.

They squelch up the creek bank, disappearing into the trees. Chloe checks the compass on her wrist, adjusting as they head north.

"So, just so I'm clear: you're saying we buried Toby Dunne in the middle of the woods with the Newell family diamonds in his pockets?" Mel asks when Chloe doesn't continue, because fuck, how is she supposed to explain this, really?

"Stolen diamonds without serial numbers," Chloe says, keeping one eye fixed ahead of them. Mel hangs back behind her just a little, they've fallen into the same pattern they did in their teens—*you have my back, I'll watch ahead*—so easily that Chloe could laugh. Old habits never die. And neither do they.

"You probably know more about how much untraceable currency like the diamonds are worth, being in your business," she continues.

God, there's nothing but pine trees everywhere. How are they going to get out of here?

"No serial numbers?" Mel asks, voice sharpening.

"They're from the thirties or something. Been in the Newell family forever. And Rick kept ranting about how flawless and special they are. Considering him and his entire family have been chasing after me for six years, I'd guess he wasn't exaggerating."

"*All* the Newells? But they're—"

"Not criminals?" Chloe asks sarcastically.

"They're a century-old political dynasty from one of the red districts in California, of course they're criminals." Mel sneers. "I just thought—"

"—they weren't fueled by Rick's drug money? Think again. I've spent years tracking down all the Newells' dirty work. Rick's business has been keeping the political machine running since the assembly-man's first mayoral campaign where he beat my father. That's partly why they want the diamonds. Richard III, he aspires to be more than assemblyman. He's eyeing the Senate. He needs money for it."

"Why the fuck did Toby steal them in the first place?" Mel asks.

"Hubris? A way to screw Rick over for underpaying him? Maybe he had some magpie in him and liked shiny things. I don't know, Mel. I didn't ask him before we kicked him off a cliff."

"All the Newells are after you?"

"Yep. Though Junior's the only one who's seen me in years. Right before I stabbed him."

"Junior," Mel says. "Dick Junior? The one running for mayor? You stabbed the shoo-in for mayor?"

"I still can't believe Dick Junior is running for mayor," Chloe says. "An emu is smarter than him."

"But not better looking." Mel shrugs. "He's got guns, he's got good looks, he's got it all wrapped up and he hasn't even done anything but make a few posters. Now, about that stabbing?"

"He deserved it," Chloe says darkly.

"I have no doubt," Mel says.

"And he survived."

"Obviously. You do not sound thrilled about that."

It starts to unfold like a Slinky in Mel's brain, all the little pieces of the last few years falling together. She can see it so clearly now.

"Oh, I bet all the political favors the assemblyman gets will go away so fast if the family gets exposed. It's not even weed, which Sacramento might hand wave!" Excitement spears through her. "This is great."

"I have no idea why it would be," Chloe says. "You don't want to mess with the Bag of Dicks, Mel. They want to kill you, too."

"The Bag of Dicks?" she echoes. "That's . . . a moniker if there ever was one."

"Don't let the fun name fool you. Rick's dangerous, Dick Junior is foul, and Richard III is powerful. And don't get me started on Big Daddy Newell."

"Big Daddy?"

"What they call Richard I. He's over eighty and they're all still running around, trying to impress him, just like their fathers did . . . straight into early graves. That's why they're all named Richard."

"They call him—" Mel stops herself and her horror. "You know what? Never mind. So Rick wanted the diamonds back and he thought you had them."

Chloe nods.

"Why didn't you just sic your dad on him?"

"Because Rick only knew parts of the story. He knew about me, but he didn't know about you. He'd put it together . . . but only kind of. He thought it went down *after* the car accident, because Toby's cell phone pinged in Grants Pass and that's where his truck was found."

"Because I drove it all the way there and then hitched all the way back to fuck with the timeline and the search," Mel says.

"Well, that ended up saving you from Rick *and* the cops, because it took him three years to realize I had an accomplice. When he first came for me, he thought I killed Toby on the way to Grants Pass somewhere, not that he chased me—us—into the woods at home. That's the only reason I was able to get away from Rick after he confronted me. I made him drive up the 5 long enough that he needed gas and as soon as he pulled over, I ran.

"But he never suspected you. He didn't know about you. Not the whole time he was accusing me. Not once when he was threatening me and my family and everyone I'd ever loved. I had to keep you safe. I tried to keep everyone safe."

"So you ran?"

Shit. Mel had been so in her head those last few weeks before Chloe left, trying to get her and Ted moved into the new apartment and away from Bob for good, *finally*. She'd been worried about so many things—about getting on her feet, about being independent, about Chloe forgetting her once she got to college—she hadn't seen the crisis until they were both in it.

"He threatened Olivia first, to get me into his truck. He threatened my parents. The twins. He even threatened to go after the Hendersons." Her voice dips horribly on the Hendersons' name. "If he knew about you, he would've threatened you, too. He would've gone after you first, if he knew how I felt—" Chloe stops. "I had to run."

"You must've been terrified."

"I was. For you. For everyone."

"Are you *sure* Toby had the diamonds on him?"

"Yes. Because I didn't check his jacket pockets," Chloe blurts out.

"What?"

"When we buried Toby. His phone and keys were in his jeans pockets. I found them first. I was so relieved I had them that I didn't think to check his jacket pockets. So my working theory is that we *did* bury the diamonds with him. Because if they were in his truck somewhere, it would've been in the police report when they found it."

"And how many diamonds—how much—what kind of money are we talking about here?"

"About ten million, according to Rick. Maybe more when you consider they might be sold on the not-so-legal market?"

"Shit," Mel says, shuddering to a stop.

"Eloquent."

Mel glares at her and picks up her pace, still trying to make sense of this tangle and not slip in the browning pine needles at the same time.

"Okay, why didn't you just tell Rick where the diamonds were if you were sure they were on Toby?"

"Well, one, I had no assurance he wouldn't just *kill me* after I told him. Two, even if he didn't kill me, what was I supposed to do, hand over the diamonds *and* proof that I killed Toby? And three, which is kind of the most important one: I couldn't bring Rick to Toby's body because I don't know where we buried him."

That brings Mel to another halt. Chloe frowns as Mel stares at her like she's grown a new nose or something. "You—you don't know?"

"I don't remember," Chloe says. "It was dark. We'd gotten all turned around in the woods. By the time we headed out, I'd spent hours hiding and fighting him and even more hours burying him. I was exhausted. Excuse me for not making note of the landmarks."

"Why didn't you just ask me?" Mel bursts out, ignoring the other pretty good reasons for not leading a drug dealer on the hunt for stolen diamonds to said diamonds without some sort of backup plan.

"What are you talking about?" Chloe asks, brows knitting together. "You told me, right after Nat Parker accused you, that no one would ever find Toby. That *you* couldn't even find him again if you wanted to and *you* buried him."

"Shit," Mel says. "I did say that."

That sick churn of realization in Mel's stomach is like acid, burning at her organs as Chloe's face darkens with realization. "Are you telling me you were lying?" she demands. "That you *do* know where Toby's buried?"

25

MEL

AFTER THE PLANE CRASH

"Look—" Mel says, the guilt knotting her throat because *shit*, she did tell Chloe that. "When I told you I wouldn't be able to find Toby's body back when Nat was closing in, you were so freaked. You were *crying* and I was sixteen and I really didn't want the girl I liked to cry. I was just . . . trying to be reassuring."

"Oh my god!" Chloe hisses, because she can't exactly scream. "I've been on the run for six years, and now we're heading straight toward these bastards and you've known where Toby was buried this whole time?"

"If you had told me what was going on, I could've enlightened you! This is on your fuck-all communication skills and teenaged panic, Chloe! *You left me!*"

"I didn't want to!"

"You still did. You left me with all the pieces, your friends and family were going crazy and I couldn't do a goddamn thing about it because they didn't know who I was. The twins were fucking *broken*. Especially because their dad died a month later and their college plans went out the window. And you were gone. Their best friend was *gone*. All they were left with was *me and I was no good.*"

Chloe sags against a pine tree like she needs it to help her stay up. "Don't say that," she says. "You're perfect. You are the most loyal person I know. You fight for everyone you love."

"I would've fought for you!" Mel almost screams it.

"That's why I had to go!" Chloe says, just as loud. "I had one chance, when Rick stopped for gas on the way to Grants Pass. I ran and I kept running. I knew that he'd be too distracted chasing me to keep digging. I did it so you didn't have to fight. You've spent your entire fucking life fighting people! To keep yourself safe, to keep me safe! I didn't want that for you! I wanted you to settle down. I wanted you to have a life."

"But I didn't settle down," Mel says, her voice thick. "I pined for you. Those first weeks . . . the only reason I got out of bed was because of Ted. He was taking care of me back then, not the other way around. I couldn't even tell him why. And then the weeks turned into months and then years, all because you didn't check to see if I knew where we buried him! You should have asked me," Mel says, so angry she can't even breathe. "You should've asked me. I would've taken Rick to the body. We could've avoided years of this! We could've had *years*, Chloe."

"He would've killed you," Chloe says hopelessly. "I would've made the same choice I did before. Don't you get it? I wouldn't have risked you even if I was sure you knew where Toby was. I would've run all the same. I could never put a target on your back. The Dicks had no idea you existed. I loved you more than anyone else and you were safer than anyone else, but the only way you stayed that way was if I ran and they never found out about you. I would've run a thousand times to make sure you were safe."

"Fuck you," Mel says. "You made a choice for me, you chose a whole life for me that I didn't want. That I never wanted, because from the second I really knew you, all I wanted was *you*." She wipes at her face angrily, ignoring the tears. "I never wanted anyone but you. I couldn't get over you in a few months or a year like a normal person. No, you know what I did, instead? I became a PI. I became a person who had all the skills to find you . . . and then I didn't. Every day it was a fight in me, not to look for you. My mental game of chicken. *Is this the day I break?* I could never let you go. So you don't get to say you'd make every single choice the same like it's some righteous thing because look where it got us! Right where you didn't want us to be. All of it was for shit! We're right back where we were before, in the fucking forest running."

Chloe glares at her.

"You leaving me shaped me. Your choices, they made me. I am who I am because of you! Because I love you!"

"Don't say it like a death sentence."

"Isn't it?" They're yelling at each other here in the middle of the woods, and anyone could hear but no one comes. Mel swears to God, if someone comes running, she's gonna shoot them just to keep them from interrupting her from dealing with this finally. She's trembling so hard she thinks she might shake out of her skin. Her entire body hums with that terrible mix of adrenaline and danger and . . . "You wrote letters and postcards to your parents but never me. You never tried once to come back!"

"That's not true," Chloe says. "I tried, once. To come back."

"You did?" Mel stares at her, trying to suppress the angry *Then why didn't you come for me?* that wants to come out. But her heart twists when Chloe continues.

"When my grandpa died . . . I couldn't miss his funeral . . . but I never made it to the church. They found me, it was like the Newells had planted spies all over the county just in case I finally showed. I had to learn the lesson the hard way: to never, ever come back."

"You were just gonna let them ruin our lives forever."

Chloe says nothing.

"Six fucking years, Chloe!" she yells because if she doesn't remind herself, she might grab her and kiss her.

"I was trying to protect you!"

"Look where that got us! Crashed in the damn woods! Killing men right and left! Just like we're sixteen again!"

"Technically, Toby was just one man and I would argue he was more of a boy—" She cuts off when Mel stares at her. "Okay, your point is taken," she mutters.

"What am I supposed to do with all this?" Mel asks, trying not to reel, but fuck, this is a lot. Even for her brain.

"Survive," Chloe says. "Survive so we can figure this out."

"Figure *what* out? Us? Or how to get out of this mess with the Dicks?"

"Both," Chloe says.

"You're really wanting to take multitasking to another level here," Mel says.

"Do you believe I love you?" Chloe asks, sounding so hopeless it breaks whatever's left of Mel's heart. She hadn't even realized there was enough intact for that to happen.

"I know you loved me," Mel says.

"I *love* you. Present tense. Not past. Everything I've done, I've done to keep you and everyone I love safe."

"It didn't work," Mel says, and now she's the hopeless one. "You just made us suffer, because we didn't have you."

"You have me now," Chloe says.

"Do I?" Mel asks. "For how long? Until your Bag of Dicks comes round the mountain and kills us both? Or—if we survive—until you run again? Because don't tell me that you were planning on staying. If we hadn't crashed, you were going to blow town as soon as you said your goodbyes to your father."

"You're right, I was going to leave," Chloe says. "But now . . ." She looks at Mel, the distance between them suddenly feeling impassable, even though it's less than four feet. "Now . . ."

"You can't even say it," Mel says, okay, maybe she dares it, because she's an ass and she's frustrated and she knows her. "You can't even fight for me." She knows how to load her like a weapon and make her pull the trigger. So she seals it with the killing blow. "*Coward.*"

And just like that, Chloe's blue eyes spark at the challenge of the insult and Mel's broken heart thuds, still trying to keep blood in it through the carnage that is Chloe Harper.

Mel never can leave well enough alone.

Chloe pushes off the trunk of that tree and Mel's moving, heart-blood spilling and fuck it all, because when they collide, it's on the edge of vicious, too sharp and too much and she tastes like salt and citrus, she haunted her for-fucking-ever and now . . . *finally* . . . Chloe can't run anywhere but to her.

Chloe slides her hands under her shirt, curling into the soft skin of her lower back, trying to anchor her. To keep her.

She kisses her like it's the last fucking time because it very well may be. The greed to touch is overwhelming—what a way to go. When her hand comes up to press her thumb against that spot behind her ear that always made her squirm when they were younger, the *sounds* Chloe makes. It vibrates against Mel's lips as she pulls her closer, so hard they stagger backward steps, and then Mel's pushing her against the pine tree, because if they don't get some outside support they're gonna end up on the ground.

She still tastes like lemons. Mel never could eat one without thinking of her.

"I couldn't let them get to you," Chloe says against her lips, a blur of a sound that she can barely make out. "I just couldn't. Not after—"

Mel just swallows the citrus-bitten words, her entire being focused on getting closer. On giving more.

For a moment, it is blissfully, beautifully quiet in her mind. It's just sensation. Chloe's hands on her skin. Shivering touches that are almost too sensitive, too much in the wake of the before-memory.

There were kids before. They're not anymore. They know the risk. The consequences.

The fucking glory that is *this*.

She is love-drunk and stupid. She always was when it came to Chloe. But as her hands dip into the waistband of her pants, Mel's fingers resting against the precious softness of her hip, it's like her brain comes back online, just for a shuddering flicker.

I tried once. To come back.

She bats the thought away as Chloe's hand grips her ass. What a fucking glorious feeling. The strength of her, combined with how pocket-size she is . . . it's deceptive in the best way. And wildly distracting.

But Mel's brain can't keep quiet. Maybe it is a fucking curse. It feels like one right now.

When my grandpa died . . .

It can't be. But just as soon as it crosses her mind she thinks: *Who are you kidding. How did you not see this?*

Mel jerks in Chloe's hold.

"What? What?!" Chloe looks around wildly, like she expects the Dicks to be coming.

But no.

It's her. Her and her realization. She didn't see it before. Not back then. How could she have missed this?

Now it's all she can see. A connect-the-dots moment that ends in a pool of blood.

Heat crawls up Mel's face that has nothing to do with taste and touch.

"What's wrong?" Chloe blinks at her, her lips pink and her eyes hazy as her hands fall away.

For a second, Mel just looms over her, hands framing her against the tree. She pants, partly because, well, yeah, she's desperately horny. But mostly, she's lost her breath in realization.

"You said Rick figured out you had an accomplice three years ago," she says slowly. "And then you said you tried to come home once. When your grandpa died."

She wants to step away. She *needs* to step away. Because if she doesn't . . .

If she doesn't, she might just explode.

But she doesn't move. Neither does Chloe. Mel's hands curl into fists above Chloe's head as the pieces fly around in her brain, battering against each other, trying to fit.

"Your grandpa died three years ago," she says. "The same time

Rick found out you had an accomplice. And you tried to come back. *Three years ago.*" She pounds her fists against the tree. "You know what else happened three years ago, Chloe?"

Chloe doesn't flinch. But the stricken look on her face—it says it all.

"Did you think I wouldn't make the connection? That you could just lie to me?"

Mel wants to scream. But she wants answers more.

"Is one of them responsible?" Mel demands. "Your Bag of Dicks? Did one of them do it? Did they think *she* was your accomplice?"

Oh god. Did she take Mel's place? It was supposed to be Mel. Mel was Chloe's accomplice and if they thought it was her . . .

"I don't—"

"Do not lie to me!" Mel says. "You have no idea how hard—" And then she stops herself, because she does know, doesn't she?

She knows the truth. Was she there? Did she show up too late?

Was she responsible?

"Tell me," Mel says. "Right now. I want the truth. When I went through her phone records, there was a Colorado number I could never track down. Was that you?"

Chloe nods.

"She found you."

"She found me," Chloe says.

"She never told me."

"She wanted to keep you safe," Chloe says. "Just like I did. She figured it *all* out on her own. That journalist streak screwed us both in the end. She's the one who uncovered all the stuff the Newells were up to. The Dicks—they didn't know about you. They thought—"

"—it was one of the twins who helped you kill Toby."

Chloe nods. "It made the most sense. They were my best friends."

"Mine too," Mel grits out. "What did they do to her, Chloe?"

Chloe licks her lips, the quiet and her reluctance wrapping around them.

"Never mind, don't answer that. I know what they did. *I saw the blood.*"

"Oh, Mel." Chloe's face breaks as tears shimmer in her eyes.

Mel's voice rises and cracks on the question. "Where the hell is Whitney's body?"

26

MEL

THREE MONTHS AFTER CHLOE RUNS

The last thing Mel expects to see is Whitney Teller standing at the bottom of her apartment complex's stairs, two coffees clutched in her hands like some sort of peace offering. Her first thought is: *What the hell?* And her second is: *At least it isn't Gigi.*

Whitney looks wildly out of place in the bad part of town. Her linen pants don't have one wrinkle in them and Mel doesn't even know how that's possible. But leave it to Whitney to bend fabric to her whim. The bracelets around her wrists aren't just Cartier, they're vintage. Inherited. From her grandmother, Mel suspects.

Mel doesn't pause when she spots her, though she wants to. She thinks about going back inside her and Ted's apartment, but she promised Ted she'd get outside today. He's been worried enough about her since Chloe left. She's just started getting out of bed on her days off instead of staying in her bedroom, crying.

"Don't try to run away," Whitney says.

"I wasn't," Mel says. "I have stuff to do."

"Coffee?" She holds a cup out. Mel glances down, seeing the barista's scribble on it. It's her order, which is a spooky attention to detail that she'd expect from what she knows about Whitney from school and Chloe.

"Should I consider it creepy you got my order right?" Mel asks. "You stalking me or something?"

"Don't pretend," Whitney says. "I need some answers."

Mel's about to ask, but Whitney continues, "Where is she? Do you know?"

"She?"

"Don't play dumb, Mel. Where the hell is Chloe? It's been three months. She's only called her parents twice. She didn't show up at UCLA like she was supposed to. They're *freaking* out. Especially after that postcard."

"Postcard?" Mel echoes.

"They got a postcard last week. Sent from New Jersey of all places. 'I'm fine. Don't look for me. I need space. Love, Chloe.'"

New Jersey? What was she doing in Jersey? It's close to New York. She could've caught an international flight out. She could be halfway across the globe by now.

God, Mel was never going to see her again, was she? The pit that kept growing in her stomach was so big it had to be organ-crushing at this point.

"Tell me where she is!" Whitney demands. "I don't know what kind of game you two are playing—"

"Why do you think I'm involved?" Mel demands.

Whitney rolls her eyes and crosses her arms, her perfect sleeveless turtleneck and vintage Cartier making her look like she walked out of a nineties Calvin Klein ad. Around her neck, that little gold acorn necklace she always wears swings.

"I know, Mel," Whitney says, in that way that says *everything.* That sends Mel's stomach dropping all the way down to her fucking ankles and then out of her body and down to hell.

"About you and Chloe? I've known for over a year."

"Know what?" Mel asks, because clarification is necessary where *you and Chloe* means several things. Some of them good. Some of them downright tragic. And some of them terribly criminal.

"I knew you two were together," Whitney says. And it's some relief, that it's *that* and not the other mess.

"I saw you two," Whitney tells her. "I came round to the house last year and Chloe's mom told me she was out in the barn. So I went up there and you two were—" Her cheeks turn red, and so do Mel's because that's mortifying considering what she and Chloe got up to in the hayloft. "I never told anyone I saw, not even her," Whitney continues. "Her life, her business. But now I've got no choice. Are you two running away together or something? I know the Harpers are old-school but do you two really think they're gonna shun you because you're together?"

Mel wants to deny it. She wants to tell her she was imagining things. That there was some other brunette she caught Chloe with in the barn. She opens her mouth to do just that.

What croaks out instead is: "I have no fucking clue," right before she starts crying like a fucking baby.

Whitney clucks her tongue, moving from annoyed and angry to soothing and sympathetic in such a seamless display that it has Mel reeling. Which is the only excuse for what happens next: through the tears, Whitney puts her arm around her and kind of guides her up the stairs and toward her apartment and just lets herself inside after she plucks Mel's keys out of her hands.

The audacity, really. But that's what the Teller twins are known for. Steamrollers, both of them.

Whitney guides her into the studio apartment that's more like a castle to Mel and Ted, their bunk beds tucked in the corner, with the bookshelf that Mel made out of two-by-fours and cinder blocks. Ted likes to walk Marigold in the morning, so he's not here, thank god.

Whitney sticks out like a beautifully dressed thumb in the midst of Mel's shitty little kingdom. But she doesn't even make a face, which is nice of her.

Mel's got to get her shit together. Crying like this? Dead giveaway. Absolutely humiliating. She can't wriggle her way out of this.

Whitney just goes into the kitchenette, realizes there's no paper towels, and grabs the one dish towel Mel got from the dollar store, thrusting it at her like an offering.

Mel takes it, swiping under her eyes, trying to breathe deep and shuddering instead. She goes over to the bottom bunk and sits down. Ted likes to sleep on the top bunk, tucked up near the ceiling. He says it feels safe. It works out, because Mel needs the bottom one. She needs to be able to roll out of bed and fight. Just in case.

Whitney crouches down in front of her. "What do you know?"

Nothing. Everything. Maybe a little bit. But Mel can't figure out what those bits are because her heart is fucking broken.

Chloe just left. No word. No sign.

"I don't know anything," Mel says. "Chloe didn't say anything. She was going to come back next month to visit after she got settled in at college. We made plans to meet." *We made plans for a life. We made plans for forever.*

"You really didn't know she was leaving."

"If I knew, don't you think I'd be with her right now?"

They stare at each other, once girls who never really knew each other and now women facing the same horror.

Mel knows all about how horror bonds you.

"Oh god," Whitney says, sounding so small that it breaks Mel a little more and she's plenty broken already. She doesn't need more of it. "What are we going to do?"

And for the first time in a very long time, Mel is honest with a person who isn't Chloe Harper.

"I have no idea."

27

MEL

"Where is Whitney's body?" Mel's voice pitches up in desperation. Birds scatter from the pines above them.

This time, Chloe does flinch. Mel has to push off the tree to keep from reaching for her. It's still instinct to comfort her.

Remember the car, remember how Nat tried to protect you from seeing, from having Whitney's blood in your head, but you do, and it's not just in your head, it's on your hands. It's on you.

"I can't," Chloe whispers.

"Because you don't know? Because you weren't involved?"

The barest shake of her head condemns her. Mel's so angry she thinks she might faint. But she can't, because of the looming danger and the Bag of Dicks. Men are coming for them. The same ones who took Whitney. Who killed her. She's got to stay in control.

But it comes spilling out all the same. "You knew this whole time— you let them *suffer.* You let the Tellers bury an empty coffin? Gigi spiraled into fucking *delusion* after. She still believes—"

"Mel, please. We need to move. You need to—"

"All I need to do is find Rick Newell and slit his throat. And then I'll find Richard and Dick Junior and do the same and after that, I'll move on to Big Daddy. An eye for a fucking eye."

Chloe's eyes widen. "You can't—"

"That's how the coroner said she died, you know," Mel plows on, because if Chloe refuses to tell her what happened, then Mel will give her every grisly detail the investigation hypothesized. Because that's all you can do when there's no body and just blood: guess.

"The coroner said that Whitney's attacker, they must've hit a major artery. Her best bet was the throat. She told me there was no way she could've survived three hours, let alone three days. She told me it should be a comfort. That Whitney went fast."

"Stop it," Chloe says. "You've got to stop. You can't go after them just operating on pure rage."

Mel's eyes narrow. "That family deprived me of the love of my life *and* my best friends, because have I mentioned that Gigi's *totally fucked in the head* about what happened?"

"Please. You have to trust me. You can't just take on the Newells with one gun and no plan," Chloe says.

"Watch me."

And then without another word, Mel walks off.

Part IV

THE BODY

28

MEL

THREE YEARS AFTER CHLOE RUNS

It's one of her first jobs as a PI. Mel's done her hours, she's got her license, she's got the training Nat instilled in her . . . and then suddenly, they've got a missing person. Whitney just never shows up at work at the paper.

Mel would think it was something about her, that people keep going missing around her, but she's too busy fighting through the dread as the hours stretch from twenty-four hours gone, to forty-eight, to past seventy-two, and the sheriff's got nothing and Nat's mouth is getting tighter and tighter and Mel's floating through another nightmare and all she can think is: *How the fuck is this happening again?*

The last time any camera caught Whitney's car was on the 5 headed north instead of south when she was supposed to be driving into work at the newspaper. Her cell phone pinged on a tower near Damnation Peak. So Mel and Nat have triangulated the area, they're doing the work themselves, driving through the little towns, exiting off every ramp, driving down roads that turn to gravel and then dirt, searching as hope dwindles.

They find her car on the fourth day, off exit 720, thirty miles into the winding forest road that's an offshoot of the main road. It's tucked neatly under a pine tree like she parked it there on purpose, but the door's wide open.

"Let me go," Nat says as they pull up. "You stay here."

Mel regrets so much that she didn't listen. She dashes out of the car first, like she's expecting Whitney to be sitting in the driver's seat, waiting to be picked up by Triple A or something.

She notices the flies first. Then the red rusted to brown, a horror-show stain across the white leather seats of the car.

But no Whitney. Just blood.

She doesn't remember screaming, or making any sound at all. The stains are everywhere, filling every sense she has, blotting everything else out as Nat's arm hooks around her middle, trying to tug her away from it, but it's too late. Mel remembers everything she's read, every person she's met, every single horror she's ever witnessed.

She'll remember this until the day she dies.

"Look at me! Melanie!"

Slap. It's more of a tap on the cheek, really, but she's acutely aware her barometer for being hit is very skewed because of Bob.

It brings her back, which she guesses is the whole point. Nat looks guilty, though, her jaw tense as Mel's eyes finally snap to her face.

"We need to call the sheriff," Nat says.

"We have to search—she could be in the forest, she could be hurt—"

"I know. We'll call it in. No, *no*, do not look over there—"

It's too late, Mel's eyes have locked back on the car, but from this angle, her eyes catch on something. A glint of gold among the horror.

She wrenches away from Nat, grabbing hold of the acorn necklace that's been looped around the steering wheel like a taunt. "This is hers," she says. It's clasped around the steering wheel, like someone put it there on purpose.

Mel straightens, the back of her neck prickling. Nat pulls out her cell phone and starts talking urgently into it. Mel ignores her, searching the side of the road, pacing back and forth. She's got no experience with forensics, but she does have experience tracking wounded deer. If Whitney got out of the car, if she ran, there'd be a blood trail.

She spots the crush of weeds and sticks, the dark splash that could be dried blood and bolts through the underbrush, into the tree line, the ground sloping down, her speed picking up as she follows the marks. Nat yells after her, but she doesn't listen as she follows what she realizes are drag marks. They *dragged* her down here. She either fought or they struggled to pull her because the path's zigzagging instead of a straight line.

Every step she makes, she knows she's drawing closer to the inevitable: to finding the body. Mel's already trying to detach herself from it, *the* body, not *her* body. She tells herself she can handle it.

She comes to a stop at the end of the drag marks, spinning in a slow circle, looking for any sign.

But there's just a stain at her feet. Crushed grass and branches, sweet pea vines that haven't had the chance to bloom. And no more trail to follow. It's like Whitney got dragged down, then just disappeared.

It hits her, as she stands there in the sick realization, that there's something worse than finding your best friend's body.

And that's never finding it.

It's six months before she gets the acorn necklace back. The sheriff gives it to her the day before the funeral Mrs. Teller's decided to have. Whitney's mother has moved through this like she's moved through everything in her life: with grace and a kind of strength that no one should be required to display. So Mel summons up some of that strength and goes over to the Tellers' to deliver the necklace.

It's a long time before her knock's answered, and it's Gigi instead of her mother on the other side. She glances at Mel and then just turns around and stalks back into the house, her messy ponytail swinging. Gigi leaves the door wide open, so Mel surmises she's supposed to follow.

Gigi's bedroom is at the end of the hall. She throws herself on her childhood bed as Mel steps inside, nose wrinkling at more than the frilly canopy and the ballerina prints.

"It stinks in here," Mel says, keeping her hands in her pockets.

Gigi shoots her a disinterested look from the window. "No one's asking you to stay."

"I heard you weren't coming tomorrow," Mel says.

"To fake bury my sister? No, I'm not going," Gigi says. "I'm not giving up like the rest of you just because of a little blood."

Mel bites her tongue. Because it wasn't a little blood. It was so much no one could've survived. It was just a question of who took her from the crime scene: a bear, a cougar, or the human who killed her.

Mel steps toward the whiteboard that's been propped up against the window. "Been watching *Law & Order*, I see," she says, trying not to grimace as her eyes fall on the printout of how long a person can survive after losing two-thirds of their blood volume.

"Fuck you," Gigi says, no hesitation. "Why are you even here? Conspiring with my mother now?"

"Sheriff asked me to drop this off for you. I thought you might want it before the service tomorrow," Mel tells Gigi. She places the acorn necklace in the cup of her palm, the chain pooling there.

Gigi stares at it like she can't quite understand what it is. "Her necklace," she says dully.

"It was in the car," Mel explains. "I made sure that the sheriff took good care of it until he could give it back."

"It was in the car," Gigi echoes.

Mel licks her lips, trying not to let the nerves swamp her.

She's never been good with girls like Gigi. Mel always thought she was shallow and it tugs hot and shameful at her now, because watching her dissolve into grief has taught her that all she knew was the glossy surface of Georgia Teller. The depths are endless and dark and she isn't sure she wants to plumb them.

"I should go," Mel says.

"You never said her necklace was in the car," Gigi says as Mel rises to her feet. She flinches when Gigi's head snaps toward her suddenly, her eyes locking on her, suddenly clear. "*Where* was it?"

"I found it looped around the steering wheel," Mel explains carefully, hoping that Gigi won't quite understand what it means. That whoever took Whitney, whoever killed her, they took the time to unclasp her necklace in the aftermath. To leave it swinging from that steering wheel like a terrible taunt: *I'll leave you this, but not her.*

To her surprise—to her horror—Gigi smiles, full-tilt into genuine relief. The shift on her face is so fast, so all-encompassing, that Mel steps back. It's like suddenly catching sight of someone in a fun-house mirror.

Her hand clasps tight around the necklace.

"She left this for me," Gigi says. "So I'd know."

Mel swallows the bitterness down. Like dregs of tea long gone cold. "Oh no. Gigi—"

"She's coming back," Gigi whispers.

Mel could tell her she's delusional. That she's wasting energy, thinking that when she could be trying to hunt down the people responsible.

But that's Mel's job and she's failed on every level. Months of search-and-rescue teams, three different experts, and there's nothing. No remains. No sign.

Wildlife and terrain are killer out here even without foul play, one of the guys had told her soberly. *Might take twenty years to find a bone. Might take forever.*

"I'm not crazy," Gigi says.

"I never said you were," Mel says.

"I would feel it," Gigi tells her. "If she wasn't coming back, I would *know.*"

"Okay," Mel says, and Gigi relaxes into the agreement as Mel comes and sits down next to her on the bed.

"I would know if she was dead," Gigi says again, like she's trying to convince herself, too.

Gigi's fingers tighten around the necklace.

"I believe that," Mel says, because she's not going to argue. There were times when Ted was out of contact and still doing drugs when she told herself the same thing. The difference, maybe, is that she knew, deep down, that it might not be true. Does Gigi?

"She thinks you're so smart, you know," Gigi says.

"I tried, Gigi. To find her."

Gigi nods, still staring down at the necklace. She lets the chain puddle in her fingers, tilting it back and forth. "Will you wear it?" she asks. "Until you find her?"

She holds it out before Mel can protest, so Mel takes it.

"Good." Gigi's eyes slide back toward the window. "Just until we find her."

Mel clasps it around her neck, the weight unfamiliar, the moment too heavy.

And she can't help but wonder if she's made a mistake . . . or a friend . . . or maybe both.

29

RICK

"I hate tiny planes," Vinny mutters as Rick fiddles with the controls on the Skyhawk. Of course Richard wouldn't lend him the chopper he uses to get to Sacramento. Rick's stuck with the hand-me-down from Big Daddy. It's practically a crop duster. Cramming the girls in the back will put them at capacity.

"You don't trust me?" he asks. There's nothing but green below. They've got another twenty minutes before the strip comes into sight.

"Small planes have a twenty-five-times higher chance of crashing than the big ones," Vinny says.

"You google that before we left?" Rick asks.

"Yes," Vin admits after a pause. "You hear about the plane companies killing all their whistleblowers and shit?"

"But *we're* the bad guys," Ricks says, as Vinny shifts nervously beside him in the Skyhawk. Vin has to hunch to fit, really.

"Turning snitch has never been anything to be proud of," Vin says.

"Loyalty to a man or family is one thing," Rick says. "Loyalty to a corporation? Fuck that. You and I, we've got an honest life. We don't pretend to be what we're not."

"Renegades. Only way to be," Vinny agrees, looking down out the window. "You really think she's alive down there?"

"I think it's better not to underestimate that bitch any more than we have already," Rick says, one eye on the fuel gauge. They'd have just enough to get back to his place, but not enough to land the plane on the family compound. Which was perfect. A built-in excuse.

He wants his time with Chloe before Richard butts in and he has to bring her to Big Daddy. He's got plans. And knowing Junior, he'll try to stab her the second he sees her. The boy's got a full-on vendetta, all over a few pokes. It's insulting. *Rick's* the one with the proper reason for revenge, and if he has to listen to Junior ramble on about his scar again, or god forbid, *see it*, he might reach for a knife himself and finish what Chloe Harper started.

"I don't see any smoke," Vinny says. "Maybe the engine crapped out and they just went down?"

"Fuck me for trusting that Jackson Harper would take care of his own jet," Rick mutters. "You stay on top of it once we land. She could be anywhere. And she's clearly in a killing mood again."

"She's always in a killing mood," Vinny says.

Rick sucks his lips in sympathetically, eyes on the horizon. Out of the two of them, Vin's the one who's faced Chloe's wrath the most. She almost killed him last year in Montana. But then again, he almost killed her first. Rick had to fuck him up for that. The one rule he has: *take* Chloe Harper, don't kill her. And Vin almost screwed it up. He wouldn't have even tried it, if Rick had been there.

That's the problem with running a business and also trying to coordinate and lead a woman-hunt across two countries. You can't have it all. You've got to delegate. And Big Daddy wanted the diamonds, but he also wanted Richard's and Junior's campaigns funded and everything running smoothly. Rick's been coming apart at the seams trying to handle it all. Fuck, he's got some sympathy for Hill now. Multitasking is hard, and she's got to do the lion's share of it with Richard at the helm of their imported-oak ship. He always wonders if she knows about the mistresses in Sacramento—or if she even cares.

"We'll find her and the other one, we'll get them on the plane and back to my place," Rick says. "And I'll lock them up in the smoking shed and cut on the other one until Harper breaks."

"Didn't really get answers the first time that happened," Vinny points out.

"Well, I'm in charge now, aren't I? I wasn't then. So it'll work," Rick says as he catches sight of the strip ahead and begins their descent. They hit the strip a little rough—he can hear Vinny's teeth clack together as the wheels jolt and rattle, kicking up red dirt and stone as they slow to a stop.

"You okay there?" he asks.

"I bit my tongue," Vinny growls, dabbing at his mouth, his fingers coming away bloody.

"Let's hope that's the only blood that gets drawn today," Rick says, grabbing his gun and his bag. "Come on, Vin. I know you like girl hunting."

"Not this girl," Vinny says, pushing the tiny door open. "Not anymore."

"Tell you what," Rick says. "I'll let you cut on her first."

"Thanks, boss, but I'll leave her to you," Vinny says. "There's something weird about Harper."

"You ain't scared of her?" Rick asks, half laughing, but Vinny's eyebrows don't even twitch.

"It's creepy, how she survives everything," Vinny says. "You. Me. The entire family. A goddamn plane crash. You don't think that's spooky?"

"Some bitches are born lucky, Vin," Rick says. "Chloe Harper was born with a silver spoon in her mouth and one up her ass and there's a whole town carrying her name. Girl like that, fate's just gonna be on her side most of the time. That's how she got away from me the first time I had her. She won't this time. She's run out of luck."

"But what if she hasn't?" Vinny asks.

"She has," Rick says firmly.

"Where's Sean, then?"

Annoyance spikes inside him, like it always does when Vinny's got a good point. "He's probably taking a piss."

Vinny's quiet, scanning the horizon. "Let's find him. Fast. So we outnumber them," Vinny says, but Rick doesn't like how unsure he sounds. You never want your muscle to be insecure about his abilities. Strength is all Vin's got, after all. The man wasn't born with an abundance of anything else.

The strip had taken months to build—Rick had only flown out of here a few times since then. Cleaning up Junior's messes in preparation for the campaign had been taking up most of his time when he wasn't hunting Chloe and the diamonds. He was so close to being done with all of it—Junior's bullshit campaign and everything to do with the mess that was Chloe Harper. He can almost taste the triumph.

He deserves a vacation after this. He's gonna make sure he gets one, even if it's just drinking a beer and taking a piss on Toby Dunne's finally-found bones.

Checking the compass on his wrist, he points toward the south. "Jake said he saw smoke to the south before she took him down?"

Vinny nods.

"Let's go."

He keeps his gun at his side and descends into the pines, Vinny following.

Rick's gonna end up with those diamonds and that bitch dead, no matter what.

Rick's always been comfortable in nature. He'd spent his childhood on a riverbank getting up to no good, and as soon as he got his first big score, he bought thirty acres out on the Bluffs. He has the knack but not the heart for deer hunting like Richard. But hunting humans?

Well. There's a certain challenge to chasing someone down. Especially if they're good at hiding. Chloe Harper has proved to be both patient and good at hiding.

But she's got nowhere to go now. No way out of here unless it's in his plane. Maybe she's even hurt. He hopes so, but considering she's already killed Jake, it seems like she's hale and hearty after everything.

It *is* a little creepy, how she just keeps surviving no matter what. Knowing she's out there, probably lying in wait. But if she dies, so does the location of the diamonds. He's gotta stay out of the way of her goddamm arrows and get close enough to grab her or something.

Shooting her would be so much easier, but even if he tried to wing her, he'd probably shoot her straight through the heart. Harper never makes anything easy. She runs when she's not supposed to. She comes back when he's not paying attention and Junior gets stabbed and fuck it if he's ever gonna hear the end of that. She gets a PI put on her trail and that bitch actually finds her and then he has to pay off pilots to drug her and even *that* can't work out easy. No, she has to crash, survive, and then go around shooting his men.

His feet slip on the swath of pine needles littering the ground as he and Vinny make their way through the trees. Vinny's moving slower than usual, overly cautious, and it's pissing Rick off.

"Hurry up," he says, pushing past him, but Vinny points. Rick has to step right next to him to get the view he has—straight down the cliff to the creek.

Rick sighs when he sees the rusty-red water first, and then what's left of Sean's head in the creek.

"Well, that's gonna fuck up the water table," he says, trying to swallow around the bitterness. That's two guys of his she's offed just *today*. Not to mention that time she nearly killed Vinny.

Her luck better fucking run out.

"She got both of them," Vinny says.

"That's not an arrow in his head," Rick says.

"So?"

"You ever known Harper to pick up a gun when she's got her weapon of choice?" Rick asks.

Vinny shakes his head. "Those arrows hurt more than a bullet going in and getting pulled out. I think she likes it that way."

"This was the other one. The PI," Rick says.

Vinny stares down at Sean. "That's a perfect head shot."

"She was not fucking around," Rick agrees.

"You're telling me there's two of them like this?" Vinny swears. "What is wrong with women these days?"

"Fuck if I know," Rick says. "Hill's just as bad, too. All those concealed-carry classes she teaches."

"This is fucking unfair, Rick. I liked Sean! He was good for a beer after work and now—" He gestures down to the creek.

"Keep your voice down, you don't know if they're still around," Rick says.

"We should go back," Vinny says. "Fly out of here. Fuck this."

"Vinny—"

"Fuck the diamonds!" Vinny shakes his head "And . . . and fuck you!"

"Christ, Vinny, calm down," Rick says, one eye on Vinny's gun hand. "You keep shouting you're gonna draw them right to us."

"Isn't that what you want? Fuck this! I'm going back to the plane," Vinny says, turning in a circle like he's trying to remember which way it is. He stalks off in what Rick is pretty sure is the wrong direction, but Rick's a little worried about what Vinny might do if he points that out, so he just follows for a second.

"Vinny, stop!" He stumbles over a tree root and then slams right into Vinny, who has stopped, but not because of him. Goddamn it.

It's not Harper. It's the other one. The PI's a tall brunette who looks like she knows how to throw a punch.

Vinny raises his gun, but he's too late. She's already got her gun on them.

A shiver goes down Rick's spine, a strange feeling, as not much scares him.

But the look in this girl's eyes? It's dark motherfucking fury. And it's all directed toward them.

"Which one of you is Rick?" she asks.

30

MEL

"Which one of you is Rick?" Mel asks again.

She glares at the two men, waiting for an answer. Of course, only ten minutes after leaving Chloe, she runs straight into more of the Newells' thugs. She hasn't even walked off her anger at Chloe's stubborn ass refusing to tell her anything about Whitney.

The guy with the shaved head and tattoos nods to the smaller man, the one who hasn't even reached for his weapon, like he thinks he's too good to react to the threat of her. Of course it's him.

Rick is lean, ropy cords of muscles and bulging veins that make her think of steroid use. His blue eyes glitter out from a sun-worn and grooved face shadowed by a ratty baseball cap.

"You must be Nat Parker's apprentice," Rick says, like she doesn't have a gun pointed at him. "I heard she picked some kid to train up."

Mel closes the space between her and the two men. "I want your weapons tossed out of reach. Right now."

"That's not happening, sweetheart," Rick says, his hand finally settling on the gun on his hip, still too slow and easy. He's not taking her seriously.

"Your men are dead."

"I've seen that."

"You think I won't kill you, too?"

"You do that, you kill your only way out of here. Unless you know how to fly a Skyhawk?"

She swallows. She'd suspected there was no way out of here but by plane. But she hated it was confirmed. Damn it. She was gonna have to trust in the fact that he can't kill them if he wants the diamonds.

"You grow up here?" he asks.

She nods.

"Then you know. You ain't getting out of the Cascades on foot," he warns. "The bears'll get you. I picked this spot for a reason. Have you even heard a fire chopper in the air since you crashed? No. They haven't found you. And unless the crash set the entire forest on fire, they might not ever find you."

He's right. This terrain is deep back country. "I heard you were running drugs out of here," she says, to buy time.

"Chloe likes to talk, doesn't she?" Rick asks. His gaze drifts over her shoulder like a starving man looking for a meal. "She around?"

"I ditched her," Mel says.

Rick raises his eyebrows. "Harper's your job. You slacking?"

Mel steps closer. She knows it's dangerous, she doesn't care. All she can think of is Gigi in her canopy bed, thinking Whitney would come home. That fucking empty grave.

"You were wrong, Rick."

"It wouldn't be the first time," he says. "But you're gonna have to fill me in on what I was wrong about and why it's made you so mad. You don't stop glaring at me, you're gonna get wrinkles right . . . here . . ." He jabs toward her forehead and she jerks back out of reach. If there's one thing she's good at, it's dodging men's fucking hands.

"You're fast," he says.

"And you're an idiot," Mel says. "You were wrong about who helped Chloe kill Toby Dunne. It wasn't Whitney."

His head tilts, his focus fully on her. "You?"

"Me," Mel says.

"Well, holy shit," Rick says. "What the hell were you doing out there with her?"

"Until today, I thought we were just out there burying a boy, but I've been recently informed we buried something else with him."

"You weren't friends, you two. I would've known. I did research on all of Harper's little girl friends."

"That's because we weren't girl friends, Rick, we were *girlfriends*."

"I've got an aunt like that," Vinny says.

"I'm sure she's lovely," Mel says.

"You two were fucking?" Rick asks, sounding like he'd never heard of such a thing.

"Lesbians," Vinny supplies helpfully.

"Bisexuals," Mel corrects. "It doesn't matter. What matters is that we can help each other. But if you don't put that down"—she gestures to the gun—"we can't."

"You want to make a deal," Rick says.

Mel opens her mouth to say *I do*, but something hisses by her shoulder and Rick hollers, dodging back at just the right second as the arrow embeds itself in the pine tree behind him instead of in his neck like Chloe intended.

"Goddamn it, Chloe!" Mel yells, trying to dive away and failing, because Vinny's grabbed her ankle and yanked.

Her chin hits the ground, her teeth clacking together painfully because she can't use her hands to brace her fall. She has to keep hold of the gun—

—it's no use. Vinny plants a boot on her lower back and she screams at the unrelenting pressure on her ribs as he twists the gun out of her hand, almost snapping her trigger finger in the process.

He hauls her up against him as blood dribbles out of her mouth and even though she's tall, he's big enough that her feet dangle. She's plastered against him like a Mel-shield and there's a long moment of silence as Rick spins around, his gun finally out, his eyes crazy as he looks for Chloe in the trees.

"You better come out," he yells. "I'll kill her."

Mel's teeth clench as Rick presses the gun against her temple. The pine trees rustle as Chloe steps out from the shadow of them, an arrow nocked and at the ready.

Rick lets out an almost-giggle, like he can't contain himself, finally drawing her out.

"There you are," he says.

"Let her go," Chloe says.

Rick presses the gun harder against Mel's temple, another giggle burbling from his chest. "Girlfriends, huh?"

Chloe's jaw twitches.

"I was sure it was one of the twins who helped," Rick says.

"Life's full of surprises," Chloe says, but her eyes are on Mel and no one else.

"You think you can shoot me before I shoot her?" Rick asks, and fuck, Mel's gonna have a barrel-shaped bruise on her forehead for weeks if she survives this. That'll be fun dinner conversation.

"I know I can't," Chloe says.

"Sometimes guns are better, Chloe Bryce," he says.

Her lips press together at the familiarity.

"You're gonna hand that over to Vinny," Rick says, nodding to the bow. "And then we're gonna walk, nice and slow, back to the plane. And for once this is gonna be easy. Because otherwise, I'm gonna put a bullet in her brain."

"You really don't want to do that," Chloe says with deadly calm. "She's the only one who knows where your diamonds are."

"Bullshit," Rick says, but the pressure of the gun lessens a little.

"Or maybe I have been lying this whole time about not knowing." Chloe shrugs. "I guess if you want to shoot her and gamble . . ."

"Put the bow down," he says.

"Chloe," Mel grits out.

Chloe tosses the bow on the ground out of reach. Vinny slowly lowers Mel.

"Time to go," Rick says, grabbing Chloe's arm and yanking her into his side. "You stay with me."

Mel lets Vinny pull her through the trees, her eyes trailing up and down his tattooed arms. They don't look like prison tatts. This is studio work—a lot of it. There are little gold studs in his ears and his belt is real leather, even if it's worn. He cares about the details.

Rick is messy where Vinny seems fastidious. There's a stain on the hem of his shirt and a Skoal circle worn into the back of his jeans. His ball cap doesn't look like it's been washed in years or maybe at all.

The airstrip is only a twenty-minute walk from the creek. If Mel hadn't been so fucking distracted by Chloe, and then angry at Chloe, they could've staked it out. This could've gone all different.

There's no use in going down that thought path. She's got to focus in on the present. Starting a fight and trying to get away will almost certainly spell death. Rick's right—the only way out of here is by plane. That's why a drug dealer would traffic out of here.

She can't attack them in the air. They'll have to land and then she'll find a way to get away from these two before the Dicks descend.

So she needs to let him win . . . until they get back on the ground. Where would he be taking them? Not an airport. Too public. It needs to be somewhere that has room to land the plane. Either Rick's place or the Newells' place, then. Would it be better if it was Rick's? Might be less of them to deal with in the long run. If he took them straight to his family's place, she was dealing with not just him, but the entire Bag of Dicks, Big Daddy included.

"Get in," Rick says, pushing Chloe toward the plane as Vinny opens the door. Chloe casts a look at Mel, who tries—and probably fails—to convey with her eyebrows Chloe should just do what they say.

She climbs in, Mel following. The Skyhawk is cramped and it stinks of menthol and tobacco. She spots the plastic cup that serves as Rick's spittoon precariously perched between the seats. Vinny shuts the door firmly after he climbs up, looking back at both of them.

"No bullshit," he says. "You won't survive another crash. No one's that lucky."

"No bullshit," Mel agrees, mostly for Chloe's sake. "You hear that?" she says to Chloe as Rick starts fiddling with the controls. God, she hopes he was actually telling the truth about flying this thing.

"I can't believe you left me behind," Chloe mutters as the engine roars to life and Rick starts taxiing on what little dirt runway there is.

"Hypocrite," Mel snipes back.

"Both of you, shut up and let me concentrate," Rick says, and they fall silent because Vinny is right: another plane crash is not gonna help things.

Mel's stomach swoops as they pick up speed, she can feel the rattle as they lift off with a wobble and the wheels retract. She grips the edge of her seat tight as they rise and rise, finally steadying.

She fixes her eyes on the back of the co-pilot's seat, which she's directly behind, as the engine hums and the forest below grows more distant.

"The brunette won't stop staring," Vinny hisses to Rick.

Mel snorts behind him. Does he think she's got some sort of evil eye or something?

"Hey, Columbo, eyes down," Rick says, raising his voice to be heard properly over the plane engine.

"What are you gonna do, come back here and make me?" she asks.

"No, but I'll let Vinny cut on you," Rick says. "He'll skin you like you're a parsnip."

"I did always like to cook," Vinny says.

"You should've pursued that instead of shacking up with this fucker," Mel says. "You know how much trouble you're in, Vinny? Messing with planes the way you two did is a federal offense. Sheriff's not gonna look the other way on this 'cause there's a Newell involved because he ain't in charge and it means fuck all to the Feds what family you work for."

"I didn't mess with the plane!" Vinny says. "It's not my fault Jackson Harper can't maintain his plane worth shit."

"Keep my daddy's name out of your mouth," Chloe says.

"Both of you, you're screwed," Mel continues. "The sheriff's been wanting to bring you in for years, Rick. Only thing standing between him and that has been your family."

"She's right about that," Vinny mutters. "That guy calls you a scourge on society."

"Shut up," Rick says as they hit an air pocket that has him gripping the controls tightly, fighting against the turbulence.

Mel directs her gaze out the window, concentrating on the terrain below instead of on Vinny and Rick. If she sits here and thinks about which one of them killed Whitney, she's gonna end up crashing this damn plane.

It's almost an hour in the air. They skim up Salt Creek and over what has to be North County—she can see the distinctive red roof of the town's church—before they head over the mountains to the Siskiyous and the Bluffs. Mel's trying to make a mental map—there's the gray snaking path of the 5, but then she loses sight of the highway as Rick makes a sharp turn east, beginning their descent. There's a house . . . a long sprawl of land, acres and acres of it before she can spot another house.

It doesn't look like Rick has a whole lot of neighbors, but as they continue to drop steadily in altitude, she notices a piece of land that's laid out in an oddly shaped grid from this vantage point. She frowns. Was that . . . a campground?

As they get lower, she's almost sure she's right as they fly over the spot, heading northeast as a large field bordered by a dirt road comes into sight.

"Brace yourselves!"

Rick sets the plane down in the field with a few scraping bumps that have Mel sucking in her breath and remembering, oh, yes, she was in a *plane crash* less than twelve hours ago. Even if she doesn't exactly remember any of it.

"Go get the cart," Rick tells Vinny as soon as the engine's shut off.

"You sure you want to be alone with them?" Vinny asks.

"*Go*," Rick says as Vinny gets out.

"Your underling seems scared of us," Mel says as Rick turns in his seat and levels his gun at the both of them.

"Vinny's got a superstitious nature," Rick says. "And this one"—he jabs the gun toward Chloe—"she nearly got him in Montana last year. It's hard to forget when a bitch tries to shoot a man with a three-foot fucking arrow."

"Too phallic for you, Rick?" Chloe asks.

He does that almost-giggle thing again. The sound prickles against Mel's skin like hitting all her knuckles down a box grater. "I can't believe I finally got you."

"Big Daddy will be so proud," Chloe says.

His face shifts from gleeful to darkly determined so fast it makes Mel's fists curl. "Once I have the diamonds," he says, eyes flickering to Mel. "She said you had them."

"No," Mel says. "She said I knew where they were. Big difference."

"Huge," Chloe says, shifting in her seat in a way that makes Mel nervous she's planning something.

"Where is the boy buried?" Rick asks.

"It's not like I can give you the latitude and longitude," Mel says.

"A map, then."

"It would be useless. I'll have to take you," Mel says. This was true, even though there was no way in hell she was bringing him out into the woods to find Toby's body.

"Fine," Rick says. "How far is it?"

"We'd have to start in the morning. No way you want to get caught out there at night with all the bears."

"I'd take a bear over killer girls," Rick says.

"Will you put that down?" Mel asks, gesturing toward the gun. "If you shoot one of us, you're not gonna get what you want."

He lowers it. Three inches. It's progress and Mel's feeling encouraged. And then the screaming starts.

"What the—" Chloe starts to say as Rick's head whips in the direction Vinny headed off in. A cloud of dust on the horizon, followed by Vinny, driving a golf cart.

It's not Vinny screaming, though. He's driving like a bat out of hell, sure.

The birds chasing him are doing the screaming. Loudly. Piercingly. There's got to be twenty of them. Mel winces as Rick adds to the screaming with swearing up a blue streak.

"Are those . . . peacocks?" Mel asks.

Sure enough, one of them is angrily fanning its impressive plumage.

"That goddamn bitch Doris!" Rick yells, yanking open the plane door and jumping from the cockpit, gun in hand.

Mel's entire heart turns over as he pushes the door shut, but it doesn't catch and he doesn't notice when it swings back open. He's too focused on running toward the herd of peacocks screaming their tiny heads off.

"Hold on, Vin!" Rick hollers.

"Christ," Chloe breathes. "There's a whole pack of them."

Screeeammm. The sound is hellish as the stout peacock leading the group lets out an irate cry when she spots Rick. Her minions freeze at her fearsome call as she charges ahead of them, her pace picking up, her head bobbing back and forth in the golf cart's dust. Another one—a male judging by his blue belly—leaps onto the back of the golf cart, hopping toward Vinny with what can only be described as ill intent.

"Get in the cockpit," Mel orders, realizing they only have so much time. "We can run."

Chloe scrambles toward it as Vinny shouts as the feral bird pecks him and another joins. Vinny jerks the wheel of the golf cart in a valiant bid to either throw them off or mow some of the other birds down. But they keep gathering onto the golf cart until it's a mess of feathers and screams—both of the Vinny and peacock variety.

Mel climbs into the cockpit. As she watches, the golf cart skids off two wheels, the shift in weight too much, and starts to roll. The peacocks in the way don't even scatter—instead, they converge even more angrily as Vinny thrashes and spins inside the tumble and crumpling of metal.

He doesn't get up or even move in the smoking tangle. Blood trickles down his forehead before he disappears in a cloud of bejeweled feathers.

"Vinny! You goddamn hell-beasts!" Rick shoots toward the swarm of peacocks.

"Go!" Chloe says, jumping down. Mel follows, leaping out of the plane and landing with a hard *thump* in the field grass.

"There's a campground on the other side of his land," she says. "This way!"

She grabs Chloe's hand and as the peacocks' screams rise and Rick shouts Vinny's name, they run.

31

CHLOE

Chloe does what she does best: she takes advantage of the situation and she runs. But this time, she makes sure she's holding Mel tight.

There's no time to think, just to move. The peacocks will only distract them for so long. They're only halfway across the field when she hears his concerned shouts turn to a bellow as he realizes he's fucked himself once again.

Rick really should've learned by now: getting away is her greatest skill.

They hit the tree line at full tilt in the dark. Her feet find the rough trail through the trees like it's been laid out just for her. Finally, things are going her way.

"Fence ahead," Mel pants as she spots its dim shape. Chloe has to let go of her to push up the barbed wire to create a gap big enough for her to duck through, and then she does the same for Chloe.

Every run of her life has been for this moment. They tear through the trees, any second she's sure Rick will be right behind them shooting, but then she spots light through the trees. Then red. And then blue.

Tents. The campground.

"Go, go, go." Mel pushes her forward and Chloe wants to scream that she's trying to block her with her body when that's Chloe's job. It's Chloe's job to save her. To love her. To protect her. If she fails . . .

The trees clear. They dash through an empty campsite and onto paved road—the one that weaves through the grounds. Ahead of them is a log-cabin-style building labeled SHOWERS and between the two doors is a pay phone.

"There," Mel says, spotting it a few seconds after her. She drags Chloe across the road, yanking open the shower door and pushing her inside.

"Hey!"

"Stay there, I'm gonna make a call."

Before Chloe can even protest, she closes the door. Rolling her eyes, she yanks it right back open, because the lock is on the inside, obviously. Mel's already got the phone to her ear. She mouths *Go back inside* to Chloe, who shakes her head, keeping an eye on the road instead.

"It's me," Mel says into the phone. "Listen, I need you to come to the Happy Trails Campground off the 5, up near the Bluffs. Pull into spot 43 and honk three times. Got it?" She pauses. "Okay. See you in twenty."

"Who was that?" Chloe asks, but Mel ignores her, pushing her back into the shower stall and slamming the door shut behind them, turning the lock firmly. "Gigi?"

"I do not have the bandwidth to deal with Gigi trying to kill you right now," Mel says.

"Gigi will not try to—" Chloe stops. She licks her lips. Is it time? It can't be. She needs the diamonds in hand before she can pull the trigger. "Did you call the sheriff?"

Mel looks up from her slow circle of the shower room, which isn't much more than a tiled room with two coin-fed spigots set in the wall and small windows for ventilation set so high no one can see through them. Which was good for privacy but bad for area surveillance when a crazed peacock-bitten drug dealer was chasing after you.

"We need to figure out our story before we bring in the sheriff," Mel says.

"Our story?"

"Why you left. Why the Dicks want to kill us. It's not like we can tell the truth."

"We could tell some of it," Chloe says.

"Deciding which parts is kind of key," Mel says.

Chloe watches her make another circuit of the room like she can't let herself stay still.

"Does she hate me?" she asks.

Mel has the grace not to pretend like she's confused over who Chloe's talking about.

"Gigi loves you," she says. "That's what makes it hard. Because she lost you, then she lost her dad, and then she lost her sister. I have no idea how she's still standing."

"And you?"

"Do I hate you?" Mel asks.

Chloe didn't quite know if she had actually meant that, but she nods anyway. She needs to know.

Mel finally stills, leaning against one of the tiled walls. Chloe does the same, the distance not much between them, but it feels like miles.

"You were the first person to ever really try to take care of me. So no, I can't hate you, Chloe. I've loved you since the second I really knew you and I loved you all the years you were gone and I love you now, even though I know what you look like when you lie to me."

Chloe closes the space between them, standing right in front of her. "I love you and I need you to trust that I have an ace up my sleeve," she says. "Am I lying now?"

"Damn it, Chloe," Mel says, leaning forward as Mel's hand slides up her side, warm and solid and real.

Outside, a horn honks three times. Mel swears under her breath as they freeze, inches from each other.

"That'd be our ride," Mel says. "Let's go."

Chloe peeks out the shower door tentatively, but she doesn't see Rick or Vinny—pecked to bits or not—anywhere.

"Right there." Mel points to a gray truck with the words SWEET

PEA NURSERY stamped on the tailgate, parked in the camping spot across from the showers.

They run across the road and Mel yanks the truck door open for Chloe, who pulls herself inside.

"Stay low!" Mel says as Chloe ducks.

A man Chloe's only seen at a distance until now, his reddish-blond hair peeking out from his knit cap, gives them a little wave as Mel slams the door shut and says, "Go, go, we need to get out of here."

"Shit, did you kill someone or something?" Mel's brother asks.

"Did you tell him?" Chloe almost yelps.

"Drive!" Mel orders.

"Bossy," Ted says, pulling the truck out of the spot and weaving along the main road through the campground. "Who we running from?"

"Bad guys," Mel says.

"You stink. Why are you so dirty?"

"Be a gentleman and don't mention it," Mel says.

He snorts. "I'm not a gentleman, I'm your brother. Hi, Chloe." He tilts his head a little bit to meet her gaze. "You're back. I'm kinda surprised."

"Teddy, what the fuck?" Mel asks.

"Uh," Chloe says. "We've never met . . ."

"Not officially," he says, pulling out of the campground and onto the on-ramp that leads to the 5. Chloe breathes a little easier when they're on the highway.

"I know, I wasn't supposed to know," Ted says as they stare at him. "Sorry. I guess I kinda did. You two weren't really good at hiding things when you were kids, you know."

"Yes we were!" Mel snaps like anyone with an older brother who loves to act superior.

"It was obvious to me," Ted says. "Especially after she left. You cried for months. But you're back. That's good."

"Oh my god, can you speed up, please?" Mel says.

"I'm just saying you missed her! Are we going to your place?"

"Hotel," Mel says. "You got the cash from my drawer?"

"In the glove box. Gonna tell me what's going on? Gigi called. She wasn't making much sense. Something about radio contact and a missing plane." He frowns and then leans toward Mel and gives her another big sniff. "Is that smoke?"

"I am not getting into this with you," Mel says. "You'll just get upset."

He gives her a long-suffering look. And then: "Am I gonna need to bail you out of jail?"

Chloe almost laughs. "Have you had to do that before?"

Ted just smiles.

"There's more money and a lawyer's name's in the coffee can under the sink if it comes to that," Mel says.

"Fair enough," Ted says, with the kind of serene calm that Olivia would *not* have if Chloe randomly called and warned her sister she might need bail money.

"Take exit 733," Mel tells him after about twenty minutes and two road signs. "The hotel on Third Street."

He pulls up to the office and Mel dashes out to book a room, leaving Chloe alone with Ted.

"So I guess the figuring-out stuff is a family trait then?" Chloe asks.

"Nah, I'm just good with people," Ted says. "I don't notice stuff like her. Mel's good at figuring people's motives out, but that's not the same as figuring *them* out, you know?"

This observation totally contradicts his claim of it not being a family trait, but Chloe's not going to argue. The adrenaline that's been driving her since the crash is starting to drop. Her overworked muscles start to throb, the blisters she's got start to sting, the sweat and dirt and blood start to make her skin crawl. Her body's coming back to life now that her life isn't in immediate danger.

"Whoa there," Ted says, pushing between her shoulder blades with gentle pressure, urging her head between her legs. "You went sheet white. Breathe slow and steady."

Chloe closes her eyes, fighting the sudden drop as the truck door opens.

"Is she okay?" Mel's voice.

"I think she needs to rest," Ted says.

"Come on, Chlo," Mel says, taking her arm gently. "You haven't slept in ages."

The hotel room is dated, jungle flowers on the bedspreads and palm tree photos on the walls like this was LA instead of the very last sliver of California before Oregon.

Chloe sits down on the edge of the bed. It feels strange to be in a room after so many hours in the wild, not knowing if she was getting out. She didn't feel that way the first time. But it was dark the first time.

She's in the bright, punishing hotel room light now and she can see every spot of blood and dirt on her arms.

Ted and Mel murmur back and forth with each other, like they're worried their voices will hurt her ears.

"I'll leave you the truck, I can get a rental from down the street," he says, pulling out his phone and handing it to her. She begins tapping away at it.

"You've got to promise me you won't stop until Portland. I need you out of town while I deal with this," Mel tells him.

"I promise," he says.

She hugs him for a long time before he hands over his truck keys and gives Chloe another kind of shy wave.

Mel keeps her hand pressed against the hotel door as she closes it, like she can somehow keep every bad thing out. Then it's like she realizes she's being soft and human again, because she straightens, clears her throat, and methodically flips the locks and secures the slide chain. Then drags the hotel desk in front of the door for good measure. The curtains get tightly closed.

Chloe keeps sitting there, feeling useless as Mel bustles about. A knock at the door startles her out of her fog, her hand automatically going for a quiver that's not there.

"It's okay, I ordered some essentials from Ted's phone," Mel says, waiting a beat before removing the desk and peering through the keyhole. She unlocks the door, stooping to grab the Walmart bags and then ducking back inside. After she secures the room, she dumps the contents of the three bags on the bed.

Chloe's eyes skim over the prepaid cell phones and gift cards, the roll of gauze and medical tape and hydrogen peroxide, the change of clothes for each of them, along with the bag of snacks, including her teenage favorite: Nacho Doritos.

There's something about the fact that she remembered that Chloe freezes on, even though she should be focused on the other things.

"You should eat something," Mel says, tearing open one of the packages that holds a cell phone, powering it on.

"Are we running?" Chloe asks, waving at the phones and prepaid cards.

"I'm not," Mel says. "But Rick's gonna stake out my place and office, so we should stay here for now."

"Richard's got some ins with some banks," Chloe says. "That's how Vinny found me last year. Rick was using the Newell connections to trace the different banks I withdrew my trust fund from to triangulate where I went next."

"So we stay off grid as much as possible," Mel says, tossing the activated phone back on the bed and grabbing the gauze.

"Your leg," Chloe says, taking the box from her and wincing as Mel gingerly rolls up her dirty pant leg, exposing the knife wound.

"Fuck." Mel hisses between her teeth. "I'm filthy. I'm gonna shower before I try to dig out all the crud from my wound."

Chloe nods and Mel gets up, going over to the bathroom. She can't help but notice she leaves the door open a crack. Chloe closes her eyes as the rush of water trickles through the gap, telling herself it's not an invitation.

The door creaks. Chloe's eyes fly open, meeting Mel's through the crack in the door. She's stripped down to her bra and underwear, sweat-stained and grubby-glorious.

For a moment, everything stills, Chloe's heart thudding too tight under her skin.

Mel pushes the door wider, her eyes never leaving Chloe's.

Chloe never had a chance.

She goes to her.

32

CHLOE

They don't speak. They don't fall upon each other and Chloe almost thought they would. So many years, so much repression even when they were together. It would make sense. She thought she might cave the second she steps onto the tile of the bathroom floor.

Instead, it's like every move is too much to absorb. Slow-motion savoring.

Steam's starting to fill the tiny room as Mel reaches out, hooking her fingers in the waistband of Chloe's pants, tugging her forward before her fingers slide to the middle, flicking the button open.

Chloe's hands always had been strong but Mel's were clever. Gambler-quick and just as reckless. Her knuckles brush up against the skin below Mel's belly button before they trail to her zipper, the rasp of it too loud even with the shower pounding behind them as her cargos puddle to the ground. She tugs her own shirt off and kicks away her pants, down to her underwear. Chloe had long given up bras—she'd never really needed one anyway—and she shivers as Mel's gaze dips and wanders. She's sixteen and brand-new again. She's twenty-four and tinged dark at the edges.

She is all of herself with her. She is only herself with her.

It's only fair that she reaches out, stroking the length of Mel's blue bra strap, her fingers lingering on the swell of her breast. The water pounding behind her is a reminder: the grime on both of them is unbelievable, really. When she pushes Mel's bra strap from her shoulder, she exposes a clean strip of skin, almost like the dirt is a suntan. It makes her want to laugh and when Mel glances down and sees it, she does.

"Fuck, get in here," Mel says, backing toward the shower, shucking off her underwear and bra like it's nothing. She never had any qualms or shyness, Chloe had always loved her for it. Admired it. Wanted to be like that, but wasn't.

But she is now, isn't she? She can be.

She follows her into the warm stream of water—surprisingly good water pressure for a place like this. Her muscles start to unwind just at the idea of heat. When Mel tips her head back under the spray, the water pours down her dirty, freckled skin and Chloe doesn't think there's anything that's ever been more beautiful.

Chloes unwraps the tiny bar of hotel soap, tossing the wrapper somewhere, she doesn't look because she's sliding the soap up Mel's arm, suds and fingers trailing and she's letting her.

There are scars she doesn't recognize and ones that she's mapped in her mind in the years she was with her and even longer without her. She touches the new ones first, soap suds covering every inch and Mel lets her, her arms loose like it doesn't matter, even though Chloe knows it does. It's when she moves to the old ones that she stiffens under the first touch, the one on her hip that came from the night with Toby. Chloe's hand flattens against the mark, the soap trapped between her palm and Mel's hip.

Mel's eyes flutter closed, the water trickling in rivulets down her body.

"Do you regret it?" Chloe asks. "Stepping in that night? Now that you know what it led to?"

Her eyes snap open in an instant. They darken with a fierceness that squeezes the breath out of her, waiting for what comes next.

"Not for a fucking moment," Mel says, with such truth that Chloe's almost shaking from the brunt of it.

The water swirling down the drain turns a reddish brown as it beats down on them. The relief of getting clean almost rivals the relief of being here with her. Touching her.

There was a time she never thought she'd get to again.

Chloe drags the soap across Mel's collarbone. She swallows, her chest heaving as Chloe's hand travels between her breasts and only then does Mel's hand shoot out and grasp hers. That clever hand wraps totally around hers and pulls her in, until their intertwined hands are pressed between their bodies as Mel dips and Chloe rises.

It's a simple thing at first. A soft brush of lips. And then Mel's free hand settles on her lower back and Chloe moves into her at the gentle urging, and then she's pressing her into the tile of the shower, slick skin and slicker tongues, the soft tangle of hair under her fingers as she dips lower and Mel's head thunks against the shower, her cry in Chloe's mouth.

It's the only time my mind shuts up, she'd once told Chloe.

God, does Chloe want to shut her up.

When she wakes up the next morning, forget the threat of the Newells: it's her hamstrings that are trying to kill her. She blinks up at the popcorn ceiling of the hotel, trying to wake up. She turns over to the side to see the clock says 9:00 a.m. She hasn't slept this late in years.

Running for your life will do that to you.

"Morning," she murmurs, turning back over, her hand hitting cool sheets instead of warm Mel.

She jerks up. "Mel?"

The bathroom door is wide open—they were too distracted earlier to close it after their shower. She's not in there.

"Mel!"

She throws the blankets off her, jolting out of bed, looking around frantically. Did she go outside? Did she—

There's a folded piece of paper set on the dresser with her name on it. With shaking hands, she unfolds it.

Hey,

 Going to handle all this. I'll make a deal with Richard for the diamonds. You don't have to worry. Go see your dad.

 —Mel

Chloe yanks the door open, dashing outside, praying she's still in the parking lot.

Ted's truck is nowhere to be seen. She's gone.

Chloe's throat burns as she ducks back inside the hotel room, closing the door and sagging against it. Her eyes sting, she's half humiliated, half terrified. She knows she needs to lean into the terror but Mel just . . . left her. After they . . .

She takes a deep, shuddering breath, going over to the bags of stuff she had delivered. At the bottom of the snack bag is what she's looking for: the second prepaid phone Mel bought.

Pulling it out of the packaging, she spends a few minutes activating it. Her fingers hover over the familiar number, one she memorized a long time ago.

"It's now or never," she tells herself. This is why you had an emergency parachute. So that you could pull the rip cord in an emergency.

She types out the text:

This is Chloe. Meet me at the Blackberry Diner ASAP.

Less than a minute later, her phone buzzes:

On my way.

33

MEL

Mel strolls into Richard Newell's office at nine on the dot, no appointment.

"I'm so sorry, the assemblyman is very busy—" the aide at the front desk tries to explain.

"Tell him Melanie Tillman is here to see him," Mel says, with that kind of determined smile that says she's not budging. "I'll wait."

She doesn't even have time to reach for a magazine or her phone before the woman is nervously calling, "Ms. Tillman? The assemblyman will see you now."

"I thought he might," Mel says.

She's no stranger to walking into important rooms with so-called important men with a problem. But most of the time she's not the source of the problem, just the solution.

This time she's both. She just has to make him see it.

Assemblyman Newell had probably been a pretty boy like Dick Junior back in the day. His blue eyes pop against his dark hair, but too little sunscreen and too much golf under the Calabama sun had baked grooves into his skin, making his smile more menacing than charming. Mel knows his type—politically prescient, charming with a toothpaste smile that can't quit . . . until you do something to piss him off. Then you get a different man. The secret Hyde to the public Jekyll. A born-and-bred politician who can fake rural realness while he goes home to his McMansion and bitches about the white trash yokels.

"Ms. Tillman." He gets up from his desk, a powerfully built man used to weaponizing his size to intimidate. "I'm so pleased you've come to see me."

When he holds out his hand, Mel looks at it for a moment and then sits down. He doesn't miss a beat or drop the smile. Just turns and returns to his own leather-backed chair, leaning into it with practiced grace. He adjusts his cuffs, pulling them down just so.

Mel's not going to dance around the point. She's got shit to do. "We seem to have a problem, Assemblyman."

"Do we?"

"I was hired to do a job by the Harper family. To bring Chloe Harper home to see her father. And you and your family have been doing nothing but getting in the way of me doing my job."

"That's an interesting way of seeing it." He temples his fingers in front of his face, regarding her over the top.

"I'm gonna tell you some things and by the time I'm done, you're gonna see it my way, too," Mel says.

His mouth twitches at the audacity. "That would be quite the accomplishment."

"You've been operating under a false assumption for the past six years, Assemblyman. And it's caused untold damage, to your family and to those I care about."

"Is that so? And what assumption is that?"

"That Whitney Teller was the girl who helped Chloe kill and bury Toby Dunne."

Richard leans forward so minutely, she wouldn't notice if she hadn't been looking for it. "It wasn't? Then . . ." He frowns.

"I was the one with Chloe that night," Mel says.

"You." He shakes his head. "You two weren't friends. We made a thorough investigation of the Harper girl's possible accomplices—"

"Chloe and I weren't friends," Mel agrees. And just in case he's as stupid as Rick, she adds, "Being a queer girl in a small town like this, you get real good at keeping secrets. Especially when you're sleeping with the girl who comes from a family said small town is named after."

Richard lets out a huff of incredulous laughter. There's almost a glimmer of boyish charm in the looming cruelty in his eyes.

"It was always so far-fetched, Rick's story," he says. "But it was also so stupid, it had to be true. He'd never admit some teenagers screwed him over otherwise. But I always wondered how Chloe Harper turned out how she did. That girl had good breeding. But here's the answer." His eyes sweep up and down her. "*You* got into her. Influenced her. Egged her on."

Mel can't help it, she laughs. And stops just as fast because he's glaring at her like she's supposed to be impressed by his grand revelation. "I won't lie, Chloe was a righteous pain in the ass when we were kids. Impulsive *and* naive. Always doing shit before she thought it through because her daddy always saved her." She leans back in her chair, and this time, she assesses him, lip-curling at the lack of him, in the brains *and* brawn departments. "I guess you know something about that, don't you?"

Richard clears his throat, unsettled. If Rick was the black sheep, that meant that Richard was the golden child. And Junior . . . well he seemed to be the handsome idiot so far. She'd figure out if he was more than that later.

She could work with a dynamic like this. All she needed to do was play Richard and Rick off each other. There had to be resentment miles deep there, on both sides. Any good manipulative motherfucker would pit them against each other, so one thought the other was always on the way up. It'd make them work harder for approval.

They're all running around trying to impress Big Daddy Newell. That's what Chloe had told her.

She was going to take a page out of the old man's book and use that insecurity and play them like a violin. She just needed to get them both in the same vicinity as each other, which meant it was time to deliver her ace.

"There's another false assumption you're making . . . this time about Chloe."

"Oh?"

"I guess Rick didn't call to let you know last night. I told him everything, I want you to understand that. Chloe doesn't know where your diamonds are buried. *I'm* the one who had the flashlight on my key chain that night. I made note of the landmarks. Not her."

"Is that so," he says, unable to hide the eagerness in his voice.

"Rick really didn't tell you?"

Richard's mouth twitches. "He did not. Well, that does change things, doesn't it?"

"It can, if you're reasonable. You and your family's behavior has not convinced me this is the case, though."

"Well, you have been dealing with Rick," Richard says. "He's a little . . ." He sighs.

"Speaking of Rick," Mel says, looking down at her watch as it hits ten.

"—I know he's in there!" comes a muffled voice through the door, followed by the frantic murmur of the assemblyman's aide as she tries to stop him.

"There he is." Mel smiles wide as Rick comes busting through the door, trailed after by the poor, frazzled-looking woman.

There are bruised peck marks all over his face and arms. Doris and the gang had really done a number on him. Mel wonders if there's some sort of treat that peacocks particularly like and if she can bulk order it.

"I'm sorry, sir, he just—"

"It's fine, Beth. Please go take your lunch break," Richard says.

Beth disappears without another word.

"How's Doris, Rick?"

He glares at her.

"And Vinny?"

"I am gonna fucking kill you," Rick says. He glares at Richard. "What the fuck? Did you bring her here without telling me? Vinny's in the hospital because of her!"

"I did not run Vinny's golf cart off the road, your birds did."

"They are not *my* birds!" Rick says, sounding mortally offended at the implication. "They're feral!"

"Ms. Tillman came here herself," Richard says.

"I would've made an appointment, but it was urgent," Mel says. "I figured we'd get more done if we all sat down and hashed it out. Or should I have called in Big Daddy himself? I didn't want to overstep. By all accounts, he doesn't leave the family compound much these days."

"You watching us or something?"

"I am an investigator," Mel says. "I'm investigating."

"Sit down," Richard hisses at Rick. "She knows where the diamonds are. She says Harper doesn't."

"She's lying," Rick says.

"She says she told you this yesterday. Before she apparently escaped?"

"I have been fucking *busy*," Rick says.

"You've been chasing the wrong person this whole time," Mel says. "Sit down."

Rick stays standing. Mel rolls her eyes.

"I assume there's a reason you've gathered us," Richard says.

Mel folds her hands together. "The three of us are going to make a deal."

"Like hell," Rick says. "You and your bitch killed two of my guys."

"Three, if you want to count Toby," Mel says, inspecting her nails. It had taken a good ten minutes to scrub them clean. There's a speck of red dirt, still, under her thumbnail. Out of the corner of her eye, she catches a flicker of a smirk from Richard at her comment.

"Please, continue, Ms. Tillman," Richard says.

"I'll take you to Toby's body, turn the other way as you do your diamond-looting thing, and then we can part and never speak of this again," Mel says. "As soon as you take me to where you buried Whitney Teller."

"Well, fuck," Rick says.

"Language," Richard tells him.

"It's very simple," Mel says. "You give me what I want, you get what you want. Otherwise, I'm walking out of here."

"I will break every bone in your feet and then peel off your skin like string cheese before you get to the door," Rick says.

"My god, cousin!"

"Yes, have some decorum with the torture talk, Rick," Mel says, enjoying herself just a little because both of them are such pricks. "What is with you and wanting to peel me? Do you need an apple or something to get the urge out?"

"Lock the door and let me just cut on her a little," Rick says to Richard. "She'll tell us everything."

"Not another word," Richard says.

"Remember: you're in the presence of a government official," Mel says, and Richard's mouth flattens in annoyance at the reminder.

"You sent your secretary away! Just let me—"

Richard reaches out so fast even Mel's impressed at the speed. His hand closes around Rick's neck in a punishing grip, slamming his cousin's forehead into the desk with a *thunk*.

Rick slumps to the ground, unconscious. Hopefully just unconscious. Fuck, did he just kill him?

Mel's body flushes with fear, her blood rising as she tries to breathe through it. Richard just goes straight back to his chair, sitting down and readjusting his cuffs.

This was what she was scared about with him. The Hyde side. Men like him, men who can mask well enough, those are the kind of men she hunts in her job. Not obvious motherfuckers like Rick.

Men like Richard, they're the kind of men who lash out so fast and so out of nowhere you can't prepare. The kind of men who kill their wives in the afternoon and then go to the charity gala in a tux three hours later and act perfectly normal while her body's sitting in their shower.

The compartmentalization is psychotic. Dangerous. Completely unpredictable. Because you never know when the wall will fall between the mask and the murderer.

"I apologize for my cousin's . . . zeal," Richard says. "Especially when you were gracious enough to extend a deal."

"Chloe said you were the scary one."

Richard smiles. Every bit of her screams *Run from this motherfucker.* "Did she?" He seems pleased she even mentioned him.

"Psychotic, is what she said," Mel says.

"Dramatic of her," Richard says. "I am merely a man who wants his family's property back."

"Are you going to make sure he's alive?" Mel asks, nodding toward Rick's prone form.

Richard shrugs. "Does it matter?"

Mel swallows, trying to maintain a casual air. "Do *you* know where Whitney is buried? Because I'm not interested in a runaround."

"Not exactly," Richard says.

"Then we do kind of need to make sure Rick's alive," Mel says.

"I'm afraid he can't tell you where she is, either," Richard says.

"Then we have a problem," Mel says, and then it strikes her that there's one more person in the Bag of Dicks. "Unless . . ."

Oh fuck.

"I'm going to need to call my son," Richard says.

Part V

THE TRUTH

34

CHLOE

TWO AND A HALF YEARS AFTER CHLOE RUNS

She has a PO box in Moffat County, three counties over from her cabin. Being in hiding means not shopping a lot, unless it's online. She heads to the post office every few months, but never on the same day, never at the same time.

She's learned a lot, last few years. Which is why when she counts the boxes the postmaster hands over to her, she knows there's an extra one.

Something she didn't order.

Chloe goes to her truck and gets in. She's not an amateur anymore, she doesn't linger in the parking lot. She gets the hell out of there just in case someone's surveilling it.

Last year, the Newells were five minutes from finding her in Montana. She never should've taken the bait, but she'd been so lonely. And it had been so tempting, the idea of getting enough evidence to tie him to something. She'd have the rest of the Dicks to contend with, sure, but Rick was the one doing the actual chasing most of the time.

The scut worker, that's what he was. And she was just a mess to clean up for the Newells. If she forgot that, if she let her guard down for a moment, it'd be all over. Everything she's done to keep her family and Mel safe.

She pulls into a gas station, up to the pumps, and rummages through the boxes, throwing them one by one into the back as she mentally checks them off her shopping list. She pauses when she gets to a small box, big enough to house a coffee mug and not much else.

The handwriting on it is neat as a pin and just as straight, like she used a ruler.

Chloe opens it, pulling out the brass bird statue that sat on her family's mantel for as long as she could remember. It had been her grandmother's.

There's a piece of paper folded just like Whitney used to fold notes when they were in high school, a triangle with perfect sides that was taped to the statue's base. Chloe unsticks it, huffing out an annoyed breath when she sees Whitney's written *found you* on the outside.

She undoes the intricate folds of the paper, her breath tightening in her lungs with each bit of ink she reveals.

Chloe doesn't know what she expected. Anger, really. Questions about why. Maybe some sadness and worry.

She doesn't expect what she gets: no greeting, no rage, no, it's a treatise on the Newell family. She's even provided a family tree.

And then at the bottom, she's scribbled:

> I thought you might want a piece of home. Just don't ever let your mom know I took it. She'll tie some red on me and put me in front of a bull.
> I know everything. We can take them down. You just need to call me.
> —Whitney

The first thing Chloe does is drive across four counties and open a new PO box there.

The second thing she does is reread the note five times, because if the stuff Whitney's saying is true about Rick's business financing Richard's campaign, that's a connection she hasn't been able to find proof of.

We can take them down. Like they're Lois Lane or something. Does she even understand who she's messing with?

Well, yes, because Whitney's sent her the treatise.

Cold dread wraps around Chloe's spine as she stares at Whitney's handwriting, her fingers tracing the familiar creases of the paper. The Newells could be onto her already. If Whitney asked the wrong people questions, they could be watching her.

A part of her, a big part, wants to call her. To yell at her and then warn her and then disappear again. Colorado is not safe anymore, if

Whitney found her. She needs to give up her cabin. Run again, some-where farther, even more remote.

So she holds firm. She promised herself: No contact.

She starts to plan to get out of the States. To fade into this surface life of hers until she becomes more pine tree than woman. More soli-tary than lonely. Just another piece of forest. She tells herself it's poetic in a way. She tries to keep a grasp on the thought that there's some nobility to what she's doing.

But deep down she knows she's selfish. There's enough blood on her hands. The only thing that keeps her sleeping at night is the fact that Toby deserved it, that it was her and Mel, or him, that he had made it that way.

She used to think he made her this. But she's starting to realize that maybe she was this all along. And if there's more blood to paint her hands, it better be from people she hates rather than ones she loves.

Whitney's note, her stolen gift, it's a fault line in Chloe's foun-dation. One that splits her heart like the Grand Canyon when her grandpa dies.

She breaks. She heads home. She calls Whitney.

She'll regret making that call for the rest of her life.

35

CHLOE

She's late to the meeting spot Whitney arranged. Chloe makes a wrong turn and has to double back. By the time she reroutes, she's fifteen minutes past the time.

She better not yell at me for being late. She knows Whitney will. Chloe's looking forward so much her throat stings.

The road is full of steep switchbacks as she descends toward Salt Creek. She can see the curve of the turn and the road below her from this high at certain angles and that's what catches her attention: a flash of red through the trees below her.

A truck that isn't Whitney's is parked right behind hers on the road below Chloe.

She pulls to a stop instantly. Her mind screams *trap.*

But the last three years, they've hewn her from a girl who only knows how to run into a woman who knows when to charge. So she grabs the hunting knife out of her glove box and gets out of her car, moving forward low and quietly.

She spots him. Dick Junior's not even bothering to be stealthy. He's shaking. Breathing too fast, chest heaving like he's been running, and are those . . . tears? Is he crying?

Then he turns toward Whitney's car, trying to steel himself and failing and she sees his hands, the blood on them, the knife in them, and every question she has goes *poof.*

She just reacts. It's the only thing to do. She races down the road, heedless of the sound, and luckily Dick Junior seems to be in the throes of a panic attack because he doesn't even try to look over his shoulder until her knife is against his back.

"Don't move," she says as he stiffens. "I'll get you right in the kidney." She raises her voice. "Whitney!" She can't see into Whitney's car from here. Where is she? What did he do to her?

Junior tenses, muscles shifting under his shirt. He's gonna go for her.

Stabbing him's the only way to stop him, really. You have to put a lot of strength into it, even with a knife as sharp as hers. But she grew up hunting deer. Field-dressing them. She's never been a stranger to a knife.

He lets out a surprised little grunt and then she twists and he screams.

There's no time to wait. She yanks the knife—more effort, Christ, that's a lot of blood—out of Junior and runs toward Whitney's car.

She doesn't remember screaming but she must have, because a piercing sound cracks through the trees, sending birds scattering.

Whitney's on the ground, like she's spilled paint from a can, her hands weakly clutching her throat.

Chloe's torn her shirt off in a second, pressing up against Whitney's bloody hands and that's when she sees the wash of red on her side, too.

"Chloe," Whitney gasps.

"It's okay," Chloe says. "Hold this tight." She presses her shirt against the cut on her neck. It looks long, but she'd be dead if he cut deep enough to hit her artery. That's good. That's *good*. She glances over her shoulder, where he's sprawled on the side of the road, near the embankment.

God, she wants to kick him off a cliff just like she did Toby.

"I'll be right back," she tells Whitney. Her first-aid kit is in her car. She needs to get it. She traded one of her prepper friends for military-grade wound dressings last year. She just has to get it.

Whitney's hand scrabbles against hers. "No," she says. "I don't—" She lets out a shudder. "I don't want to be alone when I—"

"—you are not dying on me!" Chloe says, pressing hard against her neck. She grabs Whitney's hand, trying not to be rough, but she kind of has to slap it against her neck so she'll keep the pressure. "Do not move!"

"Where the fuck am I gonna go?" Whitney looks incredulous as Chloe leaps to her feet and runs. She gets to her car in record time and throws herself inside, turning down the curve of the road and speeding toward Junior, who yells as he sees her coming and rolls out of the way . . . right down the embankment.

She doesn't even bother to check to see if he's fallen far. She just grabs the first-aid kit from her bag and runs.

Remembering anything after that gets fuzzy. She gets Whitney in her car, because the next thing she knows, she's driving on the highway, but there's no time to call anyone to get them. She has to get to help herself.

"It's gonna be fine."

Chloe keeps saying that. She keeps lying. Anything to keep Whitney awake. Anything to keep her focus on the road, instead of on the blood all over her hands and smeared on her chest and her friend, her best friend.

She's always been her best friend, since they were five, and now she's bleeding all over the cheap car Chloe bought in Montana. She's bleeding out and the closest hospital is over the border in Oregon.

She presses her right hand against the bandage she wrapped around Whitney's throat. The wound dressing pressed to her side isn't staining through like the neck wound.

"Where's Junior?" Whitney slurs.

"He's gone. Don't worry. Just a few more minutes. It's gonna be fine. You're gonna be fine."

Whitney slants her a look. There's a terrible, knowing silence. One born from years of loving each other, from being closer than sisters, from every secret whispered since they were five years old.

"Liar," Whitney gasps out.

Chloe hates that she's right.

36

MEL

Mel has exactly ten minutes to get right with it in her head, that *Junior* was the one who killed Whitney. The silence simmers around them as she stews over it, hating that his face was likely the last thing Whitney saw.

When she hears the office door opening, something flips over inside her and settles. An eerie calm before the storm of her killing his dumb ass.

"Hey, Dad," Junior says, breezing into the office without even looking toward Mel. "I've only got like ten minutes before I head home. Mom wants to go over talking points for the debate—"

He finally catches sight of an unconscious Rick on the floor, and then to Mel. "Oh shit, you got one of them."

"Sit down," Richard says. Dick Junior obeys his father instantly. He's ramrod straight in the chair, practically chewing on his tongue in nerves.

"Do you remember that day in August three years ago?" Richard asks.

Dick Junior stares at his father. "Um, Dad, you said to never—"

"Tell Ms. Tillman what you did with that girl," Richard says.

Mel's fingers curl around the arms of the chair. She's seconds away from gouging his eyes out, but she has to wait. When the revenge is as simple as death, the execution never is. "Tell me what you did with her. Now."

"I'm not—" Junior swallows. "What'd you do to Uncle Rick?"

"We had a disagreement about Ms. Tillman," Richard says.

"I want to know where Whitney is," Mel says.

"Tell her," Richard says when Junior squirms.

"She's gone. Dad, it doesn't matter," he practically whines.

"Now, Junior," Richard commands, looking like he wants to pinch his nose and sigh.

"I threw her in Salt Creek right after a storm. You're never finding her," Junior says. "I know my shit."

Junior's scornful enough, he's almost believable. It's Richard who gives it away. He stiffens at the lie, his head whipping toward his son.

"That's not what you told me."

"What? Yes it is." Junior shrugs, red crawling up his cheeks.

At her feet, there's a groan. Rick's coming to as Richard rounds on Junior. Rick throws his arm dramatically over his eyes, squinting one eye at Mel as he takes in the scene.

"You said you got rid of the Teller girl. That you were stabbed because you gutted Chloe's friend. *I buried that bitch.* Those were your exact words, son."

"They sure were," Rick chimes in, getting to his feet. Richard rises from the desk, coming to stand next to his cousin and suddenly, they're on the same side, united in anger and even though it's not directed toward Mel at the moment, it's the scariest thing that's happened in this room since she walked into it. The patriarchal disapproval is so thick it makes every nerve in her body scream.

"You dined out on that for months, motherfucker. You telling me it's not true?" Rick demands.

It's like they've forgotten her for a moment, their entire focus on Junior.

She launches herself at him, knocking him and his chair straight to the ground, but she does it with some finesse so she *doesn't* knock him unconscious.

"Where is she?" she yells. "Where the hell did you put her?"

They twist off the chair and onto the ground, her hands slide up to his throat before he can really register what's happening—he's slow on the take, Junior.

Richard's not. He's grabbed under her armpits, trying to pull her off his kid while Rick just stands back and laughs. Mel has to really fight to stay on top of Junior. His eyes bulge at the pressure of her hands before Richard *heaves* and pulls her off him. She shrieks, hellcat furious, kicking out every way she can and when she hits something—one of them—hard enough to make him holler, she grins.

"Stop that!" Richard says with the fury of a man used to being listened to.

She kicks Junior again. Right under his bottom rib. Really hooks her boot in there.

He howls.

Richard shakes her like a rag doll whose stuffing he's torn out, dragging her behind his desk and shoving her in his chair. "You will stay there," he says.

"I bet all your dogs'll disobey you, no matter how much you train them," Mel says.

He's startled into staring at her for a too-long moment, which tells her she's right. There're some kinds of evil animals sense. Richard's got it in spades.

"Get up," he tells his son. "Rick, did you know about this?"

"Fuck no!" Rick says. "Like I'd keep your kid's bullshit secrets. I'm shaping up to be the most honest one out of the entire lot of us. I told Big Daddy when I realized the diamonds were stolen, I looked for the Harper girl for years while you all sat on your asses and apparently *this* one lied about killing a whole fucking girl!"

"I didn't lie," Junior says, taking his father's hand and staggering to his feet. He rubs at his throat, glaring at Mel. "I shot her like I said. I just . . ."

"What?" Richard demands when Junior dithers and Mel thinks

about all the things on the assemblyman's desk that she can chuck at his head to kill him. Death by stapler sounds great right now.

"I just didn't bury her. But only because Chloe showed up and stabbed me."

"You said that happened *after* you killed the girl."

"It did. I just . . . the girl was bleeding all over her car and it was a lot, so I stepped away to take a breath, but Chloe, she came out of nowhere! She was on me before I could do anything." He licks his lips, rubbing at his throat where pink is starting to rise livid on his skin. "She stuck a knife in me and then tried to run me off the road with her car and left me where no one could find me! It was a miracle I survived!"

The drag marks. The blood trails. It was *his* blood? Not Whitney's?

"Where did the girl go, Junior?" Richard says, his voice rising with each word.

I can't tell you yet. I need you to trust that I have an ace up my sleeve.

Chills down her arms. Her body buzzing back to hope. It couldn't be. She can't believe . . .

"When I came to and dragged myself back on the road, all the blood was there, but they were both gone," Junior says.

Richard's silence is the kind that comes before the detonation. Mel shivers against the spooky hush of it as Rick braces against the wall and smirks.

"There's no way she would've survived, Dad," Junior says, trying to fill the quiet. "And if she had, she would've come back! Harper tried to drive her out of there and she probably died before they hit the highway. Harper dumped her friend's body in some other part of the forest and kept moving. That's what she does."

"Fucking pitiful, Junior. This is like stolen valor, just with murder," Rick says.

"She's dead! It's cause of me! You don't survive a gut shot like that with no hospital or anything. She never came back!"

"Maybe because you shot her, you dumbass," Rick says. "You gotta make sure they don't have a pulse and are in the ground before you start claiming you killed 'em."

"Was she still alive last time you saw her? Was she breathing?"

It's Mel who asks. The question tears out of her and they all kind of stare at her like, yeah, look, it's her, she's still here and she's stuck in their little family drama.

"I—" Junior opens and closes his mouth a few times, looking nervously at his father.

"Did *you* put the necklace around the steering wheel?" Mel demands.

"What?" he asks in confusion.

"This necklace." She pulls it out from under her shirt, thrusting it in his face. "This is Whitney's necklace. She was wearing it when you shot her. She always wore it. After you shot her, did you take it off her and clasp it around the steering wheel?"

"Why would I do that?" Junior asks.

"Fucking hell," Mel says. She jerks up, out of her chair, her brain trying to claw the threads together. She presses her hand against the bump the pendant makes under her shirt.

She left this for me. So I'd know she's coming back. That's what Gigi had said. Over and over, she'd insisted that Whitney was coming back.

"Dad, I promise, the girl didn't survive," Junior says, but the more he says it, the more unconvincing it sounds.

"I have to go," Mel says, turning toward the door.

"You're not going anywhere." Rick gets in her way swiftly. "You're taking me straight to the boy's body. Now."

Mel clamps down on the panic, trying to project calm. Someone needs to. "You can't uphold your end of the bargain, Rick. So you don't get shit."

"I'm sure there's some sort of agreement we can make, Ms. Tillman," Richard says.

"Like you get to stay alive as long as you bring me to the body," Rick says.

"That does seem like a reasonable trade," Richard says, which is a terrible sign, that the two of them are agreeing.

"People know where I am, Assemblyman," she warns. "They know where I was going. And there's a detailed account of everything that's happened since I left for Canada in a safety deposit box."

"You let your brother know, didn't you?" Richard asks. "His name's Ted, correct? He's been hospitalized for mental illness, I hear. Not the most reliable of men."

She doesn't take the bait. "Actually, my brother's out of town. I called the sheriff."

Richard shifts, his eyes flick to her throat like he wants to strangle her.

"You did not," Junior says.

"I sure did," Mel says. "I let him know I'd be coming in today about a cold case after I met with you, Assemblyman. Didn't tell him *which* cold case, though. The sheriff loved my former boss, so he always picks up my calls. Even if they're really early in the day. If I miss our appointment, he's gonna come looking for me. I've made sure of it."

With every word, Richard's grim expression deepens.

"I am not Chloe," Mel says firmly, trying not to look like her heart's beating a hundred miles a minute. "I am not a spoiled, idealistic teenaged girl who you spooked into running. I'm a grown woman who spent her childhood getting the shit beaten out of her by a motherfucker who was scarier than all of you put together. And I've spent my entire professional career outthinking both dumb shits and smart ones who kill their wives for insurance money. I would not bet against me."

"I heard that was your specialty," Richard says. "You do know a killer's mind, don't you?"

"I sure do," she says, and she means it.

On his desk, his phone makes an odd blaring sound. He jerks, looking toward it. "Junior." He snaps his fingers, pointing. Junior scurries to get it for him, handing it over. As he glances down at the phone, his frown deepens into something dangerous.

"I'm afraid you're going to have to come with me, Ms. Tillman," he says.

"I told you—"

He flips over his phone, handing it to her. "This is the back entrance of my family's land."

It's a security feed, trained on what looks like a back gate. Chloe and Gigi are in clear view as they walk past the camera and out of the shot, presumably toward the houses on the Newell land.

What the hell is she up to?

"Shit," Mel says. "I guess I am coming with you."

37

A FEW HOURS AGO

She gets up that morning before her alarm, just like always. Thirty minutes of kettlebells, another thirty of cardio.

Her heart's not in it. She never knows what to do with herself when she has to wait like this. She never learned. She kept busy instead.

There are no phone calls. No texts. No news.

So she ventures out into the world. The sun seems too bright as she walks down Main Street toward the Starbucks. Everything feels odd and new.

"Gigi?! Gigi!"

She turns to see Tiffany Parker standing there, staring at her like she's grown a second head because she'd walked right past her.

"Sorry," she says. "I didn't see you."

"I was right in front of you!"

She smiles, strained and too tight. "Sorry, Tiffany. I haven't had my coffee."

"Oh, girl, I thought you broke the coffee cycle," Tiffany says. "It messes your cortisol up. Make the switch to matcha or something with some adaptogens."

"I'll keep that in mind," she says as her phone buzzes in her pocket. "I gotta go."

"Text me, we'll hang out."

"Bye now."

She crosses the street, hoping she doesn't run into anyone else, but it's a small town, so she's kind of screwed. She should've grabbed a baseball cap. She ducks into the alley between the drugstore and the Ace Hardware, pulling out her phone to see the text from a number she doesn't recognize.

This is Chloe. Meet me at the Blackberry Diner ASAP.

She doesn't question, she just texts back: *On my way.*

She doesn't hesitate—she can't when it comes to this . . . it may be . . . *finally*—she just moves . . .

Which is a mistake, because if she had looked up, Whitney would've noticed her sister walking down the street.

But she doesn't look.

She just collides with Gigi and braces for the inevitable.

38

GIGI

A FEW HOURS AGO

Gigi has long stopped startling when she catches sight of white-blond hair out of the corner of her eye. She's headed straight back to the Harper ranch this morning, so she's got other things on her mind when she nearly gets knocked off her feet on her way to grab some coffee and muffins. Food is important when waiting for bad news.

Hands close around her arms to steady her as she tilts off-balance, and that's when she knows. Even before she looks up, even before she can dare to hope.

One touch and she knows.

Their gazes meet and Gigi sucks in a breath, trying to steady herself, blinking into brown eyes exactly like hers.

Her brain short-circuits. For a split second there's silence as she stares. As she realizes: she was right, she was right, oh god, she was *right*.

"Fuck," Whitney says, and Gigi goes straight from *oh my god* relief to pure sisterly anger in a second and it feels so good, it's so familiar, so missed, and now it's back, now she's back oh god, she's *back*.

It's good that Gigi's got that big breath in her lungs because the next thing that comes out is, "*That's what you have to say?!*" ringing so loudly people a block down turn to look at them.

"Shit, Gigi." Whitney winces, pulling her back into the alley, looking over her shoulder like they're in a spy movie. Are they? Where the *fuck* has she been?! "Hi."

"*Hi*," she hisses, because apparently they're supposed to be quiet for some reason.

"Fuck, it's good to see you," Whitney says.

"I—I—" Gigi is so overcome; the entire world is spinning. She just grabs on to Whitney's hands, squeezing them tight, because she's *here*. Oh my god.

"Are you—are you okay? You gotta breathe, Gi. You're gonna have a panic attack—"

"No, I am not!" Gigi shrieks. "And if I was, it would be justified! Oh my god, I'm gonna be sick." She swoops, half bent over, trying to quell the choppy feeling of vindication. The relief, it's like someone's yanked her guts out in a vicious tug. She had been right. They'd all told her she was holding on to false hope, that her intuition meant nothing . . .

She's sobbing, she realizes distantly, like she's outside of her body.

"Breathe, sweetie," Whitney says, her hand settling between Gigi's shoulder blades and rubbing a circle, the anger and relief making her dizzy. "It's gonna be okay."

"You left," Gigi garbles out as the tears drip straight to the ground. "Everyone said I was crazy for not believing you were dead, even Momma had to give up to stay sane, but I knew—"

"I know," Whitney says. "I'm so sorry, honey. I can't even begin to . . ." She stops, her lips pressing together, her eyes bright with unshed tears. She twists her fingers in Gigi's, trying to reassure her. "I'll explain everything, okay? But we've got to get off the street."

Gigi straightens, her eyes narrowing. "Why?"

"Because I let everyone think I was dead for a reason," Whitney says. "And that reason's coming for me. We do not have time for this! Just listen to me for once in your life, okay?"

"Okay. Wait. Whoever's after you . . . were they after Chloe?" When Whitney nods, Gigi bites her lip. "I need to tell you something.

Chloe . . . she was just in a plane crash. They're still trying to find the exact location—"

"What are you talking about?"

"I don't know if she survived," Gigi blurts out. "I don't know where she or Mel are."

"Chloe's at the Blackberry Diner," Whitney says. "She texted me five minutes ago to meet her."

"What?" Gigi's heart tries to tear out of her chest for the second time in five minutes. That can't be healthy, even with all the kettle-bells she does. "What are you talking about?"

"What are *you* talking about?"

"The Harper family jet crashed yesterday. Chloe and Mel were on it. I've been running around like one of Grandma's chickens after she twisted off their heads, search-and-rescue is out there looking, the Harpers are losing their minds, and you're telling me Chloe *texted* you five minutes ago?"

"Oh my god, I can't believe you're questioning me three seconds after reuniting with me," Whitney says. "This is classic little-sister bullshit. Yes, she texted me. See?" She thrusts out the phone.

Gigi doesn't even look at the phone, she wipes her tears away angrily. "You are older than me by ninety seconds!"

"That's it," Whitney says. "We need to get to the diner. Staying out here is not good. They'll find us."

"Who?" Gigi demands, but Whitney grabs her arm and tugs her down the street, Gigi going with it because she's not letting her out of her sight for a second. She needs to call their mom. She needs to call the sheriff and rub it in his face she was *right*. She needs—

Answers. A lot of them. Right now, preferably.

There's a scar on Whitney's neck. When she turns her head toward Gold Street, where the Blackberry Diner is, Gigi catches sight of it. She sucks in a breath, reaching out, and Whitney flinches away, and it's hurtful, but not even close to the worst thing her sister's ever done to her, what with the whole *faking one's death*.

"I can't believe you faked your death," Gigi mutters as she trots after her. Maybe she can superglue their hands together. She's always walked so damn fast, even when there was no reason to hurry. *Whitney was born in a rush,* Momma used to always say with a rueful smile.

Oh god, Momma's gonna have a heart attack, seeing her.

"I didn't—" Whitney stops. "I didn't plan on it," she finally says as the Blackberry Diner comes into sight, the chain-saw bear statues cavorting with their comically large blackberries all around the pathway leading up to the door. "It just happened."

"Faking your death doesn't *just happen.*"

"I was in between a rock and a hard place," Whitney says.

"That means it was Chloe's fault," Gigi says, her resolve hardening. She's been suspicious for over a year that Chloe had something to do with Whitney's disappearance. She just had no proof. Now she has confirmation *and* her sister. Which means there's nothing holding her back from strangling Chloe Harper.

Mel. A nasty whisper wiggles through her head. *Whitney didn't mention Mel.*

"Where's Mel?" Gigi asks.

"She's probably with Chloe, come on," Whitney says, tugging her through the aisle of bears and their blackberries. They always freaked Gigi out a little and she's spent every Sunday after church at this diner since she was a kid. "Be nice," she tells Gigi, like she can read her mind. "You'll regret it otherwise, once I explain."

They push through the double doors as one and it makes Gigi want to sob and howl and never let her go, but then she catches sight of a twenty-something Chloe in the empty back room of the Blackberry Diner and she just points at her. "You," and yes, maybe she is shouting a little, and maybe Whitney is trying to hold her back, but she's got *years* of anger and grief to work through here. Nothing's gonna stop her.

She wrenches out of Whitney's grip, stalking toward the booth. "You are *dead,* Chloe Harper!"

Chloe flinches, like she knows their different inflections—it was always so hard to play switcheroo with her—and before Chloe can react, Gigi flings herself into the booth, closely followed by Whitney.

"We ran into each other on the street," Whitney says when Chloe shoots her a questioning look.

"You couldn't have laid low?" Chloe demands.

Whitney rolls her eyes. "I needed coffee." She jerks her thumb at Gigi. "Gigi says everyone thinks you and Mel were in a plane crash, so . . ."

"We were. It's fine. Moving on," Chloe says.

"Moving on? From a plane crash?" Whitney leans forward and sniffs her. "You smell like smoke."

"I took a shower. We're gonna need a few minutes," she tells the waitress who approaches tentatively after Gigi's fit.

"I'm gonna kill you," Gigi says.

"Fair," Chloe says, and Gigi softens a bit at her lack of dodging. "But maybe later?" Chloe looks at Whitney. "Mel knows where they're at," she says, way too mysteriously.

"You're fucking kidding me," Whitney says. "This whole time?"

"This whole time. And she's about to do something really stupid and we need to save her," Chloe says.

"What's she done? What's going on? I want answers and pancakes, right now. And you need to call Momma," Gigi adds to Whitney. "Do you know what you've done to her? She had to pick out your *headstone*. She visits your not-grave on our birthday. It's been hell."

"It was the only way to keep everyone safe," Whitney says.

"Bullshit," Gigi says. "What the hell have you two gotten yourselves into?"

39

CHLOE

Twenty minutes, a stack of pancakes, and three coffees later, Chloe finally says, ". . . and that's it."

"That's it," Gigi echoes, like she's trying to absorb it all, what with the self-defense and the running, and the drug dealer and the former-mayor-turned-state-assemblyman all trying to kill everyone over buried-with-a-body diamonds. "*This* is why you were so weird the last two years of high school? It wasn't because you liked girls, it was because you *murdered* a boy with the girl you liked?"

"Keep your voice down," Chloe says, looking over her shoulder. The back room of the Blackberry Diner is thankfully empty. That's why she chose it. "First, I didn't like Mel until *after* I got to know her. And it was self-defense."

"Of course it was! You're way too precious to kill anyone who isn't going to kill you."

"I am not precious."

"Precious, righteous, whatever," Gigi says. "And now Mel's run on you." She laughs. "How does it feel?"

Chloe suppresses the urge to throw the blackberry-shaped salt-shaker at her. "Can we focus on the fact that she's heading right into danger? We need to pay the bill and get going."

"Do you know where she's at?" Whitney asks.

Chloe sets the note down on the table.

Going to handle all this. I'll make a deal with Richard for the diamonds. You don't have to worry. Go see your dad.

"Maybe we should just let Mel broker a deal," Gigi says tentatively. "She's good with that stuff. She's a professional—"

"Absolutely not," say Chloe and Whitney as one.

"The assemblyman is psychotic," Whitney says.

"You said the one who was the drug dealer was the problem," Gigi says.

"Rick is crazy. But Richard is focused and ambitious and he'll do anything to get what he wants. Mel currently has the thing that's keeping him from ascending to new political heights. If he has the diamonds, he has the money to run for Senate or whatever," Chloe says.

"He wants to run for Congress, not Senate," Whitney says in a long-suffering voice. "You keep confusing them."

"It doesn't matter. We need to do something fast to save Mel."

"If she's going to meet with the assemblyman, we should go to his office," Gigi says. "That's where she'll be."

"If we do that, then he's got all of us," Whitney points out. "He'll take advantage of that."

"Oh, I forgot, he thinks you've been murdered by his son," Gigi says sarcastically. "I am going to *ruin* Dick Junior for hurting you. He is not going to be worth the paper his election posters are printed on after I'm done with him."

Whitney looks genuinely touched by this.

"I think we need to bypass the Dicks completely," Chloe says. "And go to the only person they listen to."

"Big Daddy?" Whitney asks.

Chloe nods.

"Anyone who insists on being called Big Daddy is not a rational person," Gigi says.

"He's a lot more rational than his progeny," Chloe says, signaling for the check.

"It's risky," Whitney says.

"Why aren't we calling the sheriff, again?" Gigi asks. "This is his job."

"If Rick gets cornered, he'll try to shoot his way out and take everyone with him," Chloe says. "We've got to deal with this the way the Newells do: inside the family."

"It's how they work," Whitney says. "I've spent years researching them, Gigi," she adds when her twin continues to do the scrunchy-skeptical-eyebrow thing.

"There's nothing stopping them from killing all of you as soon as they have their diamonds!" Gigi says.

"That's where you come in," Chloe says. "You've got to stay behind."

"I will not! If you think I'm letting my sister out of my sight after what you—"

"Gigi, she's right," Whitney says. "We need someone who knows everything if it all goes wrong."

"And you'll need to deliver this to the sheriff . . . if you get my signal," Chloe says, pulling out an envelope.

"What's this?" Gigi asks.

"An explanation of the last eight years," Chloe says. "Every bit of it."

"You want me to hand deliver your confession of self-defense and how you then fled from the family who figured out you were a killer to the sheriff?"

"If I text you *acorn*, then yes, I want you to do just that."

Gigi swallows, looking down at the envelope and then up to meet Whitney's eyes. "You left me, you left Momma *because* these guys are so dangerous . . . and you want me to just let you walk right back into their clutches?"

"I didn't start this," Whitney says. "But I got caught by the landslide of it just the same. So I need to finish it." Her face hardens. "I need to make sure Dick Junior pays. And I need you to trust me."

Gigi takes the envelope and puts it in her purse. "I don't trust either of you," she says, trying to ignore the pain that flinches across Whitney's face. "I love you. But you faked your damn death. And you helped her." She glares at Chloe. "And you both left me and Mel to pick up all the pieces. So I'm not doing this because of trust. You need to earn that back. I'm doing this because *Mel* needs my help. You two may have been partners in crime the last three years, but Mel and

I have been partners in hunting *down* crime. So if I don't get a text from you, Chloe . . . if you don't let me know on the hour *every hour* that you two are okay, I won't just give your confession to the sheriff. I will bring the entire department to come break down the Newell family's door."

Chloe grins. "Yeah, I know, Gigi. I'm counting on it."

40

CHLOE

"My mom is gonna kill me," Whitney says as they get in the car.

Gigi stands on the sidewalk, watching them drive away, her arms crossed, the envelope with Chloe's confession clutched in her hand.

"Your sister is gonna kill me," Chloe says, pulling onto the street and heading toward the 5.

"Gigi will get over it. My mom won't," Whitney says.

"At least there's already a headstone for you."

Whitney snorts. "Fuck, I didn't think—" She stops. "I thought it'd be another six months, at least. Until we found the source behind all the moving of the money. I thought there'd be time to prepare to come back."

"Mel kind of messed up our plan," Chloe says. "It's good to see you, by the way."

"How was seeing Mel again?"

"How was reuniting with your very irate, murderous sister?"

"Seeing her was the best thing I've seen in years," Whitney says.

Chloe's quiet, the desperate thread in Whitney's voice killing her, because she's the whole reason behind the separation.

"Seeing Mel . . ." She stops, hands tightening around the steering wheel. "I don't know what I'm supposed to do. It got bigger . . . loving her. How is that possible? It shouldn't be *more* than before, when we've spent so much time apart. But it is. It's more. *She's* more."

She's everything.

"There's a whole saying about absence and the heart growing fonder," Whitney says. "It's better than your heart getting harder."

"I didn't tell her," Chloe says.

"About loving her? I think she knows," Whitney says.

"I meant about you being alive."

Whitney's eyes narrow. "Why not?"

"I was worried Rick might torture it out of her," Chloe says. "He had us until he decided to go on a peacock-squashing rampage. You're the one advantage I've still got, that the Bag of Dicks thinks I've been working alone and that you're dead."

"You should've told her," Whitney says.

"I should've done a million things better," Chloe says. "But I'm not gonna regret trying to keep you in play. You've had my back for years."

"I'll always have your back."

The past three years, they had fallen into a sort of shorthand during their mutual hiding. As soon as Whitney was healed up, Chloe had left Colorado behind. And Whitney had stayed and gotten to work untangling the Dicks' finances and misdeeds. She wasn't going to hide forever and Chloe couldn't stop her, so she had to help.

"What's the plan here?" Whitney asks. "We're just going to appeal to Big Daddy's sense of . . . what? Because if we make the wrong move—"

"—he'll feed us to the pigs," Chloe says. "But I'm sure we're right. If Richard or Rick are moving money through that shell company without Big Daddy's knowledge, that's the smoking gun to turn him against them. We've got the proof the money's being moved."

"And if we're wrong about the shell company? What if it's been Big Daddy all along?"

"Then maybe the pigs will be quick," Chloe says. "But if we run . . ."

"We leave Mel and Gigi in danger, instead of keeping them safe." Whitney sighs.

"Moment of fucking truth," Chloe agrees.

"God, I hate these guys."

"So let's get them in trouble with the only person they're scared of," Chloe says.

The Newell property had a few entrances. There was no way they were going through the front. They wouldn't get past the intercom.

"Back entrance should be right down there," Whitney says, looking up from the sketch of the property lines she has on her phone, pointing to the road on the right. Chloe takes it, the road sloping down, shadowed by pine trees. "So, the plane crash?"

"The Newells paid off the pilot, I think. We were right—Rick's got a new strip in the Siskiyous to fly out of. That's where we were supposed to land, but we went down maybe five or six miles from it instead. Rick found us. Took us out of there in his little plane."

Whitney looks her up and down. "And you're not in a hospital because . . . ?"

"I couldn't even get you to a hospital, you think that's what I was prioritizing when Rick's on a rampage? He finally got ahold of me and then lost me because he's got a peacock vendetta."

"Technically you got me to a doctor," Whitney points out. "Kind of," she says, her nose wrinkling at the memory of the cattle vet they'd ended up at that night. "God, I can still smell the manure. Also, I do not get this peacock thing, but you can fill me in later. After we survive."

"Looking forward to it," Chloe says as the gate comes into sight down the road. As they stop in front of it, her fingers tighten around the wheel as the lump in her throat grows. "Maybe you should stay here," she says.

"Remember the last time I was hanging out alone around a car and a Newell showed up?" Whitney asks. "We stick together."

But Chloe keeps hesitating, that familiar fear thrumming to life inside her. She dreams about Whitney's blood on her hands more than anyone else's. If she gets her killed now, after Gigi found her again, she'll never forgive herself.

"Come on, Harper," Whitney says. "You started this. But we're ending it together."

She walks past Chloe and hops right over the fence.

Chloe's got no choice. She follows.

41

MEL

"Stop looking at me like that," Junior says, shifting in the back seat.

Mel just folds her arms and keeps staring. She's not memorizing him, but learning him. Because when this is over, when she's sure Chloe and Gigi are safe, he's gonna try to run from her and the sheriff.

And she plans to kill him first, before the sheriff or anyone else can get ahold of him.

She'll bury him with Toby if she has to. It's a good spot to put someone, after all.

"You two behaving back there?" Rick asks, sounding way too pleased with himself.

"She's being a bitch."

"Not saying a goddamn word over here," Mel points out.

"Your eyes are the definition of 'shooting daggers,'" Junior says. "Fucking chill, will you?"

"I don't think I will," Mel says, still staring at him. She likes that she's unsettling him. She's already suffering, being in the car with all three of them. Talk about a nightmare. Junior's cologne is way too strong. She needs to crack a window, then she needs to save Chloe and Gigi, kill Junior and then the rest of them, and then she needs to get some goddamn answers about Whitney.

"You do have a very intense gaze, Ms. Tillman. You could direct your attention forward," Richard says, making it sound like a benign request and a threat all at once.

"I could," Mel agrees, continuing to stare Junior down.

"Fucking women," Rick says.

"Indeed," Mel says, and he snorts like she's actually funny.

"I expect civility in my car," Richard says. He's got that end-of-his-rope tone back, and Mel is curious what will happen if she pushes him. She needs to know what she's dealing with.

Rick's crazy, but Richard's the scary one. That's what Chloe had said to her.

"Considering this is a car full of killers, I think you're gonna have to alter your expectations," Mel says. Out of the corners of her eyes—still fixed on Junior—she can see a tic in Richard's cheek muscle.

"I didn't kill anyone," Rick says.

Mel snorts.

"Well, in this current scenario," he concedes.

"Stop engaging her," Richard tells him. "My god, cousin."

"You're engaging her, too!"

"I'd like her to stop engaging me," Junior adds, and Mel just settles back as they fall into the same pattern as they did in the office: talking over each other, blaming each other, no fucking loyalty.

Her plan is unfolding just fine, despite the hiccups and revelations. All she has to do is get Chloe and Gigi out of the line of fire and then bring the fucking fire down on the Newells—once and for all.

42

RICK

The damn PI will not stop trying to kill Junior with her eyes. It's downright disturbing, and Rick's not even on the receiving end of it.

"We'll get guns at the house, then go out on the Gator to find them," Richard says as he pulls onto the gravel road that leads to the lodge.

"More golf carts? Are there feral peacocks roaming around here, too?" the PI asks slyly. Rick turns around to glare at her. She smiles, showing way too many teeth. She's a biter, that one. Rick can tell. The kind of woman who'd pull a Tyson.

"Sorry to disappoint, but I keep my land managed," Richard says.

"It's not your fucking land. It's Big Daddy's," Rick says.

Richard ignores him. "Big Daddy didn't pick up when I called; someone's gotta go down and see him."

"Not me," Junior says instantly.

Rick snorts. "I'll deal with Big Daddy," he says as the lodge comes into sight. Hill's Tesla is parked in front. Fuck. She'll ask questions if she sees they've got a hostage. "What are we gonna do about the little lady?" he asks, nodding toward the car as they pull up.

"I'll deal with her," Richard says, but Rick's thoroughly unconvinced, considering his wife's got more balls than him seven ways to Sunday. "Guns first."

"If you shoot Chloe or Gigi, I'm not doing shit for you," the PI says.

"You are not in any position to deny us, Ms. Tillman," Richard says coolly.

"Watch me," she spits, with way too much deadly promise for Rick's comfort. Harper may be creepy-spooky with her nine lives, but this one?

This one's got a murderous streak *and* a torch for Harper. Fucking cannonball combination, if you ask Rick. Love makes you do crazy things—add in a predilection for murder and investigation, and you've got a dangerous individual.

He shivers at the thought of how neat the head shot Sean took was. How far away was she when she did that? How much time did she have? It couldn't have been long. Sean was good.

But she was better.

"Come on," Rick says, getting out of the car and going over to her side to grab her. He throws the door open and then tries to yank her up, but she jerks out of his hold.

"Tell your minion to stop manhandling me," she says to Richard.

"I am not his minion," Rick says.

"Rick, just stop, she's not going to run. There's nowhere for you to go, Ms. Tillman," Richard says, and Rick's cheeks heat as she smiles at him, way too knowing.

God, he never thought he'd find someone he dislikes as much as Harper, but this one's giving her a run for her money. And all within less than a day of knowing her.

"Let's go," Richard says, snapping his fingers at Junior, who scrambles up the steps of the lodge and grabs the doors.

Rick doesn't bother to take his cap off this time. Fuck Hill's rules.

"Richard, is that you?" her voice carries from the kitchen. "What are you doing home?"

"Forgot a few things," Richard says. "I'll be in my office."

But before he can move, Hill comes striding into the foyer, a dish towel in her hand. Her eyes widen slightly when she sees Rick's with them, along with the PI.

"Who's this?" she asks.

"My name is Melanie Tillman," Mel says, before anyone can come up with a goddamn excuse.

"We've got work to do," Rick says firmly, before the PI says something dumb like *I'm being held hostage*. He'd never hear the end of it. Every Thanksgiving Hill would say *Remember that time you took that girl hostage? Oh and pass the peas*. Hill doesn't like anything shady near her or her precious Junior. She'd explode if Rick suggested burying the PI and Harper somewhere on the property.

"You should stay in the house today," Richard says.

Hill frowns. "What are you talking about?"

"Just stay in the house," Richard repeats, a threat of *Fucking do as I say—or else* in his voice.

"I have to take your grandfather his lunch. And I have—"

"Just take the lunch down to Big Daddy and *stay* there," Richard instructs. "Don't go outside. And don't open the door to anyone but me."

Hill stares at him for a long beat, her arms folded, her expression inscrutable.

"Just trust me and do as I say," Richard says.

"For once in your life," Rick mutters.

Hill glares at him. "Fine," she says. "*Fine*." She whirls on her heel and stalks off.

"I will never understand why you married that piece of work," Rick says.

"That's my mother," Junior protests.

"You have my sympathies," Rick says. "Come on. Guns then the Gator. Harper's probably hiding in the woods." He slides a glance at the PI. "That's what she's good at."

"She also seems pretty good at shooting your men," the PI says. "And look who's left." She gestures at the three of them. "Not the brightest bulbs, if you ask me."

"We're not tulips," Junior says scornfully.

"Oh my god, shut up," Rick says as the PI snorts. She stops when he grabs her arm and tugs her down the hall as he hears Hill go out the back door with Big Daddy's lunch.

"Guns," he says again, to Richard.

Richard's rifle cabinet is in his office—how else would he play at being cowboy for the voters when really, he spent most of his time fucking his mistresses? God, Hill is a piece of work, but so is Richard. Fucking kismet, those two. Soulmates in rotten.

"Get out of my way," Richard says, pushing past them to open the gun cabinet. Irritation flares inside Rick and he steps forward to jostle Richard, dropping the PI's arm.

"Where's the AK-47?" Junior asks.

"Someone let you have an AK-47?" the PI asks incredulously. "This fucking country."

"Greatest country in the world," Richard says, knee-jerk automatic like there's a string on his back that you pull and he'll spout patriotic bullshit.

The PI snorts again. Maybe Rick will feed her to Big Daddy's pigs. He'll have to pull her teeth out first, though. The pigs eat everything but the teeth. He learned that the hard way. Once he was done, he'd have Harper beat on the body-disposal front. *Fuck you, I can disappear someone, too.* It would serve her right.

"Sit over there," he says, pointing to the leather armchair before turning to the rifle rack. "You do not need an AK-47," he tells Junior. "You just stand back and let me and your dad pick."

"I get my time with Harper! You promised," Junior whines as Rick regards the gun rack. Of course, Richard goes for style over substance. Maybe he should raid Hill's gun safe instead, but she probably actually has hers under biometric locks and he'd have to cut her hand off or something to get it open. No way she'd let him in herself.

"Rick's right," Richard says.

"I think that's the first time you've ever said that," Rick says.

"He'll end up shooting himself with the AK," Richard says under his breath, picking out a .22 and handing it over to Junior. "Rick, take this one." He reaches for a shotgun and hands it over.

"Where are the handguns?" Rick asks.

"The rifles will do," Richard says, taking his own gun off the rack. Rick recognizes it. It's one of Big Daddy's bolt-action Remingtons.

"Fuck off with that. You need more than one gun to take on Harper. Or did you forget she likes to pop out of nowhere? That's how she gutted your boy."

"She didn't gut me."

"She should've," Rick says. "Done us all a favor."

Junior drops the rifle to swipe at him, which is so stupid, because Rick *doesn't* drop his gun. He raises it, setting the barrel right on Junior's chest.

"Don't you fucking dare," he says.

"Rick," Richard snaps, so angrily that Rick's a little surprised that much fatherly instinct has been summoned, but then he sees where Richard's looking.

The office door. It's cracked open.

"Oh that bitch," Rick says, jerking the gun out of Junior's face.

The PI is gone.

"All I fucking ever do is chase after women," he says, and then he takes off, Richard and Junior at his heels.

43

CHLOE

Chloe and Whitney's walk across the fields to the main house on the Newell compound leaves them sweaty, but thankfully it is not hilly or dusty. Chloe is so sick of cliffs and slopes and red dirt. She can still feel it in her pores, no matter how much she scrubbed. She wants to sleep for a week. Preferably next to Mel.

"I want to know more about the plane crash," Whitney says.

"I told you, it doesn't matter—"

"It does. Explain it to me," Whitney says.

Chloe rolls her eyes. "We crashed maybe six miles from the landing strip. The food they gave us in the air—it was drugged. I don't remember the plane going down. All I remember is waking up in the smoke and one of Rick's guys pulling me out of the wreckage."

"Are you sure the plan wasn't to fake an engine malfunction and then land on the strip and it got messed up?"

"Why would they drug us then?" Chloe asks. "Rick was expecting to take us off my dad's plane and onto his. We weren't supposed to be conscious during any of it."

"Good point," Whitney says.

"It was just bad luck," Chloe says. "My dad's sick, he's not gonna be checking the mechanic reports like he usually does. My mom doesn't know anything about planes. Maybe someone overlooked something with the engine."

"I don't think so," Whitney says as they swish their way through one of the hay fields.

"What do you mean?" Chloe asks.

"Because when Mel found you, there was more movement from the shell company's accounts," Whitney says. "A one-time payment of four hundred thousand dollars to Bayview Aviation that I traced to an IP address on the Newell compound. Bayview Aviation is the company that provides the mechanics for the private flights out of the airport you flew out of."

Chloe stops, staring at her. "That doesn't make sense," she says. "If someone paid off one of the Canadian mechanics to mess with the engine . . . that's assassination."

"Assassination is only for public figures," Whitney supplies helpfully.

"My point is, why would the Bag of Dicks pay someone to bring the plane down mechanically when they'd already paid the pilots and crew off to drug us and land on Rick's strip? They don't want me dead. They think I know where the diamonds are."

"I know," Whitney says. "That's what makes it weird. Something's not right here."

Chloe can see a house down below—Big Daddy would be living in the main house. That looks like it's his.

"Maybe we were wrong," she says. "Maybe the shell company *is* Big Daddy's. Maybe . . . maybe he's sick of their bullshit. Sick of chasing after the diamonds?"

"If Big Daddy's gone rogue . . ." Whitney gulps. "Are we sure we want to talk to him?"

"If he does want to kill me, might as well put our cards on the table. Maybe it'll change his mind."

"I hate gambling," Whitney says, picking up the pace as they make their way toward the blue house in the distance.

It only took a few more minutes to get to the front door.

"Do we ring the bell?" Chloe asks.

"It can't hurt to be polite," Whitney says.

Chloe presses the bell. The chime is loud enough she can hear it echo through the house. A minute passes. Then another.

Whitney cranes her head toward the driveway. "Truck's here," she says.

Chloe glances that way, seeing the dust-covered truck tucked under the carport.

"Maybe he's a man who prefers a knock," she says, before rapping on the door loudly.

Still no answer.

"Windows," Chloe says, and they walk off to check. The curtains are all drawn tight.

Something starts a slow drum inside her, a beat that's off from her heartbeat, a *rat-a-tat-tat* that tells her *danger*.

"Maybe he's on a walk or something," she says, even as she goes back over to the front door and tries the knob.

It's unlocked.

Chloe pushes the door open, the darkness of the foyer making it hard to see inside. "Mr. Newell?" she calls, raising her voice slightly.

"Are we really just gonna walk inside?" Whitney hisses.

Chloe shrugs and does just that.

"Mr. Newell," she calls again, stepping into the darkness, looking in the dimness for a light switch. She finds it, flipping it on. There's a boot tray in the foyer, boots with long-flaked-off mud set in it. A buffalo-check barn jacket covered in a thin layer of dust like it's been waiting too long to return to the barn. "Big Daddy?"

Whitney follows close behind as they venture farther into the house. They pass by a living room with a stack of *The Harper's Bluff Gazette* on the coffee table and deer heads mounted above the fireplace. Down the hall there are family photos lining the wall as Chloe ventures farther. Her footsteps echo as a thought creeps inside her: *This house is empty.*

The door at the end of the hall is half-cracked and when she pushes it open, sunlight spills out.

An empty hospital bed sits in the middle of the primary bedroom, stripped of its sheets.

"What the hell?" Whitney mutters behind her.

Chloe runs her finger over the dust on the bed, holding it up to the light. No one's been in here for a while.

"I don't think it was Big Daddy who paid off the mechanics to mess with the plane," she says.

"Who else—"

There's movement at the bedroom door. Whitney startles back.

"Hill," Chloe says, catching sight of her, and suddenly Chloe understands everything.

Hillary Newell steps into the bedroom from the hallway.

"Oh my god," Whitney says when she sees the gun in Hill's hands.

Chloe almost starts laughing, because she never paid much attention to Hill. She'd kind of written her off as an ambitious trophy wife—she clearly had underestimated the ambition. And then she realizes the gun in Hill's hands, it's bright pink. Like Barbie's First Dream Gun. And she can't stop the laughter this time because if she gets killed by a deadly embodiment of the pink tax, she might rise up just to die again from the absurdity.

"You're trespassing, Harper," Hill says, shutting the bedroom door behind her with a neat kick of her cowboy boot. "Breaking and entering. I'd be well within my rights."

"Shit," Whitney mutters.

"How do you know who I am, Hill?" Chloe asks. "We've certainly never met."

Hill swallows. She's slipped up and now Chloe can see it, almost like she's Mel. All the little threads that she and Whitney couldn't untangle.

"My husband and I have a very trusting relationship," Hill says. "I know everything when it comes to you. There are no secrets between him and me."

Whitney snorts. "Does that mean you know about Vera the side piece?"

"I thought the mistress was Fern," Chloe says.

"That's the backup mistress," Whitney says. "Remember? He's got a little ménage going."

"Right," Chloe says, her eyes settling back on Hill, who's stark red instead of white, which means she probably did know about the mistresses. Or at least just expected them from a man like Richard. "I can keep on going with the dirty secrets."

"There are a lot of them," Whitney adds.

"I want you both to leave, before I call the sheriff."

"You won't do that," Chloe says, stepping forward. It's a gamble and it's also a guess, what she's about to say. "Because then the sheriff's going to ask to talk to Big Daddy. And he's not here, is he?" She licks her lips, trying to ignore the pounding in her heart. Because if she's wrong, she's probably gonna get shot. "How long has Big Daddy been dead, Hill?"

Hill goes white then and Whitney mutters *holy shit*, because she's putting it together, too. When the Newells started moving money, they had thought Rick had gotten a new supply chain going. But if it had been *Hill* moving money because Big Daddy kicked the bucket . . .

"Did you kill him?" Chloe asks a little incredulously because that man seemed as hard to put down as herself.

"Of course not!" Hill snaps, sounding almost offended.

"He got sick, didn't he?" Whitney asks. "Thus the hospital bed."

"Did you keep it a secret?" Chloe asks.

"He had a stroke," Hill says. "He didn't want anyone to know. Richard was in Sacramento working for months. I was the only one home. I'm *always* the only one here. I'd never hurt him. I *took care* of him. Honored his wishes. I loved him like he was my own grandfather. I'm no killer."

"You're pointing a gun at us," Whitney says.

"She stabbed my son!" Hill jabs the gun toward Chloe. "You think I'd forget that?"

"Junior deserved it," Chloe counters.

"That doesn't matter! Your sister never mattered." She whirls on Whitney.

Whitney's eyes widen at the mistake. Chloe makes another step toward Hill, trying to edge in so Whitney's not in the line of fire.

"Only family matters. You two are not family!" Hill's last words end in an almost shriek.

"Thank god for that," Whitney says grimly.

"I took care of Big Daddy until the very end," Hill says. "I did what he asked of me. I kept the stroke a secret. I paid everyone I needed to off. If Richard knew . . . if *Rick* knew . . ." She shakes her head. "And don't get me started on the second cousins out in Yreka. They're practically *feral*. And it's not like anyone noticed, did they? Because *I* was the one who spent time with Big Daddy, who cared for him. They were all too busy running after *you*. You and those goddamn diamonds."

And there it was.

"*You* were the one who paid to bring the plane down," Chloe says.

"Do you know how much time and money they've wasted, chasing after you?" Hill demands. "I have mutual funds that are a better investment than you! But it became all about their goddamn bruised male egos, and I am sick of it, do you hear me?"

"Considering you're shrieking at the top of your lungs, *yes*," Chloe says. She's positioned herself so she's almost totally blocking Whitney from the gun now. That's good. Can she tackle Hill? It'd probably be a bad idea. She's a woman unraveling right in front of them.

"Hill, you're right," Chloe says as she sucks in a breath to shriek some more. "You're *right*, it's been a total waste of time and money. Because I don't know where the diamonds are."

The room goes silent.

"You're lying."

"You've got a gun on me! No one knows we're here. I've got no reason to lie. I came *here*, didn't I?"

She frowns. "Why are you here?" she demands. "Why aren't you running again?"

"Well, I was gonna try to cut a deal with the head of the family, but since he's passed away . . ." Chloe licks her lips. "Looks like there's a vacancy."

Something flickers across Hill's face. Chloe recognizes it: hunger. No one spends almost half a million dollars to bring a plane down without a plan to seize power in some way.

"My family means everything to me," Hill says. "I would never betray them."

"I get it, you know," Chloe continues. "I come from ranchers. Families ruled by men are kind of bullshit when you're a daughter. My grandpa used to lament that my daddy broke tradition by having girls. Like I couldn't take on running the ranch. You're never smart enough, or strong enough, not to them."

"You are not going to get me with some boss-bitch speech, Harper," Hill says. "You're going to take me to the diamonds and we'll be done with this, once and for all."

"You're planning on giving them the diamonds after all this?" Whitney asks.

"Richard needs a war chest for his run," Hill says.

"Oh, come on," Whitney says. "He's cheating on you! With two different women! I'm pretty sure you wrote all his early campaign speeches *and* you're writing Junior's. I recognize the style."

"You didn't even trust your husband enough to tell him his father had a stroke," Chloe says.

"But you're just gonna hand over a bag of diamonds to him? Just like that?" Whitney asks.

"He is my husband," Hill grits out.

"So?" Chloe says, and for some reason, this question seems to hit Hill like a Taser zap. She stares at her, stunned, the gun lowering a little.

"Really, what's wrong with a boss-bitch speech?' Chloe says. "Being the boss is great. Isn't that what you've been doing ever since Big Daddy died? Maybe even before? You were handling everything for him. For Richard. For Junior. For the whole family and no one appreciated you or let you in on anything, sounds like. So you did what any practical woman would do: you seized the opportunity."

"I did what had to be done."

"Yeah. Like the boss. Why are you denying the exact thing you are? Why are you letting them treat you like the Jackie when you could be JFK?"

"Jackie lived. He did not."

Whitney snorts. "Okay, you've got a point there," she says. "What! She does!" she says when Chloe glares.

"We're done talking about this," Hill says firmly. "You're going to take me to the diamonds, Harper."

"I don't know where they are!"

"But I do."

Hill startles, the gun swinging toward the door and the voice as Mel steps inside the bedroom.

44

MEL

"You should put that down," Mel says, closing the door behind her. That's probably a bad idea, but she does it anyway. Better to contain the situation.

Hill makes no move to do what Mel says.

Mel looks her up and down, which seems to piss her off. "Cute gun. Drop it."

"I will not. You're trespassing."

"Stop that," Mel says disgustedly. "Your husband brought me here. You met me in your foyer. And I'm the only one who knows where the diamonds are, so shooting me is a real bad idea."

"Where is he?" Hill's voice sharpens. "Is he with you?"

"The entire miserable lot of them are up at the lodge arguing over which guns to pick to kill us with. Your son wanted to use an AK-47. Great job, raising that one. He's an idiot."

"He is gifted in unique ways," Hill says.

"Pretty but psychotic is not exactly a gift," Mel says.

Getting away from the Dicks had been surprisingly easy. She wonders if they've even noticed yet. Or if Junior's grabbed the AK-47. What kind of idiot lets someone like Junior near that kind of firepower?

She takes in the empty hospital bed. "You kill Big Daddy or something?" she asks Hill.

"I am not a killer!" Hill shrieks. Nails on a chalkboard, fuck, it's a wonder Junior has any hearing left.

"Great to know," Mel says, standing straight in front of the pink gun.

"Mel," Chloe growls. "She's a crack shot. And Big Daddy died from stroke complications . . . three months ago."

Three months? A laugh burbles out of her throat before she can stop it. "Are you telling me that these fuckers have been running around trying to impress a dead man?"

"Apparently," says Gigi.

"What are you doing here?" Mel demands. "You call me whipped. But you come running as soon as Chloe . . . comes . . . calling—" Her words slow to a stop as Gigi's head tilts.

Gigi doesn't tilt her head to the left. She tilts her head to the right. *Whitney* tilts her head to the left.

"Holy fuck!" Mel yells, and this time, Hill does startle at the outburst. The gun drops and fuck it all, Mel has to dive for it instead of processing that it's *Whitney* not Gigi. It's the responsible thing to do. Goddamn it.

Hill lunges for the gun at the same time, their heads smack with a dull *thud*, the woman howls, and Mel barely blinks because you get your head smashed into the side of a trailer enough, nothing takes you down. She swipes the gun with her foot and grabs it, righting herself, pointing it at Hill's chest. It's a nice weight. Cute color.

And then she remembers. "Whitney?!"

She gives a meek wave. "Hey."

"Wait, that's not the other one?" Hill demands. "Junior killed you!"

"He tried. But luckily, like everything else he attempts, he sucked at it," Whitney says.

"Junior didn't kill you," Hill says, almost to herself. "He's not—he didn't do anything!"

"He slit my throat and shot me, so not exactly. But yes, I live to tell the tale."

"He's not a murderer," Hill breathes, the relief spooling tension off her like a pulled thread. "There isn't a body somewhere with his DNA all over it."

"Now that we've established Junior is not a killer, we're gonna go now," Mel says.

"No."

It's not Hill, but Chloe who says it. She steps forward, into Hill's line of sight, taking both of her hands.

"Hill, listen to me," Chloe says. "Because any minute, Richard and Rick are gonna come busting through that door and swing their metaphorical and actual dicks around, and Junior will listen to them, not you. As soon as they find out Big Daddy's dead, they're gonna get their hands on his will, and you and I both know that man didn't leave shit to you."

Hill nods faintly. Whatever Chloe's doing, it's working, so Mel shuts the hell up and just watches.

"No matter how much money you moved, no matter how well you hid it, they'll find it."

"After all, we found it," Whitney says.

"And whatever you moved, it's nothing compared to what you get if *Junior* is the sole inheritor because Richard and Rick are in jail. Because we both know your son's gonna hand all that hard work of running things over to you if you give him a big enough budget for his girls and his toys. He handed his whole campaign over to you, didn't he?"

"I was the best person for the job."

"All you have to do, to get all that money and all that power, is just agree with everything I say." Chloe leans forward. "Don't you want to be selfish, just once?"

Hill takes a shaky breath, the indecision wavering across her face. "Junior didn't kill her," she says, like she needs to remember that.

"I know you wanted to keep Junior safe. And Richard . . . he'll throw Junior to the police if he has to. You don't cape for a man like that. You fuck him up."

Hill licks her lips, her eyes gleaming. "I—"

She's wavering. Mel can tell. Is there a way to push her over the edge?

"Do you hear that?" Whitney asks, just as the sound of sirens becomes clearer.

"Oh Christ," Chloe says. "I forgot to text Gigi!"

45

MEL

"The sheriff will be at the gate," Hill says, moving toward the bedroom door and yanking it open. Mel scrambles to follow her, Chloe and Whitney close behind as she stalks to the kitchen where a small television with the security feed is. Sure enough, there are four sheriff cars grouped in front of the gate.

"Incoming," Whitney says, peering out the back window. "The Dicks are heading toward us."

"Can we open the gate from here?" Mel asks. She'd rather have the sheriff on his way down the road right now.

Hill's brows scrunch together as she wavers.

"The sheriff and I already had a conversation this morning," Mel says. "He won't just go away."

"It's now or never," Chloe says urgently to Hill.

"They're my family," Hill says, but it's weak coming out of her mouth.

"Rick is gonna end up using Junior as a human shield if he has a shoot-out with the sheriff," Chloe says.

All the blood drains out of Hill's face as the blunt truth hits her. She reaches over and flips a switch on the wall labeled GATE and then she dashes toward the back door, yanking it open. "Junior!" she yells.

"Mom?" He lopes ahead of his father and uncle.

"Get in here!"

The shrieking, it seems to work, because he hightails it inside. She slams the door shut, locking it.

"What the heck, Mom?" Mel hears him ask from her spot in the living room. "Dad needs to get in. We've got an intruder on the property."

"Get in the kitchen," Hill orders, peering out the window at her husband. He waves at her. Her face hardens. And then she marches down the hall to lock the front door, too.

"What the fuck!" Junior yelps when he sees Chloe and Whitney standing in the kitchen.

"Hi, Junior," says Chloe.

Whitney smiles as his eyes settle on her, confused until she draws a slow finger across her neck. His sputters like he's choking on his tongue. "Long time no see," Whitney says, tossing her hair over her shoulder, exposing an ugly scar on her neck that makes Mel's stomach sicken.

"You—you—"

"Didn't die. Aren't you lucky."

"I'd kill you if you had killed her," Chloe says.

"That's so sweet," Whitney says.

"I mean, Mel would've probably gotten there first. But I would've helped her clean it up."

"Fuck you, you didn't tell me she was alive even when we were fighting," Mel says, following Hill back into the kitchen. "And I can do my own cleanup, thank you very much."

"Hey, that's my mom's gun," Junior says.

"That would make putting a bullet in you pretty funny," Mel says. "I could use a laugh."

"Do not shoot my son," Hill says, glaring at her until Mel tucks the gun in the back of her jeans. "Not if you want me to go along with whatever plan you've got."

"Mom, what is going on?" Junior says.

"We turned your mom, Junior. She's one of us now," Whitney says.

"What?"

"Junior, I'm going to need you to listen to me very carefully," Hill says, coming to stand in front of Junior, putting her hands on his shoulders. "Big Daddy is dead."

"What!"

"Is that the only word he knows?" Whitney mutters to Mel, who keeps stealing glances at her, trying to reassure herself yes, that's Whitney, not Gigi with weird scar makeup on her neck. She can't believe it, even though the proof's in front of her.

"Big Daddy's dead, and your father and uncle will be put away for a very long time after what they've done."

"Mom—"

"I know everything about Harper, Junior. *Everything.*"

He swallows hard. "I was just doing what Dad told me!"

"You almost killed someone. Do you know what that could've done to your political career?" Hill snaps.

"Yeah, Junior, real politicians pay other people to do their wet work," Chloe says.

"I'm gonna—"

"—you will not do anything to her," Hill snaps. "You are going to stay behind me, agree with everything we say when we talk to the sheriff, and you will get out of this, do you hear me?'

"Listen to your mom, Junior," Whitney says. "Otherwise . . ." She trails off, tapping her scar.

"Mom, this is crazy," he says. "You don't understand what these women have done."

"I know exactly what they've done," Hill says. "And I know what you've done. So I'm doing what I have to in order to protect you, as your mother. I will always protect you. So sit back and *behave* and when this is all over, you'll have the entire Newell inheritance at your feet."

He blinks.

"I think it's actually getting through his thick skull," Chloe says.

"Men really do fail upward," Whitney says.

Mel rolls her eyes. "Are we done?" she asks, just as pounding on the back door fills the kitchen, followed by Richard's muffled voice, calling Hill's name. She flinches at the sound.

"It's fine," Mel says, hand going to the gun. "Sheriff's almost here." She keeps one eye on the camera feeds as the vehicles disappear down the gravel road, heading toward the main house.

"How are we playing this?" Chloe asks.

"I told the sheriff I needed to meet with him about a cold case. I didn't say which one."

"Well, I sent Gigi with a confession to give to him," Chloe says.

"A confession? About what exactly?"

"Keep your mouth shut and find out," Chloe says, as the sound of sirens grows louder and louder and then gets cut off abruptly.

"Living room," Whitney says, moving toward it. They crowd in front of the window, peering through the curtain cracks.

Richard stands there, relaxed as you pleased, talking to the sheriff, his rifle set on the ground like he'd been ambling around on a wild boar hunt instead of a girl hunt.

"Such a slick son of a bitch," Chloe mutters. "I'm done with this. Hill, do we have a deal? You and Junior for Rick and Richard?"

"We have a deal," Hill says.

"Great. Just go along with what I say then, and remember: my birthday's June tenth."

"What does that—"

Chloe's already marching over to the front door and opening it, stepping outside.

"Fucking hell," Mel says, grabbing Hill's arm and dashing after Chloe because *she's* the one with the goddamn gun.

"I'm coming!" Whitney says, hurrying after them.

". . . as you can see, there's no issue," Richard's saying to the sheriff. He glances over his shoulder to see them filing out of the house. "There's my wife," he says, gesturing toward Hill. "She's just . . . having her book club. Right, honey?"

Hill stays standing next to Mel, folding her arms bitterly and saying nothing.

"Chloe Harper, as I live and breathe," says the sheriff. "I was certainly surprised when Georgia brought me your letter."

"Nice to see you, Sheriff," says Chloe as Whitney steps out from behind Hill and into view.

The sheriff practically chokes on his own mustache, he sucks in such a startled breath. He whirls toward his tinted-window SUV as Gigi slowly gets out of it and walks to him, as if confirming he's seeing what he's seeing.

"Oh fuck," Rick says as his gaze bounces between the twins.

Richard says nothing, but that vein in his forehead begins to twitch. Mel swallows, eyeing the rifle at his side.

"My god," the sheriff says. "Whitney Teller."

"Like I said in my letter, I can explain everything," Chloe says. "Why I ran away, who attacked Whitney and left her for dead, and how I found her. I even know the person responsible for bringing down my family's jet on Thursday. It wasn't engine trouble—it was sabotage."

"And what does any of this have to do with Toby Dunne's disappearance?" the sheriff asks.

"On the night of June tenth, Mel here convinced me to take my BMW on a joyride. We crashed, remember?"

"I do. Your parents were very worried when you disappeared from the party."

"We told everyone we got lost in the woods trying to get back to the road," Chloe says. "That's the truth. But we didn't tell anyone about what we stumbled across in the forest that night."

Mel's heart thumps. Is Chloe doing what Mel thinks she's doing? Is she that crazy?

Or is she that smart?

"Mel and I watched Rick and Richard Newell kill Toby Dunne and bury him in the woods the night of June tenth."

"What the fuck! You did not!" Rick yelps.

"That's ridiculous," Richard says.

"Mel and I ran before they could see us—or so I thought. Somehow, Rick figured out that I had witnessed their body dump. When I was eighteen, he threatened me and my entire family if I didn't leave town."

"Sheriff, surely you're not entertaining this," Richard says. "My family are long-standing members of this community—"

The sheriff shoots a look at Rick and Richard's mouth closes, that vein bulging on his forehead.

"She's lying," Rick says.

"There were several eyewitnesses who said the Dunne boy's truck was at your place on and off that summer," the sheriff says. "Even his momma said she thought he'd gotten in with a bad crowd. I brought you in for questioning myself, didn't I, Rick?"

Rick presses his lips together.

"This is absurd," Richard says, as he looks over his shoulder at Hill. "Go get Big Daddy," he says. "Sheriff, my grandfather is going to want to talk to you about this."

Junior's eyes bulge at the mention of Big Daddy as he casts a nervous glance at his mother . . . and keeps his big trap shut for once in his life. A little thrill runs through Mel. Shit, this is really gonna work.

"Richard Senior is welcome to come out here and talk to us, too," the sheriff says. "But I want to hear what else Chloe has to say."

"Go get him," Richard hisses at Hill between gritted teeth.

She doesn't move. Richard's hands clench the barrel of the rifle. The sheriff's hand goes to his gun belt, casual but at the ready. Mel's grateful he seems to understand this situation could devolve into a shitshow at any second.

"I ran because I was scared," Chloe says. "But after three years of isolation, it was too much. I reached out to an old friend."

Whitney smiles at her. "When Chloe reached out, I started investigating the Newell family. But I wasn't careful enough," she says. "Richard and Rick didn't want anyone digging into their business because that's how I found out Rick's drug money was funding Richard's political campaigns. They discovered Chloe and I had arranged a meeting and attacked me on Salt Creek Road before she could arrive. They gave me this." She touches the scar on her neck. "And this." She lifts up her shirt, exposing the bullet scar.

"I never touched you! Junior is the one who gutted you!" Rick says.

"Junior?" Whitney echoes innocently. "No. It was the two of you. Richard held me down and you slit my throat." She presses her hand against her scar. "It was terrible." Her voice cracks.

"Sheriff—" Richard tries.

"Chloe saved me." Whitney mows his protest down sweetly. "She found me on the side of the road and realized what had happened."

"How did you survive?" the sheriff asks. "The blood—"

"Dr. Victor Howard of Scott Valley can verify that we showed up at his place the day Whitney went missing," Chloe says. "He was my dad's cattle vet for years. He was closer than a hospital."

"Dr. Howard fixed me up, but I knew that if Richard and Rick thought I was alive, they'd come for me because of what I knew. So I hid, just like Chloe," Whitney says. "We were so scared they would target our families. They'd already gone after me because of my connection to Chloe. I knew that if they thought I survived, they'd hurt my family to draw me out. I couldn't let that happen."

"I cannot believe you are entertaining this nonsense," Richard says. "My cousin has long been needlessly harassed by the sheriff's department. My grandfather is a pillar of our community, and I am a dedicated public servant. I have never even seen this young lady until today apart from her missing person posters. Sheriff, I insist that you leave. Before I have to go inside and get my grandfather. This is his property."

"Feel free to go and get Richard Senior," the sheriff says. "I'd love to get his take on this."

"Fine, I will," Richard says. "He won't be happy that he has to sort this out with you, Sheriff. He expects more from the law enforcement. Especially with the donations he makes."

It's a clear warning that the sheriff doesn't seem interested in bowing down to.

"I'll wait," he says.

Mel looks at Hill. It was now or never.

"You can't," Hill says.

"—and he will be aggravated to hear about this behavior from you of all people—"

"What was that, Mrs. Newell?" the sheriff asks.

"You can't talk to Big Daddy," she says.

"Nonsense," Richard says. "Go get him, Hill."

"Why not, Mrs. Newell?" the sheriff asks gently.

"He's not here," Hill says.

Richard's head snaps toward her, startled. "What are you talking about, you said you were bringing him lunch."

Hill takes a deep, steeling breath.

"Mom?" Junior warbles behind her and for some mystifying reason it seems to give her strength.

"Big Daddy passed away from complications of a stroke a few months ago," she says. "You can verify this with the McCloud Funeral Home, who took care of the cremation according to Big Daddy's will and the Smith Nursing Service who assisted me in his hospice care the last few weeks of his life."

"What the fuck are you talking about?" Rick hollers. "The old man's dead?!"

Mel is surprised he sounds slightly emotional about it.

Richard says nothing for a moment. The vein in his forehead is doing all the talking for him.

And then, he lunges.

But he's not going for Hill—he moves past her so fast he knocks her to the ground in his haste to get to the front door, yelling Big Daddy's name. One of the deputies scrambles after him, but it's no use. He's already dashing into the empty house, screaming like it's the end of the world.

"Did you kill him?" Rick demands.

"Hillary!" Richard bellows, stalking back out of the house like a thunderstorm. "*What have you done?*"

"Stay right there," the sheriff says, stepping between Richard and Hill. "And lower your voice."

"My grandfather is dead!" Richard says. "Dead! She knew and didn't tell me! Arrest her!"

"Calm down," the sheriff says. "I understand this is a very sensitive subject. Mrs. Newell, can you explain this to me, please? What happened?"

"I've been Big Daddy's caretaker for many years now," Hill says, ignoring Rick and her husband. "I know it seems complex, but he was so dedicated to the family, to my husband and son's careers . . . he begged me to not let them know about the stroke. He was sure he'd recover. He was such a tough man, I was sure he would, too. So I respected his wishes. He was worried it would distract Junior from his campaign and that my husband would be more focused on family matters instead of representing our fine district in Sacramento. He was selfless until the end. I couldn't deny him."

"This is very unusual, Mrs. Newell," the sheriff says.

"I was obeying his wishes," Hill says firmly. "And you know Big Daddy . . . he was a man you listened to."

"He was quite a man," the sheriff agrees.

"You are *dead*," Rick yells.

"One more outburst out of you, and I'm putting you in a squad car," the sheriff tells him.

"I was going to tell my husband, but then . . ." Hill trails off, her eyes cast down, the picture of regret and womanly realization. "Miss Harper contacted me. At first, I dismissed her as a crazy person. I knew Rick was trouble, but I tolerated him because every family has bad apples. It's not my place to change that. I never dreamed my husband was capable of such terrible things. But then Miss Harper told me the date of Toby's disappearance and I remembered something."

She wrings her hands, looking genuinely distressed. "My husband—he came home on June tenth absolutely covered in dirt and blood. He told me at the time he had been at Rick's, helping him sort out some issue on his land. I just assumed it was a wild boar or a peacock problem. I didn't make the connection to the Dunne boy's disappearance back then . . . until Miss Harper contacted me to explain what my husband had been up to the last eight years and how he was targeting her for the last six. And that's when I started putting his strange behavior together . . . not just around the disappearance of Toby Dunne, but when Whitney Teller went missing."

"Hillary!" Richard says. "What are you doing?"

"Oh, you fucking bitch," Rick says, going for his gun.

Hill rears back, into her son's arms. To Junior's credit, he does protectively hold his mother away from the line of fire.

Mel starts to reach for Hill's pink gun at her back, but she doesn't need to. She hadn't known the sheriff had it in him, but maybe losing out on punishing a guy like Rick Newell for so long gave him some fire in his belly, because that man moves way faster than he should be able to at his age. Rick slams down to the ground and the deputies swarm him and Richard like angry bees. The rifle's snatched out of Richard's grip before he gets cuffed alongside his cousin.

"I have done nothing!" Richard bellows. "It's Rick and Junior you want! Rick's the one who employed Toby, and Junior attacked the Teller girl! I have touched no one, hurt no one, I am a *government official!*"

Chloe shoots a look at Hill like, *See? Told you.* Hill just holds Junior tighter, her eyes colder by the minute.

"We're going to need to have you all come in," the sheriff says to all of them standing there, watching his deputies drag Rick and Richard into the SUVs. "Make some statements. Figure this the hell out. Chloe, have you even spoken to your parents? Whitney, did you call your mother?"

"We've been a little busy trying not to get killed by those two," Chloe says.

The sheriff sucks in his lips and part of his mustache, contemplating them, Hill standing between with Junior.

"I'm not sure what to think here," he says. "Especially with no body or proof."

"I've got proof," Whitney says.

"And I can show you where they buried the body," Mel says.

46

MEL

"Can you draw me a map to where Toby was buried?" the sheriff asks.

He's had her in the questioning room for three hours. She's gone through being hired to find Chloe, the plane crash, the running, the being caught, the running again. And now they're at the Toby of it all.

"Not really," Mel says. "It's been a long time. I can guide them myself to the spot," Mel adds. "I'd say it's about a two-hour hike in and out, in the daylight."

He nods. "It'll take a few days to get together a recovery team."

"I'll be here," Mel says.

He takes a deep breath, settling back in his chair. "This is quite the story."

"I've learned that life's full of crazy shit and crazier choices in my line of work," Mel says.

He gives her the stare of a man who knows there's something not entirely right here, but he can't figure out what it is when he's been handed everything on a silver platter. She knows that whisper in her head well: *This is too easy.*

If only he knew exactly how fucking hard it was, getting here.

"Nat thought the world of you, you know," he finally tells her.

Mel ignores the ache in her chest.

"It's one of the reasons I'm putting so much faith in you here, Tillman."

Mel's mouth flattens. "You should put faith in me. I've helped you solve two cold cases today, Sheriff, plus the cause of a plane crash. You've got the men responsible for all of it behind bars and not just eyewitnesses but survivors of some of the crimes, and I'll lead you to proof of the one guy who didn't survive the Newells. I'd call this a win."

"I might just call it that, too," he says. "*If* Toby's where you say he is."

"Am I good to go?" Mel asks. "Or do you have more questions?"

"You're good to go. As long as you show up to help guide search-and-rescue. We should have a team by Thursday."

"I'm not going anywhere," Mel says. "See you Thursday, Sheriff."

She walks out of the room, heading toward the lobby. The sheriff barks at the gawking deputies to get back to work as she passes.

Mel makes her way down the steps of the building, the summer sun hitting her full force.

It's bizarre to spot two white-blond heads on the sidewalk, instead of just the one she's used to. The twins both turn toward her. Gigi's clutching Whitney's arm like she doesn't want to let go.

For a second, she marvels in the sheer aliveness of her. Never for a fucking second did she think she'd survived.

"I can't believe you're here," Mel says in wonder. She lowers her voice. "I can't believe you never told me about the Newells."

"Join the club," Gigi snarks.

"It took Chloe months to even respond after I found her," Whitney says. "I intended to bring you in on it, Mel. I promise, I was gonna make Chloe talk to you when she came home the first time. I just . . . well, I got my throat slit before I could."

"Junior is not getting away with that," Gigi says. "Why couldn't we incriminate him, too?"

"We needed Hill to back us up. We'll talk about revenge later," Whitney says.

"I looked everywhere for you," Mel says. "But I—fuck, I gave up." The guilt is monumental, even though Whitney's standing there, whole and alive and seemingly not too worse for wear. But she knows looks can be deceiving. Three whole years gone. It's not fair. To any of them.

"It's okay," Whitney says.

"No," Mel says. "It's not. I should've believed—"

"We're good," Whitney says. "It's not like you would've found me, babe. You were looking for a body and I wasn't dead, I was just in Colorado."

"I knew you weren't dead," Gigi says sulkily. "And everyone thought I was crazy."

"You can tell me 'I told you so' until the end of time," Mel says.

"You better bet I'm going to," Gigi says.

"We all did what we had to with the information we each got. And look: we're here." Whitney reaches out, hugging Mel, holding her too tight to be comfortable. Mel's never been a hugger, but her eyes burn as she breathes in the familiar Chanel perfume.

"Do you think it's gonna work?" Mel asks in a quiet voice in her ear.

Whitney nods against her cheek before pulling away. "It's gonna work," she says. "Chloe should be out in a minute. But we gotta go. My mom . . ." A smile splits her face. "I get to see my mom," she says, her voice cracking.

"Go," Mel says, knowing how much that means. "I'll wait for Chloe. We'll talk tomorrow."

"You gonna be okay?" Gigi asks.

"Are *you* going to go kill Junior? Because I will very much not be okay if you do that."

"Whitney said I couldn't," Gigi says.

"We'll talk about that tomorrow, too," Whitney says, in a way that has Mel grinning. There's no way Junior's gonna get away with winning the election, not when he has slitting Whitney's throat to answer for. But Whitney had a way of ruining people without even picking up something as sharp as a nail file. That was the power of words and legacy local journalism and a PI best friend.

"Get out of here. Say hi to your mom for me."

She watches them get into the car, which still seems just incredible and impossible, the two of them reunited.

Mel sinks down onto the concrete steps of the sheriff's department, staring up at the fading sun, trying to breathe around that feeling in her chest.

That sense of finally being *done*.

"Hey."

She turns to see Chloe at the top of the steps.

"Hey."

Chloe takes the steps slowly, like she's gonna scare Mel off.

"My truck's three blocks over, at Richard's office," Mel says. "Drive you home?"

The wariness fades a little in her eyes. "I'd like that."

They're quiet the whole walk to the truck. Mel thinks that the second they get inside, the privacy of it will spill forth words and excuses and explanations. But instead, the quiet grows as she drives down Main Street and then turns on Pine to head toward the freeway and the ranch.

Thirty minutes of silence and when Mel turns onto the drive without being told, the tires crunch on the loose gravel. The gate's wide open, like the sheriff called ahead to let them know they were coming. The lights are on in the windows, roses climbing up the white posts of the porch. Mel's never seen it in daylight, she realizes, as they pass by the field that had been a parking lot that night, the maze of cars and Toby's bullshit sealing her fate.

Mel slows to a stop in front of the house. "This is you."

Chloe looks at the gently glowing windows, then back at Mel. "Come with me?"

Mel doesn't answer for a long moment. Chloe doesn't deflate—it's like her body refuses to. She gets out of the truck and Mel thinks that's it . . . until she circles around and opens the driver's door, extending her hand. "Come on."

Mel lets her pull her out of the truck and up the steps. The only explanation is she's exhausted and too emotional. She has spent hours in the company of either dangerous or annoying men. She just wants a snack and a nap.

"Feels weird to knock," Chloe murmurs, almost to herself before she does it. A dog barks, footsteps come so fast they have to be running, and a gray-haired woman rips open the door like she's ready to face a tornado.

Chloe kind of is one, so it makes sense.

"Hey, Mom," Chloe says.

Mrs. Harper lets out one of those choked-back noises that's a sob and a laugh and a wail all at once. A heart sound, one that comes from deep, deep wounds itching to life so they can finally heal.

Mel steps away as Mrs. Harper grabs Chloe close, holding her so tight Chloe immediately starts to squirm.

"The sheriff called—I almost didn't believe it. You're just always surviving crashes, aren't you, Chloe?" Mrs. Harper asks, brushing Chloe's curls off her face, cupping her cheeks like a child.

"Is Daddy—"

"He's resting in the downstairs bedroom," Mrs. Harper says. "He's having a good day. But he's been so worried. I didn't know how to explain—"

"I'll explain," Chloe says. "I'll—" She glances down the hall, licking her lips nervously.

"Go talk to him," Mel says, remembering how her eyes had shone in the van to the airport, asking about how Mr. Harper was, if Mel had seen her father.

"Mom?"

"Go," Mrs. Harper says. "I'll make some tea."

Chloe drifts down the hall, disappearing around a corner, and Mel smiles, trying to make it not look strained.

"Please, come in," Mrs. Harper says, gesturing Mel inside.

"Mrs. Harper, I'm Melanie Tillman. I'm in charge of the Parker Agency after Nat passed?"

"Yes," she says. "The PI. You—you're all right?"

"I'm fine," Mel says.

"I don't understand how the plane could have gone down."

"I'm sure your daughter will explain everything," Mel says.

"Isn't that your job?"

"My job was to bring her to you. So. Job's done," Mel says, strangely bereft at the idea. She has no real reason to be here. She should go.

But she finds herself sitting at the chipped enamel table in the kitchen, taking the tea that Mrs. Harper fixes her.

"I recognize you," Mrs. Harper says, as she settles down across from her at the table, her hands wrapped around her own mug.

"Excuse me?"

"I remember you. When you were a teenager. My husband found you on the back forty. I was on the porch when he marched you off the land. He said you were a hitchhiker, just camping out."

Mel stares at her teacup, heat crawling in her face even though it was years ago and meaningless in the grand scheme of things. But teenage shame and small-town bullshit really does run deep in her veins.

"You weren't a hitchhiker," Mrs. Harper says.

"No, ma'am."

"You and my daughter . . ."

There is so much in the silence that comes after *daughter*. A wealth of denial and what-if wondering and *Is she actually . . .* questions.

Mel meets her eyes. Only thing to do. "We go way back."

There're questions in Mrs. Harper's face that she won't ask. Not to Mel, at least.

"Well," Mrs. Harper says, staring at her hands, cheeks staining red like she already knows. "You brought her home."

Mel has to stare at her own hands then, the emotion welling up. Because Mel got Chloe home and Chloe got Whitney home and it was done.

It was finally done.

"Yes," she says. "I got her home."

47

CHLOE

Her father sleeps, the tear tracks still glossy on his face. Chloe can hear her mother moving around in the kitchen, so she takes the back stairs up to her room. She'll have to go through the full story again for her soon. She just needs a minute to breathe. She needs to let her heart break a little over how skinny and sickly her father looks. How close she was to never seeing him again.

There's something strange about being in this house. This entire day is like stepping back into something she didn't mean to leave for so long and now everything's moved off-center slightly. The same, but also different.

She pushes open the door to her childhood bedroom, coming to a stop in the doorway, partly because Mel's sitting there on her pink gingham bedspread, and partly because that pink gingham bedspread is *still* on the bed.

"Christ, they kept it the same," Chloe says, stepping inside.

"Like a shrine," Mel agrees. She plucks at one of the lacy pillows. "I don't remember you being so into pastels."

"I just let my mom pick out what she wanted back then," Chloe says.

"Your dad?" Mel asks.

Chloe tries to smile, but she knows her face is crumpling before it even reaches her eyes.

"I know this is hard," Mel says. "I used to drive Nat to chemo."

Chloe nods.

"But you got here," Mel reminds her. "You don't have to just say goodbye and run."

"I can barely remember what it's like," Chloe tells her. "To not run."

"I think your mom clocked me," Mel tells her, flopping back onto the pile of pillows.

"As . . . ?" Chloe asks.

Mel raises her eyebrows, pointedly looking at Chloe.

"Oh," Chloe says. "Shit."

"She'll have questions," Mel says.

"Tons of them," Chloe agrees, coming over and kind of hovering over her own bed, waiting until Mel scooches in invitation.

She's so close, Chloe wants to reach out, but she's not sure she's allowed. The uncertainty is like a broken bone, something hidden under the skin and aching.

"I used to think about this," Mel says. "Being in your bedroom with you. Your mom making me tea. Talking to me like a boy who came to see you."

"I used to dream about this," Chloe says. "When I was living in this bedroom, and when I was gone."

Mel keeps her eyes fixed on the ceiling. "You could've told me. About Whitney."

"If you knew and Rick got it out of you . . ."

"If I recall correctly, I've had the shit beaten out of me *way* more than you," Mel says. "You think I couldn't have withstood Rick?"

"I wasn't going to risk the one person who knew the truth when the two of us were stuck," Chloe says. "You don't know what it was like, finding her there."

"I know what it was like, finding the crime scene," Mel says.

Chloe shakes her head, because it's not the same. "The only reason Whitney survived in the first place was because I have type O blood so we were able to use mine for a transfusion."

"Remind me to send flowers to the vet," Mel says.

"He'd like that. He kept it a secret, this whole time. I never knew why."

"You're convincing when you have to be," Mel says. "Look at what you did today."

She still can't believe she pulled it off. She wouldn't have been able to without Hill. Without Whitney and Gigi. Without Mel. All of them, united, it was the only way it worked. An insane gamble, a one-in-a-million shot, and she hit the bull's-eye. No more Dicks. No more danger. "Are you mad?"

"That you swept in with Whitney and a duplicitous not-so-trophy wife to save us all? Yes. I'm furious I'm not going to jail."

"Can you stop being sarcastic for one second?"

Mel takes a deep breath, slowly sitting up.

"We need to talk about what happens next," Chloe says. "When the sheriff discovers all the diamonds on Toby's body, he'll have more questions for us and the Dicks."

"He won't," Mel says.

"What are you talking about? You said you were taking the recovery team to the body—"

Mel reaches out and takes Chloe's palm, curving it into a cup, before reaching into her pocket. She drops something into it, it nearly bounces off her, she's so startled.

Chloe feels the veins in her temples throb as she stares at the diamond shining against her skin.

"Mel," she says. "You . . . you had them this whole time?"

"Of course not," Mel scoffs to her relief. "I've had them for like . . ." She checks her watch. "Less than a day."

Chloe frowns, counting back in her head. "You mean . . ."

"I went out there the night we . . ." Mel says. She almost drifts into it, the memory of pressing Chloe against the shower tile. Scratchy sheets and much softer skin, the floral scent of hotel soap and the taste of lemon—of Chloe—no longer haunting, but enveloping.

"I couldn't sleep after, okay?" she says when Chloe looks up at her, open-mouthed.

"So you decided to go on a postcoital *grave-robbing* trip into the woods to help encourage your melatonin production?"

"Beats a moonlit stroll."

"You think you're hilarious, don't you?" Chloe says.

Mel shrugs, slumping back to lying down, her feet still firmly on the floor like she's afraid Chloe's mom will come barging in at any second, which is maddening and adorable. God, she can't believe she loves her.

"Where are the rest of the diamonds?" Chloe asks, lying down next to her.

"In the glove compartment of Ted's truck," Mel says like that's a perfectly rational place to stash ten million dollars' worth of stolen gems. "I was gonna use them as a bargaining chip with the Dicks and Big Daddy, but then you and Whitney pulled a fast one on everyone and Big Daddy was dead and Richard was entirely unreasonable and Rick is Rick, so now, well—" She gestures at the diamond. "I'm not really sure what to do with them. We can't exactly turn them over to the sheriff."

"Certainly not now that we've told a diamond-less story to him," Chloe says.

"And if we tell Hill we have them, Junior will find out."

"Can't have that," Chloe says, head spinning. "What about the grave?" she asks suddenly.

"What about it?"

"You dug him up. Won't the dirt look all messed up—"

"I didn't have to dig very much," Mel admits. "I think we kind of sucked at digging deep, back then. It was a pretty shallow grave."

"It seemed like we dug forever," Chloe says.

"We didn't even have shovels," Mel points out. "And it's supposed to rain tomorrow."

Chloe tilts the diamond back and forth in her palm. "I can't believe I'm holding the reason I had to run for so long."

"We could fling them off a cliff into the creek, but I thought that would be a little dramatic," Mel says. "And wasteful. But we need to get rid of them somehow."

"I might know some people," Chloe says, not quite believing they are having a conversation about fencing diamonds in her childhood bedroom, surrounded by flannel gingham. "They could take them off our hands."

"I hoped you would. The sooner they're out of here, the safer we are. Because once the sheriff gets Toby's body and the Dicks find out the diamonds aren't there?" Mel shakes her head. "We'll hear their wailing from Canada."

"They can't do much but scream and cry anymore," Chloe says.

"You took care of that, didn't you," Mel says.

"You object?"

"More like I'm impressed," Mel says. "I walked into Richard's office ready to make a trade so I could bring Whitney's body home, and instead you brought Whitney home alive and breathing and eliminated every threat but Junior."

"Whitney's got plans for Junior," Chloe says.

"She didn't pick up murder skills while she was gone like you, did she?" Mel asks suspiciously.

"She's got a different kind of destruction in mind," Chloe says. "The pen being mightier than the sword, and everything."

"That should be interesting," Mel says. "Who's gonna be mayor when she's done with him?"

"Probably Whitney," Chloe says, and Mel laughs like she's joking, but she's really not.

Chloe lies back on the bed, so that when she turns her head she's only inches from Mel. She wants to reach out, but if she slides her hand across Mel's stomach, under her shirt like she wants . . .

She doesn't know if it's okay. If *they're* okay. But lying next to her again is such a profound relief, she tries to just revel in it.

Was this what it would've been like, if they hadn't had to hide because of Toby and this small damn town? Lying on her bed at sixteen with the girl she was falling for, pink gingham all around them, no bodies, no hiding, no secrets between them, no *us against a cruel world*.

She shakes her head, trying to quell the thoughts. There's no point in dreaming of what-ifs that fit into back then. There's only now.

There's only her. Them, if there is a them.

"So what do we do?" Mel asks.

"With the money?" Chloe asks.

Mel nods. "We'll need to launder it carefully."

"We could pay it forward," Chloe says. "Open a peacock rescue."

For a beat, Mel stares at her, her mouth twitching, trying to hold it in. Chloe waits. It's like her entire life depends on getting that smile.

"Doris does deserve to have her good deed rewarded," Mel says finally.

"It's the least we could do for her and the gang," Chloe says.

"They'd need both of us, though, to keep an eye on them," Mel continues.

"They're quite the ostentation of peacocks," Chloe agrees slowly, wondering if Mel's saying what she thinks she is. Her hand falls in the space between them, brushing up against Mel's.

She doesn't pull away. Chloe's heart leaps.

"I thought the collective of peacocks was a *muster*," Mel says.

"I like *ostentation*," Chloe says.

"I prefer *muster*," Mel says.

"Clearly this peacock-rescue idea is doomed from the start then." Chloe shrugs, starting to get up. "Just like us."

Mel's hand closes around hers, tugging her back down, and there's that smile. Hard-won and reckless. "You think you can get away from me that easy?"

Something fizzes inside her chest, bubbly like champagne as Mel pulls her closer.

"I mean, if you're going to call our peacock army a *muster* . . ."

"Armies muster! They don't ostentate!"

"Technically, to a peace-loving individual, war *is* ostentatious and unnecessary."

"Please shut up," Mel says, and before Chloe can protest, she kisses her.

Chloe's not exactly objecting. Her blankets are as soft as she remembered, and Mel's skin is even softer.

When Mel pulls back, she stays close, so close that their noses brush. "No more running," she says, the hurt in her voice more than Chloe can bear. "And no more killing," she adds, like she's trying to lighten the load of it, these six years of losing and growing they had to do without each other.

"No more running," Chloe agrees. "But I've got to have, like, a hall pass."

"A hall pass for murder?"

"For self-defense. What if Junior reacts badly when Whitney takes him down?"

"Then we'll go to the sheriff. Like a normal couple whose friend is in danger."

"Like a normal couple laundering millions of dollars of diamond money?"

Mel sighs. "Okay. You can have a murder hall pass. As long as you loop me in this time and don't keep secrets."

"I'll add that to the list. No more running. No more killing, except for the hall pass. And no more secrets."

Mel's quiet for so long that Chloe feels compelled to say, "We're not doomed, you know. Far from it. We can survive anything."

Mel leans forward.

"Indestructible, huh?"

Chloe drifts closer.

"Undeniable."

Mel smiles.

"Inescapable."

Their lips are about to brush when a voice calls up from the hall. "Chloe, honey, are you and your girlfriend hungry? I made sandwiches."

Chloe freezes like a guilty teenager. Mel trembles, silent laughter shaking her shoulders.

"She made sandwiches," Chloe says.

"*Girlfriend*," Mel says. She leans forward, kissing her quick and easy, unlike any other touch they've had because nothing has ever been easy. But maybe it is now. Maybe it will be.

"Let's go," Mel says, getting up and holding out her hand.

She doesn't hesitate. She takes Mel's hand. She walks down the creaky stairs with her, no doubt, no worry, no more fear, no more secrets, no more running.

And every step down those stairs into their future, she thinks:

Indestructible.

Undeniable.

Inescapable.

ACKNOWLEDGMENTS

I always did solo sports as a kid, so it wasn't until I started publishing books that the team spirit really got its hooks in me. A book in trade publishing can only go so far with just the writer; it can never get over the finish line without a team of passionate creatives behind it, and I was very lucky to work with the team behind *No Body No Crime*.

I must extend my most heartfelt thanks to the following people who helped get the book over that finish line (sprinting as if feral peacocks were in pursuit):

My lovely editor, Brianna Fairman, whose sharp eye and editorial instincts whipped our first draft into beautiful shape. I'm so happy we got to work together—it was so fun!

My agent, Jim McCarthy, who was puzzled about my zeal regarding the feral peacocks at first and entirely prescient about everything else. Your early notes on this really brought the Bag of Dicks to life, and I had so much fun writing them, so I am eternally thankful.

The amazing and dedicated team at MCD and Farrar, Straus and Giroux, including Sean McDonald and Benjamin Brooks; our wonderful interior designer, Songhee Kim; managing editor, Debra Helfand; production editor, Bri Panzica; production manager, Nina Frieman; and publicist, Tracy Locke; and the incredible copyediting and proofreading team: Chandra Wohleber, Vivian Kirklin, and Carla Benton, who fixed all my continuity errors (of which there were many).

My cover illustrator, the brilliant Zoë van Dijk, who has given me an absolute dream cover. Thank you so much for adding your artistry to this novel.

Daphne Durham, who originally saw the spark of worth in this, a book where I gather everything I usually take seriously and poke fun at it. I'm very grateful to you.

My mom, who is definitely responsible for introducing me to the trio of terror that is rural life, rural politics, and feral birds. You always provide excellent novel fodder, Mom.

My dear friends, all of whom had to listen to me gleefully talk about feral peacocks for several years: Charlee Hoffman, Dahlia Adler, the entire crew at the Trifecta, the delightful group over in All the Baskets, and my very sweet DND group. The peacock talk will now (thankfully) cease, unless I randomly get attacked by a muster of them—you never know.

Tess Sharpe was born in a mountain cabin to a punk-rocker mother and grew up in rural California. She lives deep in the backwoods with a pack of dogs and a group of formerly feral forest cats. She is the award-winning author of many books for kids, teenagers, and adults, including *Barbed Wire Heart* and the *New York Times* bestseller *The Girls I've Been*.